AYDEN

MELISSA BELLE

Cover Art: J. Hunter Designs

ALSO BY MELISSA BELLE

MAX

LIAM

Bonus Wild Men Stories

WILD MAN (Colton and Sky prequel novella)

WILD VALENTINE (Ayden and Bella short story)

Sign up for Melissa's Newsletter to get a free story and to receive alerts and updates on upcoming book releases.

ABOUT

Bella

I promise to keep my hands to myself tonight.

No matter how much I want Ayden Wild, I will not, should not, absolutely cannot, have sex with him.

Ayden's always been my lifeline. My lighthouse in a raging sea, guiding me home again.

Warm, safe, rock solid, erect....Oh GOD, I just can't stop myself.

Ayden's always been hot, but this summer, his body's distracting me so much I forget what we're talking about.

So I keep my ass glued to my barstool, and I flirt with the guy next to me. He's not Ayden, but he'll have to be my distraction.

But Ayden's acting...different. Like he wants something but he's not telling me.

Ayden

Bella Wesley is driving me crazy tonight.

She's letting that douchebag flirt with her, and buy her drinks, and ask her out.

I should be the one she's looking at that way. *I* should be the one holding her hand. And *I* desperately want to be the one taking her into my bed.

But we made a pact to strictly be friends. To make sure we'd get each other through the dark times. And we did.

It doesn't mean I didn't want her every damn moment since then. Of course I handled it the only way I knew how—I dated everyone but her.

So I know a distraction when I see one.

But if I tell Bella how I feel now, right before I leave town, it could screw everything up.

And if I don't?

I'LL REGRET IT FOR THE REST OF MY LIFE.

To my husband, for your unyielding belief in this story, and for never letting me give up on telling it. I love you.

CHAPTER ONE

Bella

Plus One.

The two words every single woman dreads when she opens up a wedding invitation from her ex-boyfriend and sees he's trying to be chivalrous. Kind. Possibly generous. You can bring a plus one. Sure, you can. I'm getting married, so I'm clearly not threatened, and I've obviously moved on. Have you? If you have, then you'll have no problem filling in the space next to your name with a "plus one."

I stare at the gold embossed envelope in my lap. My work shift has just ended, but I stay sitting inside the safety of the Lucky Bay Pool Hall cashier's booth because I need the privacy.

With shaking hands, I reread the thick embossed page inviting me to attend the wedding of my ex-boyfriend and his new partner, about to become his husband. And I stare at the blank space where my plus one is supposed to be.

Then, because I'm a masochist right now and old memories are center stage in my mind, I flip through my phone until I find the online video that went viral and altered the course of my life.

Me—grainy but clearly me, naïve and barely twenty-two—on stage with my guitar at a bar in Los Angeles. Happy as can be, my long blond ponytail swinging behind me as I strum the chords to the song I'd just finished writing the night before. The camera shifts to Trevor, my boyfriend at the time, making out in the crowd with someone, someone who clearly isn't me. Max. My manager. Who I trusted.

The camera shifts back to me, and my horrified face as recognition sets in because *somebody put the spotlight on my boyfriend and my manager in the crowd.* I'll never know who did it, who literally shined the light on the lie that was defining my life, but I'm actually grateful to the misguided angel. Because if I hadn't found out, and Trevor and I had kept dating and built a future like we'd planned...well, my life would be in a far worse hell than it is.

I still remember staggering home alone to my threadbare apartment that night. I was teary-eyed and lost. But then Ayden called. Ayden Wild, my best friend and lifeline since I was three years old. He asked me what was wrong, and I poured my heart out. He let out a string of curse words when I told him about Trevor.

"I'm getting on the next flight out," he said immediately. "I'll be there as soon as I can, Bella."

I glanced at the wall behind my bed, at the postcard of the stately Lucky Bay lighthouse effortlessly withstanding the rough Maine seas. Ayden had sent me that postcard a month earlier—he had told me to tack it up so I could look at it whenever I felt homesick. The town lighthouse felt like my sanctuary, calling me home when I was feeling so lost. That lighthouse reminded me of Maine, and comfort, and Ayden.

And that was the moment it hit me. "There's nothing here for me anymore, Ayden." My voice choked up as I realized for the first time how true that statement was.

"I'm here for you, Bella." His voice was rough and sure, and I clutched at the phone like I was holding onto him. "I'm here."

When I didn't say anything, he added in a tone so low I barely heard him, "I dare you."

I dare you.

Like always, Ayden gave me exactly what I needed from him.

Shivers ran through my body, and he added softly, "Come home."

And I did. I hustled my way out of Los Angeles, lost any momentum of gaining a record deal, and landed back home in Lucky Bay, Maine, where I've been hiding inside of a cashier booth for the past three years. Life's been better. But I look at the video whenever I need to remind myself that life can also be much worse.

At the familiar tap-tap on the half-open cashier window, I say, without looking up from my phone screen, "Oh my gosh, Ayden, you won't believe what I just got in the mail..."

"Bella."

Ayden's tone is edgy, and I jerk my head up.

His ridiculously gorgeous ocean-blue eyes look back at me. His trademark navy baseball cap with the red B in the center can't mask his somber expression; his mouth is turned down in a frown, and his handsome face is etched with tension.

"Hey!" I reach to my right for the door handle to the booth. "What's up?"

"I need to talk to you," he tells me in a rough tone. "Do you have class tonight?"

"No. Our summer schedule is different."

"When you're done working, can we go to the beach?"

"Of course. I'm done now." I shove Trevor's wedding invitation into my purse and stand up.

We leave the pool hall, and the chilly ocean breeze hits me like it always does. Glad for my cream cardigan that hangs over my jeans to mid-thigh, I inhale the salty air as we head across the wooden boardwalk toward the soft white sand. We pass by the shops and businesses that line the town square, nearly all of them closed and locked for the night.

The lights on the boardwalk guide us along and also give me a clear view of Ayden next to me. His unruly black hair peeks out from underneath the back of his cap, and his chiseled jaw is set in a firm line, so I know he's worried about something. His worn blue jeans fit him perfectly as always, and he strides confidently next to me in that easy way he has. I get a nice glimpse of his ass when his long strides take him just ahead of me. Carrying a brown paper bag in one hand, he shoves his free hand inside the front pocket of his dark hoodie and glances back at me with a sexy half-grin.

"Almost there, and we'll talk."

"But you're okay?" I ask him softly as we cross the sand and walk closer to the breaking waves of the Atlantic Ocean.

"I'm fine, Bella," he says quickly. "I'm good."

Thank God.

Once we get further away from the boardwalk lights, Ayden flicks on his phone flashlight and leads me around the jutting rock formation so we can't be seen from the line of shops. We keep walking until we reach our favorite spot on this part of the beach —the place where we can see the lighthouse from a distance but where we're away from everyone in town. It's just Ayden and me and the breaking waves.

As soon as we take seats on the sand, our backs against the rocks, Ayden turns off his light, and we sit in silence while our eyes adjust to the moonlight. It's shining brightly tonight and casts an even stronger glow over the water. Ayden shifts so he's facing me.

"Remember our most recent 'I Dare You?'" he asks me.

My mind starts spinning. Ayden and I started our "I Dare You" game when we were kids. Whenever one or the other of us feels stuck—from me deciding if I'm ready to snorkel in the tidal pools for the first time to Ayden struggling to choose his love of land-scaping over his family fishing business—we turn the difficulty into a dare.

Of all the times we've played the game, neither of us has refused a dare yet. It's almost like a challenge thrown down, and we're determined to carry it through. But the biggest reason we don't turn down a dare from one another? Trust. I trust Ayden with my life. I know he'll only choose a dare that he thinks I really need in order to move forward. And I do the same for him.

Right now, though—I'm actually not sure what dare Ayden means. Because the only one I've challenged him to recently felt like such a long shot—

"Wait—you mean when I dared you to apply to that job in California that Jaley told you about? The one where you'd manage an entire crew on your own?"

Ayden's straight white teeth press into his full bottom lip as he nods.

I lean closer to him. "Did you actually do it? You sent them your resume? You never said anything, so I figured that was our one dare gone wrong, and I never brought it up again."

His mouth lifts up in a grin. "You dared me. When have either of us ever turned down a dare from the other?"

I widen my eyes. "And??"

He reaches for the paper bag by his feet and pulls out a bottle of Lucky Bay wine from the only winery in town. "And I got it. You're looking at the new manager of Santa Monica Gardenscapes and Design."

I scream and throw my arms around his neck so vigorously he bangs his head against the rocks.

"Oh my God!" I reach behind him and start rubbing his thick dark hair underneath his baseball cap. "Are you okay?"

He's laughing too hard to answer me.

"Ayden? You're okay?"

He effortlessly pulls me onto his lap and holds me close. "I'm fine," he says in my ear. "I appreciate the enthusiasm."

I shift back to look at him, and our eyes lock.

And for one strange, out-of-body moment, I swear Ayden Wild is about to kiss me. His ocean-blue eyes are raw as they hook into mine, and his breath halts.

Ayden and I are just friends. Best friends, for sure, but *only* friends. On purpose, so we don't fuck up what makes us so good. So we don't lose the one and only person either of us has always been able to count on.

Right now, though, Ayden's hot eyes are on me, and I'm

clutching at his shirt, unable to tear my gaze away from his. He reaches behind me and tugs at my ponytail, using the leverage to bring me even closer to him.

I'm surprised when I feel my body start to come alive with heat, and the crashing waves somehow sound a long way off.

But then...

Ayden shakes his head, almost like he's trying to clear it of any craziness, and gently lifts me off his lap and back to the empty spot next to him on the sand.

"So." He clears his throat. "About the new job. It's far away from Lucky Bay, obviously."

I try to calm my racing pulse. "Yes. We'll be living on opposite coasts from each other again."

"Right. I wanted to make sure you were the first to know and that you heard the news directly from me," he says, his tone unusually gentle. "It starts in mid-July."

"Mid-July." I say it quickly. "Well, this is only June, right? So we've got some of the summer to hang out together."

He reaches out and his thumb strokes my cheek quickly. "Right. I've got to go out there for training in a few days, but that's just Wednesday through Saturday. Other than that, you're stuck with me until I move."

"I know you wouldn't leave Lucky Bay for the first time ever if this weren't something you really wanted."

He nods, his gaze searching mine. "Something I really *needed*. I wouldn't leave otherwise."

Something about the way he says it...

"What are you not telling me?" I ask him, worry filling my head. "I thought you were trying to challenge yourself by proving you could manage a crew year-round. And that's just not possible in Maine with how short the landscaping season is. Plus, they have great landscaping design schools out there, and you always said you wanted to get your degree. But your face—clearly there's something more going on."

He just shakes his head. "Later. Right now, I want to celebrate on the beach with my best friend." He holds up the wine and reaches into his hoodie pocket, producing a wine opener. "I know you moved away years ago, but we all know boys grow up slower than girls."

I laugh at his silly joke. "Very true." I reach out and hug him again, and his strong arms wrap around me tightly. "Congratulations," I say into his sweatshirt.

"Thanks."

His voice vibrates through my body as I hold onto him, and I swallow down my emotion. Ayden certainly isn't the reason I left L.A., but he's sure as hell the reason I dared to come crawling back to Maine. And he's the only reason I wake up here with a smile on my face.

I think I definitely need some alcohol right about now.

Ayden and I aren't big drinkers. But he must have known his news would unleash feelings that neither of us is necessarily ready for.

I gesture to the wine bottle gratefully. "Let's celebrate your big news."

Ayden effortlessly uncorks the bottle and hands it to me. "Ladies first."

I take a big sip of the full-bodied, slightly fruity-flavored wine. "This is my favorite."

"I know."

I hand him the bottle, and he takes a swig. And then another.

He scoots closer to me. "Come on. Get buzzed with me."

I giggle. "You know it doesn't take much to get me drunk, Ayd."

Ayden

Two hours later, the bottle of wine is empty. And I can't stop touching Bella. Every time a strand of blond hair slips out of her ponytail, I brush it out of her face. Which means I get to touch her soft skin—her cheeks, her neck, and the soft curve of her ears, one of which holds three tiny diamond piercings, and the other ear two. Those diamonds are my undoing right now—I have to hold myself back from nibbling at Bella's earlobe and making her moan.

What in the ever-loving fuck is wrong with me?

Bella Wesley and I are just friends. The truth is, she's far more than a friend—Bella is everything to me, and she always has been. Which is exactly why I make sure to keep her in the friend zone. Why I *need* to keep her in the friend zone. This decision is not up for discussion; it's a choice we both made and hold to, no matter what.

"Ayd?" Her voice is huskier than normal, the way it gets when she's been drinking. "You okay?"

I wrap my arm around her shoulders, and we sit silently on the beach, just staring out at the black ocean.

"I'm going to miss this place." I don't mean to say that; it just slips out.

"I know."

And that's what I'll miss the most. The woman next to me, who understands what I'm saying and every meaning underneath it without me having to explain. The woman who's been there for me my entire life.

And, because I can't seem to stop myself, I bring up a topic Bella and I always make a point to stay away from. "How's the tool you're dating?"

She backhands me in the stomach, and I laugh.

"Trey," she says, clearly drawing out the name on purpose, "is fine."

"'Fine' doesn't sound nearly good enough for you, B." As much as I try to hold it back, I can't help the jealousy that creeps into my voice.

"And we're not 'dating,'" she says, putting the word in air quotes. "We've only been on two dates. I'm getting to know him. He's...you know, it's just casual."

That's Bella code for, "I don't really like this guy, but I'll date him for a while until it fizzles out and comes to an end." I try to keep from smiling. "Okay."

"How are your girlfriends?" she says in response. "Jenny, and what's the other one's name? The one who always glares at me when I say hi?"

I can't help the grin that takes over my face. "Ashley. She hates you."

"Really," she says sarcastically. "I couldn't tell. Maybe she should hate your dating style instead—you know, the fact that you won't ever commit to one woman."

"Maybe she should." I lean closer to her, inhaling her strawberry and mango scent that I normally try to ignore.

But tonight, I can't ignore anything about Bella Wesley.

And I'm buzzed enough that I let my body take over my brain. My fingers trail a slow path down Bella's bare arm until I reach her waist. I circle her hip with my hand and squeeze.

I'm not prepared for the sound that escapes her mouth. A tiny but clear moan that has my dick threatening to break through my zipper.

I drop my hand off of her immediately and we both jump up and awkwardly brush the sand from our clothes.

"Let's go to the bar," I say. "Maybe the tool and..." I can barely remember the names of the women I've been casually dating this spring. "And others will be there."

———

Bella

Ayden drops the empty wine bottle into the nearby recycling can when we leave the beach and walk the half block to Lucky Bay Bar.

God. I cannot believe I let out that sound. It was just...the way Ayden's hot hand felt when he gripped my waist—I haven't been touched like that by a man, well, ever. It was so possessive, so... erotic. And I couldn't stop my reaction. That breathy sigh I made...it *definitely* sounded like a moan, and I'm mortified. Because clearly Ayden heard. He let go of me like I was contagious.

We separate as soon as we step inside the bar, and Trey calls to me from a nearby table. As I wave at him, Jenny leaps off her barstool and tackles Ayden like she hasn't seen him in months.

"You came!" she squeals. "I thought you said you were busy."

He immediately flips his baseball cap around from back to front, one of his tells that he doesn't want to be seen. He smiles a flirty, meaningless smile at Jenny, the kind of smile he never sends my way. It's a truth that both settles me and crushes me, the way that Ayden shows me all of himself except for the part he seems to share with every other woman in town.

And I know he and I made a pact a long time ago to never cross the line, but sometimes my hormones get the best of me. Maybe if my best friend in the world weren't so freaking gorgeous, with a sex appeal that should be illegal, I wouldn't get hit with the green-eyed monster now and again. Ayden is the hottest guy in here hands down, and there's not a woman in the bar who would disagree with me.

I nod at him quickly. "See you."

Ayden's beautiful eyes that never quite mask his pain buried somewhere in the Atlantic, zero in on me. "Bella. Give me half an hour."

I gesture toward Trey. "Same here."

His gaze shifts to Trey, and if looks could kill...

The wine definitely went to my head because I nearly grab Ayden and ask him why he's always hated everyone I date, but I know the answer already. He thinks I can do better. And the problem is he's always been right.

I wave and head for Trey's table.

———

A while later, Ayden and I take seats on the same side of a private booth in the very back of the bar. Trey left for another bar, and I didn't ask Ayden how he shed Jenny. Now it's just the two of us again, and Ayden's news is sitting between us like a broken piñata after all the candies have spilled out. Neither one of us is exactly sure what to do with it.

Ayden's already ordered us more drinks. I'm definitely buzzing, and my mouth is looser than it should be for sure. But it's Ayden who speaks first.

"I can't believe you did this at eighteen, B. Seven years later, I'm going to give it a try. But here's the thing—I know this news must hurt you. Not just that I'm leaving Lucky Bay, but that I'm going to L.A."

I wave away his comment with a flick of my hand, but Ayden catches my wrist in mid-move and holds on.

"Bella. You can't lie to me. I know you're happy for me, but I also know what L.A. means to you. And it kills me to hurt you. It's the last thing in the world I want to do. And I promise I'll tell you everything...soon."

I swallow hard. Yes, the idea of Ayden going to the place I felt driven away from—where I left behind all my dreams and hopes—stings.

But Ayden Wild and I are always there for each other. Always. And I won't let my own pain change that.

"I'm fine," I say. "I'm so, so happy for you, Ayd. Anything you need, just ask me."

Relief floods his face, and the tension in his jaw disappears. "That means everything to me, Bella."

The waitress drops off a round of shots, and Ayden clinks his glass to mine. "You don't work until tomorrow afternoon, right?" he confirms.

"Right, but you have to be up in the morning," I laugh.

"Not anymore," he says with a grin as he empties the amber liquid from his glass into his mouth.

A few drinks later, and I pull out Trevor's wedding invitation and toss it unceremoniously onto the table between us.

As Ayden picks it up and reads it, his relaxed expression turns to thunderclouds.

"That fucker *invited* you?"

I try to respond casually. "You know he probably thinks he's being nice. We still keep in touch intermittently."

"I get that, but to invite you to the wedding for him and the guy he *cheated* on you with? That asshole was your manager! That's fucked up." Ayden drops the invite back onto the table like it's poisonous.

I point shakily to the "plus one."

"This—" I say. "This part makes me nuts."

He jerks his head back, almost like he's startled. "What do you mean?"

"I mean, what am I doing, Ayden?" I look at him helplessly. "I sit in a cashier's booth all week. I'm as single as I've ever been. Trey may be my..." I don't even know what to call the guy I'm really only dating because we're on the same page, the page called casual with zero strings. "My whatever. He's nothing serious. My mother is..." I suck in air. "No better. And none of the above is on the verge of changing."

Ayden brushes a stray hair off my face. "Let me help."

"You can't."

"I can always help. And I know just what you need." He raises his eyebrows at me.

Knowing where he's going, I say, "I'm not sure a dare will work in this situation."

"A dare always works. So let's put our drunk heads together and figure it out. We've got all night." He puts his arm around me. "That's what you did for me this spring when I told you about the position in L.A. You dared me into reaching for something I didn't think I could get. Let me repay the favor."

I think about it. "Like payback. But the good kind."

He kisses my cheek. "The best kind. Okay?"

I should never agree to drunk dares. Nobody should. And normally, I wouldn't. But I'm more than thrown off tonight—I'm staggering at the idea of Ayden leaving Lucky Bay. And toss in Trevor's wedding invite...forget it. I'm not thinking straight at all. So I turn to Ayden and nod.

"Okay. Dare me."

———

Oh. God. My head. Is pounding.

And what is that damn beeping sound?

Shit. It's my phone.

Without lifting my head from the pillow, I reach blindly over to my nightstand. I snag my phone and turn it over so I can squint at the far too bright screen.

Two missed calls and four texts from Ayden.

I scroll through the texts.

How fucking drunk were we last night?

Shit. What is he talking about?

I dared you to find your forever plus one? And you dared me back?

I shoot up in my bed. "What?!!"

Too fast. Searing pain tears through my head. "Crap."

I sink back onto my pillows and read Ayden's next two texts.

How is either one of us going to win a dare so stupid? I don't do relationships.

Very true.

And you don't do healthy ones.

Ouch.

But he's right.

He's so right.

OMG. What did I get myself into?

I drag myself out of bed and head for the shower. Before I go to work this afternoon, I need to figure this mess out. ASAP.

CHAPTER TWO

I'm still finishing pulling my long hair up into a bun when I knock on Ayden's door impatiently.

When there's no immediate answer, I raise my hand to knock again, but it opens just in time.

Ayden and I stare at each other through the open doorway of his one-story cottage. He's in board shorts and nothing else. His baseball cap's on backwards, better revealing his piercing blue eyes that look at me like lasers. His day-old scruff just adds to the fact that Ayden's the hottest guy in Lucky Bay and nothing—not the dark circles underneath his eyes or the way he's wincing like his head hurts as much as mine does—can diminish that fact. His muscular chest is sprinkled with dark hair that trails downward to the place I always try to avoid looking. But not today.

Today, I'm apparently so knocked off that ogling my best friend's junk is something I do unabashedly. My eyes travel down Ayden's half-naked body and stop right at his crotch.

Realizing what I'm doing, I jerk my head back up into his amused gaze.

"Hey." He shoots me a half-grin and ushers me inside his house.

I follow him through the foyer and into the open living room to the right. We take seats on the black leather couch I helped

Ayden pick out when I moved back here, his first big purchase after moving out of his mom's house.

"Nice shirt." He reaches over and gently pulls up the loose sleeve that's slipped off my shoulder, exposing my bra strap. "Sue me for laughing," he reads off my chest.

I smile. "One of my little rebellions when I was still living with my parents after I moved back here. Which reminds me, about tonight…"

He cuts me off. "Don't finish that thought, Bella."

"But Ayden, you obviously feel like shit. You don't have to help me out every Tuesday. I can go alone sometimes."

He shakes his head. "I already hate that I won't be able to go with you once I move. I'm trying to figure out what to do about that. Maybe once a month, I can work at my job over the weekends and fly back on Monday so that I'm there on Tuesday…"

"Oh my gosh, absolutely not," I say, horrified at the very idea. "Do you know how exhausting that would be for you?"

"What about if we Facetime every Tuesday night after you leave your mom's? It could almost be like going to coffee together."

"That's a sweet idea. Let's play it by ear, okay?"

"I just want to be there for you." Pain passes across his face.

"You're *always* there for me, Ayden. Please. Let's not talk about this now."

He nods toward the adjoining kitchen. "Do you want a glass of water? And I've got the best hangover breakfast all ready if you're interested."

"Bacon and eggs?"

"With hot sauce and hash browns." He's moving to the kitchen as soon as I let out a happy squeal. "Stay put. I'll be right back with our plates."

While I wait on the couch, I look out the picture window at the ocean in the distance. The tide is low, which is the perfect match to my mood this morning.

Through my hungover brain, I strain to remember last night. Me. Ayden. So drunk.

Bit by bit, memories come floating back.

Ayden saying I needed to skip Trevor's wedding.

Me saying he's right.

He was right. No way am I attending Trevor's wedding. I'm not that much of a masochist. But between the invitation, Ayden moving away, and the karaoke station set up for the first time ever in the corner of the bar—it all clearly felt like God was sending me a wakeup call that I need to move forward too.

The reality of Ayden leaving this summer was more painful than I wanted to admit, and the pleasant numbing of the alcohol was going to burn off soon enough. And then, I knew I'd be stuck with the emptiness.

Ayden was saying something about maybe he should dare me to start singing and playing guitar again. And while that was a good, solid idea, I didn't think I was ready for it.

And Ayden, like always, read my mind.

"Too much, too soon," he murmured as he tugged at my ponytail.

I looked up at the karaoke stage, and then down. Definitely too soon.

My gaze snagged on the wedding invite again but specifically on the words "plus one."

Ayden's eyes followed mine from the karaoke stage to Trevor's invitation. Then, he cupped my cheek in his hand and stared into my eyes for a long moment. A long, tense moment filled with an energy so thick I could hardly breathe. Eventually, he sucked in a deep breath and muttered something under his breath. He almost sounded like he was cursing. Before I could ask him about it, he spoke.

"I've got it," he said slowly. "The perfect dare for you, Bella."

"What is it?"

"I dare you..." he paused. "To find *your* plus one."

I turned away and covered my face with my hands. I was embarrassed to admit to Ayden that I needed help in the romance department. That's the one area our "I Dare You" game has never ventured into. As much as possible, Ayden and I have always tried to ignore each other's love lives.

"It's brilliant, if I do say so myself," he said, tapping his drink to mine. "Just to up the stakes, I'll even give you a deadline—you need to find him before I move to L.A."

It was a dare only a very drunk person could come up with. And yet, because I was as drunk as Ayden, I thought it was perfect. It was certainly on target. Because Ayden tapped directly into the heart of what I was feeling in that moment—a deep sense of loneliness. And that's what makes a drunk idea a drunk idea, right? It doesn't mean it's smart; it just means it's said without a filter. Ayden's dare was pure and direct, and it hit me exactly where I needed it to. In my soul.

I dropped my hands back into my lap and slowly turned my head until my eyes found Ayden's. His were filled with an emotion I couldn't explain if I were sober, let alone shitfaced. But I abruptly felt an intense need to give him a dare too.

"You need to make the most of the time you have left in Lucky Bay, right?" I said to him. "Anything you want to do before you move?"

He swallowed so hard I saw his throat moving. But all that came out was a gruff, "Are you saying you have a dare for me now?"

I smiled cheekily. "I do. And you're going to absolutely hate it. Really, it's a solidarity kind of thing. Your parting gift to me before you leave for bigger and better things."

He lifted an eyebrow. "What the hell is it, Bella? Spit it out."

I picked up Trevor's wedding invitation and waved it at him. "I dare you to do the same, Ayd. To find *your* forever plus one. Whoever finds theirs first wins."

Ayden jerked back from me like I'd burned him. "What?"

"Exactly. You and I—we both suck at romantic relationships. Right? We never stay in one for long, and we always pick the wrong partners. So this summer—I dare you to find the right one. Your forever plus one."

"That gives me less than two months to find the woman I want to spend the rest of my life with," he said, his tone neutral.

"You just gave me the same dare!" I said to him.

"I didn't say forever," he murmured. "I said plus one. I didn't mean to marry him, for Christ's sake. That's fucking insane."

"Why?" I asked him, waving the invite in his face. "Why is trying to find your life partner insane?"

"I didn't say that," he said, running his hand over his face in that way he does when he's beyond frustrated about something. "I just…I don't know, Bella. I don't want to play in this one."

"So you're admitting defeat then." I shrugged. "Okay. I win. Before we've even started."

"Hey, I didn't say I was quitting." He stared at me, his eyes turning from deep blue to sea green, letting me know he was feeling far more than he was letting on. "Fine. Dare accepted."

I break out of my thoughts as Ayden, now wearing a fitted royal blue t-shirt, steps into the living room and silently hands me a plate of breakfast.

He takes a seat across from me, his eyes never leaving mine.

"I remember," I say softly as I grab a slice of bacon off my plate and crunch into it. "All of last night, I mean."

"I can tell." He reaches out and wipes a piece of bacon off my bottom lip.

"I know it's not much time for us to carry out the dares," I say quickly. "But people say when you find the right one, you just know."

"You're forgetting a couple problems. I don't do serious relationships. Remember? I don't plan to start either."

I clench my jaw, my headache suddenly feeling worse. "Why not again?"

Ayden's eyes, which are always so open, shut down. "No reason worth getting into. I'm just not a commitment guy."

I don't believe a word he says, but I'm not going to push him. Because that would give him free rein to push me.

"And you date idiots."

"Hey!"

I push his chest, and he chuckles.

"You do. Ask around. You think Tari would disagree with me?"

"Trevor wasn't an idiot," I say.

"Right."

Ayden scowls like he's still angry with Trevor.

"You only met him the one time," I say, not sure why I'm defending someone who hurt me. "He's really not a bad person."

"Once was all it took to know he doesn't deserve to be within a hundred miles of you."

"I'm sure it was hard for him to be with me when he was hiding his sexual..."

"Hiding his true self I'm sure was incredibly difficult. But being with you should never be a hardship, B." Ayden takes my chin in his hand and forces me to look at him. "Don't let his invite keep fucking with your head."

"I'm not going to his wedding," I assure him. "But this whole plus one dare. That I'm serious about. While you're planning your exit from Lucky Bay, I'm going to try my best to change my habit of dating idiots."

He leans closer. God, he always smells so good. Like pine and soap and him. "Okay."

"Okay."

Our eyes fix on each other. "So you and Jenny seemed cozy last night," I force out. "How's that going?"

Ayden shrugs. "It's going. There's also..." He cuts off.

"Ashley. I know. I remember her name today."

There's always an "also" in Ayden's world. I've never seen him with just one woman. He always dates several women at a time, all casual, nothing exclusive, and none of the women seem to mind. They just want some orbit time with Ayden Wild.

"Tari said Peter told her Ashley's getting too clingy. Does that mean she's not into the casual thing anymore?" I ask him curiously.

Ayden shrugs, and like usual, he changes the subject. "Speaking of Tari, have you heard from your BFF this morning?"

I furrow my brow. "No. Why do you ask?"

He hands me his phone. "Scroll to the text I sent Peter last night."

I open Ayden's text to Peter, who happens to be married to Tari. The four of us have been best friends our entire lives.

I skim through Ayden's obviously drunken rambling, something about the greatest wine in the world, followed by...

"You asked *Peter* to help you find your plus one?"

"And you texted Tari begging for the same thing. Once you and I established what shitty daters we are, we apparently decided to enlist the help of our friends. Peter, as you can read, readily agreed. Because he's an ass, and he wants to watch us crash and burn, I'm sure."

I glance at Peter's text back to Ayden.

Sure, buddy! This will be a fun fucking summer.

I grab my head. "Oh, crap."

"Yeah. Pretty much."

My thoughts return to Ayden's news.

He's moving.

To the city where I left my dreams behind.

And I make a decision.

"I want to see the dares through," I say to Ayden, ignoring the way his eyes widen in surprise.

"Bella." He takes off his baseball cap and turns it over in his hands. "You can see yours through. But I can't. My very philosophy on relationships ruins any chance of the dare succeeding."

I shake my head. "See, that's what makes this dare so much fun. If you fail, it will be the first dare from me you've ever not won at, and if you succeed, well...you've got yourself a second problem. Because then you'll have to decide if she's worth giving up your bachelor status—and your beliefs—for."

Ayden narrows his blue eyes at me, and I struggle to keep the eye contact. I don't know why, but something about the way he's assessing me...I'm suddenly warm and tingly all over.

"I'll accept your dare-back on one condition," he says abruptly.

Why do I have the feeling he's about to turn the tables on me?

"Okay."

"We help each other. Not just using our friends for that because I doubt we could shake Tar and Peter even if we tried, but you and me"—he points from himself to me—"we agree to assist one another."

"What do you mean?"

"We help each other choose our forever plus ones. You know... the guy you're planning to find that you can't live without? I'll give you a thumbs up or down. And you'll do the same for me."

I stare at him, but he looks back at me with a completely blank expression.

God, this is such a shitty idea. Ayden and I get along much better when we don't involve each other in our love lives. And Ayden's such a goddamn player. Women love him so much—he's going to have way more options in his lineup. I could be busy this summer just helping him pare down his list.

"I don't know..." I say hesitantly. "That feels very..."

"Very what?" he says immediately.

Very intimate. *Too* intimate.

But I can't let him know that. So I square my shoulders and look him straight in the eye. "Very fair." I hold out my hand for him to shake. "Deal?"

The flush in his cheeks is the only sign of his distress.

Ayden takes my hand and shakes it, making sure to stroke my skin with his callused thumb.

I grit my teeth, refusing to react.

"Deal," he says.

I bite my lip without meaning to, and Ayden's gaze travels to my mouth. And now I'm clutching his hand, which is still holding mine.

He squeezes my hand back. "May we each get exactly what—or I guess I should say exactly who—we want."

Right. Because if I'm honest with myself, the only man I really and truly can imagine having a future with is sitting right across from me. And I just *dared* him to find another woman to marry. I really am a hungover idiot.

———

Ayden

Fuck.

I thought for sure Bella had come over to call the whole thing off. I only threw out that dare last night because a) I was drunk off my ass, and b) when I looked at Bella's face, she seemed so...lonely.

She needed a lifeline. So I threw her one.

Then I woke up this morning and realized the full impact of what I'd done.

To dare Bella Wesley to find a boyfriend, when I can barely stand to look at any guy she's ever dated, was beyond stupid.

I assumed she'd wake up and decide a dare was no way to try to find a romantic relationship.

But she's holding firm. That must mean this dare—this whole finding her forever plus one crap—means a lot to her.

And I can't admit to her how much the idea of her finding a forever guy guts me.

The entire time we're talking, I have a ridiculous urge to tell her I'll be her plus one this summer. Or for always if she'll have me. But I don't. I can't. We made that pact when we were thirteen years old for a reason, and we've held onto our promise to make sure we'd get each other through the dark times. I still remember the solemn vows Bella insisted we exchange:

"*I, Mirabella Wesley...*"

"*I, Ayden Wild...*"

"*Promise to be your best friend, through thick and through thin, through good times and bad, through richer or poorer, till death do us part...*"

"*I promise to be there for you always, to defend you against all others, and to stand by your side...*"

"*I promise to never cross the line with you in any romantic way that would make things awkward or messy, alter the scope of our relationship, or potentially endanger our friendship..."*

"Boyfriends and girlfriends will come and go, but we will be forever..."

And we have been. As best friends. To make sure I was never tempted, I've dated nearly everyone in town but her. And over the years, I've gotten exceptionally good at never looking at Bella like the stunningly gorgeous woman she is.

I've never been good enough for her, anyway.

She looks at me sometimes like maybe she thinks I am, but she'd be proven wrong. I've never claimed to be a saint. And Bella deserves far better than what I can give her. She deserves the best. Not a landscaper with no savings, a long list of past dalliances, and the inability to promise forever. Bella deserves her forever guy, and I can't be that. For her or for anyone.

My paternal line has a penchant, even if unintentional, of shipping out early. Maybe we *are* cursed like they say in town. My father's untimely death caused my mother to suffer every day since, and I made the decision I would never take the risk of hurting anyone like that. So I only date casually, and Bella could never be a casual anything. Like we decided over a decade ago, turning our friendship into something more is off-limits.

Which is why I need to keep dating other women this summer. Casually like always. Nothing serious and nothing long-term. That way, nobody gets hurt. I'll go along with our double dare, but I'm not going to actually look for anything serious. No way.

CHAPTER THREE

Bella

By the time I leave Ayden's, I'm on the edge of being late to work. I rush home, grab my psychology textbook, and walk to town by the water.

As I'm heading across the town square, my phone beeps.

I groan when I read Tari's text.

I won't bug you while you're working and no doubt hungover as hell, but the four of us are going out this week! And you have to fill me in on what went down last night with Ayden!! Do you really want to dare him to find "the one?"

I start tapping on my screen. *No, I don't want to do that. I was drunk and screwed up after Trevor's invite. And I can't back out now.*

Of course you can.

No, I can't. Ayden and I never quit on dares.

There's a long pause, where the dots appear and then disappear before, *We'll talk tomorrow, honey. Have a good night,* appears on my screen.

I put my phone in my pocket and open the door to the nondescript clapboard building with the tilted *Lucky Bay Pool Hall & Live Music* wooden sign nailed across the front. I step inside and head straight for the cashier's booth about ten feet from the bar.

I call out a hello to Preston as he pours a drink for a customer and slide inside my booth. This place has been home for the last three years.

When I left L.A., I lived at my parents' for the first six weeks, just long enough to realize I had to get a job, any job, in order to be able to move out of their house. I walked into town and approached the first place with a Help Wanted sign. It happened to be the Lucky Bay Pool Hall. Marguerite asked me if I could shoot pool, and I said I'd never tried. She asked if I minded the smell of alcohol, and I said no. She smiled. "Scott just quit and we need someone to work the late shift tonight. Are you free?" I was free, and that was it.

In a few months, I saved enough to move into a rental house, the one I still live in. But I missed L.A. I still miss it. I've tried to bury my feelings, tried to convince myself I'm happy with the way things are now, but the truth is that I'm not.

I smile at Preston as he leaves the bar and stops outside the open window of my booth. "How are you?"

"Good. I'm down for a vacation, though." He pulls the elastic out of his short ponytail, and his dark brown hair falls messily around his neck. "Can you work tomorrow night?"

"I'd like to, but I have class." I hold up my textbook. "Last course of my college career."

"Nice. Then you'll leave us for some stuffy office job."

I make a face. "God, I know that's what I'm supposed to do. Is it wrong to admit I don't actually want to get a job like that?"

Preston smiles. "You could become a psychologist. It's your major, right?"

"It is, but I'd need to get an advanced degree if I wanted to seriously pursue it as a career. And I don't love psychology that much. I really like learning about the different disorders, though. It's super informative, especially with..."

I cut off, not wanting to talk about my mother.

And Preston, even though he knows—the whole town knows—

kindly changes the subject. "Bella, you look like shit," he says as he takes a closer look at my face. "What's up?"

"I'm so freaking hungover," I admit, and he laughs.

"You? I don't think I've ever seen you drunk."

"Yeah, well, Ayden got us a bottle of wine, and then there were shots..."

"Ah." He nods. "I heard he's moving."

No secret stays a secret for long in Lucky Bay. Not harmless ones like Ayden moving and not more painful ones either.

I chat with Preston for a few more minutes, and then a group of customers comes in and he returns to the bar.

———

The rest of my work shift drags, and by the time I clock out, I'm exhausted. My headache is still with me, and I'm so dehydrated. I feel like I could drink a gallon of water and it wouldn't be enough. A drunk group of college guys accidentally spilled beer on me, and my shirt still hasn't fully dried.

But before I go home to shower and mercifully fall into bed, I have something I need to do, something I do every Tuesday night without fail. And if Ayden wasn't by my side every single week, I may have cracked long before this.

He's waiting on the sidewalk as soon as I step outside the pool hall. He immediately hands me a bottled water, and I'm so grateful I hug him.

"You must be exhausted," I say. "Why don't you just drop me off tonight? I can stay the night there and..."

"No fucking way." Ayden takes my book and purse out of my hands, and we start walking to his car. "I'm staying with you. Like always."

He loops my purse over his shoulder so he can open the passenger door for me, and the image of my dainty feminine bag slung across Ayden's muscular chest makes me smile.

He waits until I'm inside before he hands me my purse and book and shuts the door behind me.

He walks around to the driver's side, and we pull out of the diagonal parking space in the town square and turn for the wealthiest neighborhood in Lucky Bay.

It's a drive I could do in my sleep. Seven minutes from door to door.

Ayden turns onto Gold Dust Drive and keeps going until we reach the very end. He jumps out to hit the gate code and then returns to the car, and we pull up into the large, circular driveway.

Ayden parks off to the side of the driveway and we both get out. As we walk up the front walkway lined with blooming viburnum, I glance up at my parents' two-story brick mansion filled with windows, and my chest tightens with dread. I never know for sure that she's okay; I just always hope she is.

I let us in quietly with the key I keep on my keychain.

Ellie greets Ayden and me the moment we step into the foyer. "Good evening, Ms. Wesley, Mr. Wild. She's upstairs. I brought her dinner."

I nod and smile at the white-haired maid who's been with my family since I was a teenager.

"Thanks Ellie."

She tips her head. "I'm on my way home. I'll be back in the morning."

"Have a good night," we tell her as she slips out the door.

I don't bother calling out a hello, because I know Dad's still at the office and Mom's...well, she's in her own kind of hell.

Ayden's already headed for his usual spot in the den. He pauses to hand me my textbook.

"Maybe you can get some work done," he says.

"Maybe. What will you do?"

"Bella." He kisses my head. "We've been doing this for three years. Don't you think I've got a system?"

I chew on my lip. "But I don't think I've ever really asked you what you do to pass the time."

"I do whatever feels right. Tonight, I'll probably just watch television. Sometimes I text. Or I listen to music on my phone." His eyes search mine. "Why are you worried about me? What you're about to go deal with"—he points upstairs—"is more than enough. Don't worry about me at all. Okay?"

"Okay." I wave goodbye to him and head for the winding staircase.

My parents' bedroom door is opened a crack, and I knock softly before I step inside the room. I pause and let my eyes adjust to the darkness. The shades are drawn and all the lights are off except for the dim light from the adjoining bathroom suite, which casts a low glow over my mother's still form underneath the covers.

I walk over and sit down in the rocker positioned by the head of the bed.

I don't have to look closely to know that Mom's wearing the same lily-white, neck-laced nightgown she always wears, and that her dark hair, always so perfectly done up in a tight bun when in public, is loosely knotted at the nape of her neck. My mother's one of those women who, no matter how down in the dumps she is, doesn't go a second without makeup. Sure enough, when she opens her eyes to look at me, her thick black mascara and liner are the first things I see.

My throat aches at the empty look in her gaze, and I bite back the tears.

"You didn't have to come by." Her voice, clipped as always, comes immediately through the silent room.

"I know." I ease back and forth on the rocker and carefully survey her nightstand.

A pill bottle, single glass of red wine, and a half-eaten plate of food. Nothing else.

I reach for the bottle and quickly count the number of pills left. Only seven less than last Tuesday.

Thank God.

I take the glass and go to the bathroom where I dump the rest of the wine down the sink. I turn on the faucet and run the cold water until I've rinsed the red stain away.

By the time I sit back down in the rocker, Mom's sufficiently pissed off.

"You don't need to count them, Mirabella." Her eyes, always so receded, narrow as she glares at me. "I'm not a fool."

"Of course you're not," I say in a light tone. "You're in pain."

She harrumphs at me, and I ignore her and lean over to help prop her pillow against the massive oak headboard.

"What if I didn't want to sit up?" she asks me curtly.

"Then I'll fix them back again," I say sweetly.

Dealing with my mother when she's like this is a lot like what I would imagine it's like to deal with a petulant child.

Except she's not a child; she's a grown woman. Who used to act like my mother.

Now though, Lucy Wesley is a mere shadow of herself. Six days a week, she keeps it together in front of the town. She attends Lucky Bay legion meetings; she plays bridge with the wives of my father's colleagues; and she works in my father's law office several days a week. She's always flawlessly put-together and perfectly coiffed. Inside though, she's filled with darkness, and not a single type of anti-depressant has turned the tide yet. And every Tuesday, the same day of the week she discovered my father having an affair for the second time, she disappears into a shell of pain.

She settles back against the pillows, half-sitting up now.

"You smell like beer, Mirabella."

I gesture to my shirt. "A drunk customer. Next week, I'll make sure to pack a change of clothes."

"So. What are we going to talk about tonight?" she asks me.

"Whatever we want to," I say. "Or nothing at all. I'll be here until you fall asleep. Okay?"

Her expression softens so subtly I think maybe I imagined it.

"Fine." She crosses her hands over her middle and goes silent.

"Do you want to chat about the party you're throwing for dad?" I suggest.

"Not now, Mirabella." Her voice is so tight I think it may snap.

"Right." I nearly slap myself for forgetting. "I'm sorry."

Any other day of the week, the topic of the party would bring a much-needed smile to her face. But on Tuesdays, it's the worst thing I could mention. On Tuesdays, my father is simply the man who cheated and the reason Mom believes she's lying in bed right now.

I resist the urge I have to smooth a loose hair away from her pale cheek. My throat tightens again, and I swallow down the grief I feel every time I see her this way.

I settle further into the rocker and glance down at the psychology book in my bag, wondering if I should tell her about my upcoming exam. Except then, Mom will bring up how I dropped out of school three years ago and am just now getting around to graduating. That's always a topic worth avoiding.

I close my eyes and try to remember my mother from another time. One of my fondest memories as a child was watching old Perry Mason movies with her. Those fun times stopped when things went bad, but...maybe we can have some fun again tonight.

"Well," I say. "I could tell you about this psychology class I'm taking. This week, we focused on abnormal psych, and I learned some interesting stuff about criminal behavior."

Nearly imperceptibly, Mom turns her head toward me.

"Did you know that my professor used to work for the FBI?" I ask her.

"No." Her voice lifts slightly. "Does he talk about his experience there?"

"Not often. But this week he did. In fact, he told us about this time he was shot at while hunting down a hardened criminal."

"Really." Mom turns completely toward me now. "What was the case about?"

"He couldn't go into details. Except he said the man who shot him had been wanted for years. I think he was a spy."

Mom gasps. "I saw something like this on TV once."

I smile. "I'll tell you all the details my professor shared with us, and we'll try to unravel the mystery together."

The tension in my mother's face eases, and I feel like the weight of the world lifts off my shoulders. For just a moment, I have my mother back. And even if it's just for an hour, that's worth everything.

———

Mom takes longer to fall asleep than usual. I wait until I hear her breathing even out, and then I do what I always do—I wait another fifteen minutes to make sure she's really asleep. Sometimes she jerks awake and can't settle.

But tonight, thank God, she stays sleeping.

I stand up from the rocker quietly, grateful it doesn't creak. I tiptoe across the bedroom floor and out the door, closing it quietly behind me.

When I reach the downstairs, I stop short in the open doorway to the den. The sight in front of me makes my heart lurch.

Ayden's asleep on his back, his hands resting over his stomach. He never did shave today, and his dark scruff is so sexy my hand itches to reach out and touch it. His hat's off and lying next to him on the couch cushion, and his mouth is slightly parted. I step closer until I can kneel down next to him.

I glance over at the TV and reach for the remote to turn off the movie, some popular action flick Ayden and I have watched together more than once.

I put the remote down on the coffee table. As I go to stand up, Ayden's hand reaches out and circles my wrist. I turn back to find his clear blue eyes open and focused on me.

"Hey," he says, his voice raspy with sleep.

"Hey, sleepyhead." I reach out and brush his mess of dark hair off his forehead. "Sorry to wake you."

With his hand still around my wrist, he tugs until I'm lying next to him on the couch.

"How'd it go?" he asks quietly.

I rest my head on his chest, the sound of his strong heartbeat a welcome respite to the storm that feels like it's continuously blowing through my parents' house.

"It was actually pretty good. We talked a lot."

"Good."

I exhale. "Ayden, I'm scared."

He shifts so he can see my face. "Why?"

"What if she's never going to be happy again? Ever since I moved back, I keep thinking I can help her. I even went to a therapy session with her once."

"You did?" Ayden's lips part in surprise. "You never told me. Not that it's my business, of course."

"I wanted to tell you, but my mom's ashamed about going at all. She didn't want anyone to know she went to therapy with her daughter. It wasn't very productive though. You know I'm just worried about her."

He rests his chin on top of my head. "I wish I knew what to suggest, Bella. I hate seeing you so twisted up inside over her pain."

Just like always, his words alone soothe me. Knowing that he cares, that I don't have to explain why I'm so invested in my mother's life. His body next to mine is warm, and it's here.

He runs his hand down my back, gently rubbing in circles. I know the gesture is meant to be comforting, but when he reaches the middle of my back where the ridge of my bra strap pokes through, his hand stills.

Clenching my teeth together, I lie motionless as Ayden quickly shifts his hand to my hair. He tugs at the elastic of my ponytail until it drops onto the floor next to us, and my hair falls loose around my shoulders.

"Taking this out will help your headache." His hand rakes through my hair, and the sensations that course through me—

holy shit, goosebumps pop up all over my body, and now I'm drooling.

That's right—I actually drool on Ayden's t-shirt.

Fuck. I try to wipe it off without him noticing, but when I feel his body shaking, I know I'm busted.

He's still laughing when I force myself to look up and catch his eye.

"We all drool, Bella," he says, and I smack him in the arm.

"Shut up." I try to stand up, but his strong arm holds me in place. "It felt nice. I love having my hair touched. Apparently a little too much."

His ocean blue eyes are like freaking lasers as he scans my face. "Bella—"

When his cell phone vibrates on the coffee table, we jump apart. I sit up as Ayden reaches for his phone.

"Little late for someone to be texting you," I murmur. "Is everything all right?"

Ayden's eyes drop to his phone screen. "Yep. It's fine."

I study the sudden flush in his cheeks. "Booty call, huh?"

His eyes find mine, and I force an awkward laugh as I stand. "Who was it? Jenny? Or Ashley? Or is there another woman I don't know about?"

"B." Ayden stands up and grabs my textbook before I can. "It's nothing. Okay?"

I swallow. "That texter could be the answer to your dare. Don't dismiss her so quickly."

Before he can respond, I turn toward the door. "Let's go get our coffee."

———

Ayden and I step inside Al's Coffee House in the town square. Like every Tuesday at whatever hour we manage to make it out of my parents' house, we're the only ones here.

Ayden orders us our usual—a coffee for him and hot chocolate for me, and we take seats in the corner, on the maroon couch that's seen better days but is the most comfortable piece of furniture I've ever sat on.

"Tari and Peter are pretty strung out," Ayden says in a clear effort to move our conversation back to neutral footing. "I don't know how to help them."

"Unless you can magically make them pregnant..." I start to say. I take a look at Ayden's mischievous grin. "Don't finish that thought out loud, please."

He laughs. "I just meant that I feel bad they're hurting, but I can't really relate. I mean, I'm single, and I'm not looking to have kids."

"You're still serious about not having kids?" I ask him, trying to ignore the feeling of disappointment poking at me.

"I don't know." He abruptly avoids my gaze, focusing on his coffee in front of him.

"I understand. It's hard to envision something that seems so out of reach."

"You ever think about having kids?" Ayden asks suddenly.

I halt, my cup of hot cocoa halfway to my mouth. "Not so much."

I think I'm scared to love someone that much. To feel the love of your own child is something that scares me nearly senseless. The way my mother just shut me out because of her own hurt was so all-consuming, and I don't ever want to pass that pain down to anyone else.

"Yeah." He searches my face.

"I think you'd make an amazing father, Ayden," I say softly.

Our eyes catch and hold, and heat rushes through my body.

"I can't imagine raising a child right now," he says finally. "Beers at the beach, shovel in one hand and a rake in the other...what do I have to teach somebody?"

"You've taught me a lot," I say. "It's about the love, not the way of life."

"Yeah." He shrugs. "I guess so. I'd never let my son be a fisherman, though."

I don't say anything, but then he adds, "But I guess I couldn't really stop him, could I?"

We finish our drinks in relative silence. I can't get Ayden's booty call out of my head.

And he knows it too. He tilts his head at me cockily, his eyebrow half-up like he wants to hear what's on my mind. Almost like he's daring me to.

But I'm in no mood to play games with something that could burn me forever.

My thoughts return to the matter at hand.

Ayden's moving.

And we're involved in a dare neither of us planned on.

I fidget uncomfortably on the couch and drink my hot chocolate rapidly.

Maybe Trevor's invite was like when the spotlight shined on him and Max in L.A. A second angel in disguise for me. If that's the case, I need to take this dare seriously and commit to finding a real-life romantic partner. No matter what happens with Ayden and his multitude of women, I need to focus on my own romantic issues.

Yes, Ayden's my best friend, and sometimes he feels like my soul mate. But he and I vowed a long time ago that we'd never be more than friends. And I can't take that risk. If I lost Ayden, I don't know what I'd do.

So. If Ayden's not an option, the question is—who?

CHAPTER FOUR

"Ask Ayden out," Tari whispers into my ear a few nights later as we sit at the Lucky Bay Bar. "He'll be your forever plus one. That will solve all your problems—you don't lose the dare, and you get to keep Ayden at the same time."

"I can't do that," I say as I turn on my barstool to look at her.

"Why not?" Tari says as she finishes her third whiskey sour. "I bet he's a fucking stallion in bed."

I tip my head back and laugh with her as I glance sideways at the man we're chatting about.

Ayden, standing a foot away with Peter, catches my eye and winks.

And the part of me that always melts for my best friend—well, that part melts all over again.

The four of us came here tonight to scope out potential date options for Ayden and me, and the evening has quickly devolved into light-hearted but intense arguing and drinking. Ayden hates on sight every guy Tari suggests for me, and Tari nixes all of Peter's recommendations for Ayden. And the more Tari drinks, the worse her mouth gets.

"You know what her nickname is? Town whore," she says when Peter points to Amy Allen.

I choke on my whiskey. "Tari!"

"What?" She bats her blue eyes innocently. "You know it's true, Bella. She'll sleep with literally anyone. And probably has." She turns on Ayden. "Have you ever slept with her, Ayd?"

Ayden raises an eyebrow. "I don't kiss and tell."

Tari turns my stool so we're facing away from him and Peter. "Can you believe Ayden?" Tari whispers to me.

"It's nothing new. I don't like Trey any more than he likes Amy or Jenny, and yet we still go out with them."

"How come?" she asks.

When I glance toward Ayden, Tari says, "You need to step it up, Bella."

I open my mouth to argue her.

"Lifelong best friends to lovers is just so romantic," she says.

"Tar, this isn't a romance novel. It's Lucky Bay, Maine." And life feels as real as it can get up here.

"But you deserve a man you know will have your back no matter what. Nobody else will be there for you the way Ayden Wild will. He'd take a bullet for you if he had to. You know that as well as I do. Plus, what's the harm in one date? Or one night of intense fucking?" Tari says, realizing too late by my expression that she needs to rein it in.

"You know no date, however small or brief, ever seems harmless to me. And Ayden and I...that's just not going to happen."

I sneak a glance over at Amy Allen. Her miniskirt leaves little to the imagination, not to mention her skin-tight shirt that shows more than a hint of cleavage. She's facing our group and eyeing Ayden flirtatiously. He probably has already had sex with her. My stomach plummets.

I return my attention to our circle of four and realize Ayden's focus is fixed on me. As I catch his eye, he gives a nearly imperceptible shake of his head. I exhale, trying to ignore the clear feeling of relief coursing through me.

So there's still one man in town Amy hasn't had, apparently.

Funny because I never thought of Ayden as discriminating with women.

I give him a second look.

His long-sleeved, moss green shirt brings out the mix of color in his eyes that peek out from underneath his always-there cap. He's got one hand wrapped around a bottle of beer, and he stuffs the other casually into his jeans pocket as he nods at something Peter's saying. Peter's messy blond hair falls into his face, and he brushes it away as he continues talking to Ayden. As quarterback and top receiver on Lucky Bay's varsity football squad, Ayden and Peter always made a good team. Peter likes to say that because of all the catches he hauled in, he's the reason Ayden still holds the touchdown record for state quarterback.

He also should hold the record for number of women throwing themselves at him.

As if on cue, a woman with bright red lipstick and razor straight black hair past her shoulders steps into Ayden's space. Within seconds, she's got her hand on his chest.

I bite down on my lip and avert my gaze.

Tari's blue eyes widen. "What is it?"

"Nothing," I say quickly. "It's just..."

She looks behind me and huffs out a loud breath. "Good Lord, women circle Ayden Wild like he's the only man left alive."

"They certainly do," I say in response.

She swirls her drink around as she keeps her attention focused over my shoulder. "Ayden always disappoints me when he flirts meaninglessly and dates meaninglessly. I can't imagine how it feels for you."

The thing is Ayden and I were always from two different worlds. While he was the town football star, I was definitely not a cheerleader. I was the girl who got straight A's and stood in the bleachers, watching the crowd rush the field when our team won. Watching all those girls hang on Ayden after every game was trying at best.

But I got used to it. I like to believe I became numb to it.

Until this past week.

"It shouldn't bother me," I say to Tari. "First of all, we're here to find dates, so my reaction is completely antithetical to our purpose tonight. Second, I've seen Ayden Wild with other women thousands of times. And yet, to be completely honest, recently it seems like it does. Bother me."

"You mean it bothered you less before you knew he was leaving town," Tari says. "Well, of course. Because then you thought you had time."

"Time?"

"Time for things to play out," she explains. "Time to maybe one day discuss your relationship. But now, time's running, baby. That's the problem."

Yes, that is the problem. Time is running, and I don't have a clue how to slow it down long enough to figure out my heart.

Needing space from the intensity of this conversation, I turn to Ayden and Peter. "I just don't think you can trust people in California," I say, gesturing in a wide circle with my hand. "I mean, where did they come from?"

"What the hell are you talking about?" Ayden snorts, immediately turning away from the woman still clinging to his side. The woman frowns and disappears back into the crowd.

I respond by reaching over, grabbing Ayden's cap, and putting it on my head. He grins at me and lets it stay there. I smile back at him, wondering if I keep the hat, I can keep a part of him here with me too.

"I'm with Bella," Tari says, finishing the rest of her drink. "California wasn't even in the Revolutionary War."

Ayden and Peter laugh, and Peter plants a sweet kiss on Tari's won't-shut-up mouth.

"You're right, Tar," I say to her. "Without that war, where would America be?"

"Bella didn't tell all of you before now, but it was actually her and not Paul Revere who rode the horse that night," Ayden says.

"I'm just saying from experience, that people who didn't grow up on this land—New England—are different that's all. You can't always trust them."

"What about my cousins?" Ayden asks. "You trust all of them, and not a one is from here."

"That's different," I say. "They're related to you, so by extension, they're from here. And Jenson's from Pennsylvania, so even though he's not blood, he's still from the northeast."

"Aren't there like a ton of east coasters living in California?" asks Peter.

"Yeah," says Ayden. "They get there in this really wild way. They fly on something called airplanes. They're like this machine with wings and..."

"Oh, whatever." I laugh and give Ayden back his hat. He doesn't put it on, though. He studies me for a second and then returns the hat to my head.

"So why are you going to California, Ayd?" Tari asks him suddenly.

Ayden stiffens. Clearly, Tari's hit a sore spot.

"You never did really say why," I say to him softly.

"Later," he says only to me. "I promise. Okay?"

The pain in his eyes scares me, but I pat his arm. "Okay."

Peter breaks the awkwardness when he brings up some story from their football glory days, and I lean forward and gently put Ayden's hat back on his head. He gives me the thumbs-up as I say quietly to Tari, "I can't believe we involved you and Peter in our mess."

Tari laughs heartily, her blue eyes brightening with amusement. "I'm happy to help, to be honest. Sitting around, checking to see if I'm ovulating and then trying—and continually failing—to conceive isn't exactly my idea of a good time. You and Ayden have provided a welcome distraction."

I give her a hug. "Maybe the appointment with your doctor will help clarify things. Maybe those tests you took will provide some answers."

"Maybe. We've been trying for over a year."

"I know. It will be okay, Tar."

"Thanks, honey." Tari's expression turns sad before she raises her hand to signal the bartender. "You know what would help me? Another round of drinks."

The flirty guy on the barstool to my right grins at me. "Let me get you another one of those whiskeys you're drinking." He signals the bartender. "Hey! Get this pretty blonde with the gorgeous hazel eyes a fresh one."

Tari elbows me from my other side. "How about him?" she says. "He's super cute."

"No," Ayden says from behind us.

"Why not?" Tari says, turning on him. "What's wrong with him?"

"He's got red hair," he says simply. "Untrustworthy."

The guy next to me chuckles. "Good luck getting a date with him around," he says to me.

Tari throws up her hands and glares at Ayden. "Then who? Find me one man in this bar who you think is worthy of taking Bella Wesley on a date."

Ayden pulls at the brim of his cap as he gives the bar a cursory glance. "I don't see anyone," he says, giving me a shrug.

I roll my eyes. "I couldn't possibly find the right man with you hawking every guy here. You're so negative, Ayd."

He abruptly braces both hands against the bar-top on either side of me and leans in so close I nearly gasp.

His eyes darken. "And exactly who have you found tonight that you'd like me to ask out on a date? Because I seem to recall that when Peter suggested a certain someone earlier..."

"Amy Allen," I say.

"Right. When Peter suggested her, you were acting pretty..."

I flush with heat, but he cuts off in time. Because I know what he was going to say. I was acting pretty...

Jealous.

And he'd be right.

I let out a slow breath of air as he drops his arms and backs up a step. He searches my face for a second, and then he leans in again and his warm breath tickles my skin.

"Let's go home," he says in my ear.

"We were supposed to help each other with our dares, remember?" I say. "We came here to find dates."

"I am helping you," he says. "Nobody here is worth your time."

"Sure they are!" Tari says from my side. "What about that cute blond I introduced Bella to? He was very friendly."

"He was very married," Peter says.

Flirty redhead next to me chuckles. I glance over at him, and he grins at me.

Ayden shoots him a death stare and shoves his hat down further over his untamed hair. "Come on. It's nearly closing time."

"But Bella's trying to find her plus one," Tari says softly.

"That's right," I say.

Ayden pulls at the brim of his cap and glowers at me. "That douche's wedding invite fucked with your head, B. Let's forget the dare. You don't need to find anybody."

"I do," I say so firmly his eyebrows rise in surprise. "Not for his wedding. Of course I'm not going to that. But it's time, Ayden. It's time for me to start dating for real. I haven't dated anyone seriously since Trevor." I pause and then say the truth. "I think I'm ready."

Ayden swallows and doesn't speak for a moment. When he does, his voice is so low I have to strain to hear him. "You've let guys hit on you tonight that don't deserve to breathe the same air as you. One of those assholes was staring at your breasts the entire time you talked."

"He was not!" *Shit. Was he?* I mentally try to backtrack to which guy he's referring to.

"He was. And this joker on your right—he's not looking for commitment." Ayden's wallet is out and he's signaling to the bartender.

"Hey!" the guy protests. "Watch what you're saying, dude." He turns to me. "Um, are you two...together?" He gestures between Ayden and me.

I shake my head. "Nope. We made a pact to never date."

He gives a glaring Ayden one last curious look before turning back to me. "Let me give you my number. Maybe we can set up a date."

I smile at him. "That would be lovely." I turn back to Ayden triumphantly. "See? He seems willing to commit."

Ayden snorts. "Right."

I type flirty guy's number into my phone, and he waves goodbye before disappearing into the crowd.

Tari's definitely feeling the effects of the alcohol now, and she giggles and pats Ayden's cheek. "You certainly *are* grouchy tonight!" she says. "Could it be because Bella's hunting for a man? Ayden, you do know Bella's been on a couple of dates this summer already, right? Just because she and Trey aren't exclusive doesn't mean she's asexual."

Ayden's eyes flick to mine, and I stare right back at him. But Tari's still talking.

"Ayd, you're such a player, and you're dating at least two women right now, yet you're acting like you wish you and Bella could..."

Peter's hand over her mouth shuts her up before she can finish.

I avert my eyes from Ayden's piercing ones, those sparkling chips of sea-colored diamonds that can read me like a book.

"You know what?" I say. "Forget looking for more guys here. I got one number, and maybe I'll call him. But I think I'll just start by going out on another date with Trey."

Ayden's eyes flash. "I thought that was just a casual thing. You didn't seem to think he could turn into a man you'd be serious with."

"Yeah, Bella," Peter says teasingly. "What about that?"

I glare at both of them. "I'm giving him another chance," I say. "I'll text him right now and set up something for tomorrow."

"I leave for L.A. tomorrow," Ayden says quickly.

"So?" I laugh. "Last I checked, you don't join me on my dates."

Tari raises her glass. "That's it! Yay! You two can double-date."

"No," Ayden and I both say immediately.

But Peter puts his arm around Tari. "That's a great idea, babe. Ayden and Bella *did* agree to help each other out, right? And, they're technically competitors. Two dares means whoever completes theirs first is the winner."

"So?" I say to him.

Peter, in his usual teasing mood, grins at me. "So, what better way to keep an eye on your competition than by going out together?"

"I'm game," Ayden says, surprising the heck out of me.

What is his angle? I know he must have one. Ayden and I have never been on a double date in our lives.

But I'm too buzzed to figure it out. "We can try one double-date, I suppose, when Ayden comes back."

"Who will be the lucky woman you take out, Ayd?" Tari asks him.

"Jenny," I say, as Ayden's eyes widen at me in surprise.

"Jenny? As in Jenny Woods, the new bartender at the pool hall?" Tari wags her finger in the air, and I bite back a smile at how she's weaving back and forth on her stool so much that her wavy hair falls into her face. "She just moved to town. So she's the new girl here. You know what that means, boys?"

Peter and Ayden look at her in mild amusement.

"That means easy." She tips her head back and downs the rest of her drink. "Don't you want a challenge, Ayden? Or are you too scared?"

Ayden chuckles, and Peter takes the empty glass out of Tari's hand. "All right, my little lush. That's enough alcohol for tonight."

But I nod. "Maybe you're right, Tar. Ayden does need a woman who will challenge him. I don't think I've ever seen that."

Peter finally convinces Tari they have to go. She throws her arms around me like she won't see me again for a year.

"I still can't believe Ayden's moving," she says in my ear. "You two definitely need to fuck before he leaves, Bella."

"Oh my God, keep your voice down!" I shout-whisper to her. "That is so not happening!"

"Why not? Use your dare on Ayden! And don't tell me you won't because of the damn pact you two made when you were kids. I don't know which one of you is more stubborn, but one of you will crack before Ayden leaves town. Peter and I even have a bet going."

"What! You and your husband bet on us?"

Tari giggles. "Peter thinks Ayden will break first, and I say it's you. Just put your lips on his dic…"

I pull her closer to me, glancing over my shoulder to make sure Ayden didn't overhear. Luckily, he's busy arguing with Peter over something.

"We'll talk tomorrow," I say as I kiss Tari's cheek. "Good night."

———

Ayden

"So how's this going to work exactly?" Peter's tone is filled with humor, and I barely resist smacking him.

"Shut up, and just help me through it," I mutter. "I need a damn date for this double-date shit you and your wife just talked me into."

"Why don't you ask Ashley?" he says. "You've already been seeing her."

"That's over," I say. "She wanted more. So I told her I can't. End of story."

"Okay. Well, what about Jenny?"

I unclench my jaw long enough to mutter, "Fine. One date with Jenny."

"I can't wait to watch this unfold," he says with a smirk. "If you and Bella ever agree to a second date with anyone in this town, can Tari and I accompany you? You know, for full entertainment value."

"Fuck off." I punch his arm. "I'm doing this for Bella. Not me. I don't plan to win. I just can't quit on her."

"But you're going to take the dare seriously?"

I shrug. "Seriously enough. But I know I won't find the right woman this summer."

"What if neither of you finds 'the one?' What then?"

Then I'll be fucking relieved the selfish part of me says.

I lift my beer to Peter's. "Then I'll move to L.A. still single. Like I planned on."

"And Bella? What about her?"

I look over at her laughing with Tari. "Bella will be fine," I say, as much to assure myself as him. "I'll make sure of it."

CHAPTER FIVE

Bella

After Tari and Peter leave, Ayden and I are quick to head for the door.

But before we make it halfway, a woman grabs him. She's got porcelain skin and curly blond hair that frames her pretty face perfectly. She gives me a look like, "I know exactly how to get his attention," as she curls her hand around his bicep and squeezes.

And here we go again.

While Ayden turns to acknowledge her, and I try to tamp down my newfound jealousy, a familiar-looking guy puts his arm around me. "You want to dance?"

I may have had too much to drink, but that doesn't mean I'll accept a dance with a man who's leering while he leans heavily on me like he can barely hold himself up. "I'm not interested," I say as I pull away.

"Oh," he says with a glance at Ayden's back. "You're with him." He snorts. "Out on the boat, we call his family cursed."

"Shut the hell up," I say as I recognize the man now. He's part of the crew for one of the lobster boats in town, but he's not on Ayden's brother's boat. "Ayden's amazing. He's the opposite of cursed."

"His father sure was. And his brother's just as much of a risk-taker, going out on the water when the tides are dangerous." The man turns in Ayden's direction and shouts to get his attention. "Good thing you don't like the seas, huh?"

"Don't you dare talk to him that way," I say, feeling my voice rise an octave.

"Bella." Ayden turns and his eyes find mine. "Let it go. He's just jealous Michael's boat has outperformed his the last five years and counting."

In that moment, the curly blonde makes a grab for Ayden's hat. She manages to get it off his head and turns for the dance floor with a loud giggle.

Ayden gives the guy a murderous glance and then storms after her.

Once Ayden's out of sight, the guy steps into me again. "You want some of me, honey?"

"Actually," I say. "I'm pretty sure I made it clear that I don't."

But the guy pins me to his chest and his arms come around me hard. I have a moment of panic as I realize how much bigger he is than me. Then I remember what I learned in the self-defense class Ayden made sure I took before I left for L.A. at eighteen: *A man's two weakest points are his nose and his groin. When you go for it, don't hold back.*

I have just enough room between us to line my knee up with his crotch and I take aim.

He sinks to the floor with a wail.

"And you weren't listening," I say.

"Bitch," he spits at me.

I don't have time to respond before Ayden's fist smashes into the jerk's face and sends him flat on his back.

"Don't you ever fucking touch her or talk to her like that again," Ayden growls. "Say you're sorry. Like you mean it."

"I'm sorry," the man gets out before Ayden kicks him in the ribs for good measure.

Now we've attracted a crowd, including the guy's equally-wasted buddy.

He swings at Ayden's face, but Ayden easily ducks and avoids the hit, sending the man off-balance and falling in a heap on the floor next to his friend.

"You should teach your crewmate how to treat women," Ayden says.

I turn on the man, prepared to curse him out, but I'm tugged back by the waistband of my jeans into the solid chest of Ayden Wild.

"Let's go," he says into my ear.

I turn around and touch his arm gently. "This isn't about me, Ayd. They're disrespecting you!"

"They can't disrespect me when they're only spewing lies," he says. He twists the brim of his cap tightly in his hand, and I know he's thinking about his father. "I'm more worried about you right now."

"Hey!" Flirty guy appears next to me. "You want to dance before you leave?"

Before I can respond, Ayden mutters something about limits and breaking points.

"Bella, say good night," he says. "If he cares about you at all, he'll realize you need to leave."

Ayden puts his arm around my waist and turns me toward the door.

———

We don't stop moving until we've made it outside the bar and down to the rocks overlooking the high tide below. At first, all I hear are the waves, big and loud, breaking against the shore.

"This is why I don't get drunk," I say to him.

Ayden, all six foot two of him, stands across from me, his gaze assessing and gentle beneath his hat. He takes my chin between his thumb and forefinger. "I like seeing you get drunk once in a while. You let go."

I flush with heat. "What's that supposed to mean? I'm fine. I know you're worried because you think this is about you moving..."

His eyes narrow like I've revealed my hand. "Is it?"

Shit. I clamp my jaw shut and go silent.

He takes off his hat and drags a hand through his inky black hair. Hair that was previously unruly is now downright wild, and I fight the urge to run my fingers through it and put my mouth on his. Knowing that idea is off-limits, I turn away from him and stare down at the water softly lit by the moon.

But Ayden catches my wrist gently and turns me to face him. He takes both my hands in his so I can't walk away. "Bella, when that invitation came, I'm sure it brought up a lot of shit. And then the shitty timing of me telling you I was leaving. I wish I'd known about the invite before I told you, or..."

"Or what?" I ask him. "You wouldn't have taken the job? Come on, Ayd. It's okay. Sure, the timing was weird, but that certainly wasn't your fault."

"I'm just saying, after all the stuff that went down in L.A., I'd be angry too."

I bite my lip, willing myself to keep my feelings private. "It's okay," I say in a soft tone. "I'm okay."

But like he often does when it comes to me, Ayden Wild lays down a challenge.

"Say to my face that you're not angry, and I'll drop it."

"Fine." I take a deep breath, and then say as steadily as I can, "I'm. Not. Angry. Okay?"

Apparently not convinced, Ayden shakes his head. "I mean in the three years you've been back, I've never once seen you get angry about it all. Aren't you pissed off, Bella? About the way you felt forced back here? And about what you found waiting for you when you returned?"

"It wasn't her fault," I say in a monotone.

"It also wasn't *your* fault," he says empathically. "You know that right?"

I mumble a few curse words and duck my head so he can't see the pain I know is taking over my face. But I've never been able to run from Ayden for long. He takes me in his arms, and when I try to pull away, he just holds on tighter.

Exhausted, I stop fighting him. I grip onto his shirt and cry silent tears into his rock-hard chest that's always been there for me but will soon be heading for the place where I chased my own dreams. Ayden and L.A. will be together, and I'll be here in Lucky Bay, Maine.

"You'll be okay," he says into my hair.

I lift my head and lock eyes with him. His blue eyes are almost green right now, and his jaw tenses like he wants to say something.

"I won't give up if you don't give up," he finally murmurs as he wipes the tears off my face.

I put my arms around him again and lean my cheek against his chest. "I just need to find my plus one," I whisper into his shirt. "And you're not on the available list."

He inhales sharply, and I know he heard what I said. For a second, I think he's going to answer me.

But he doesn't, and I keep holding onto him.

———

Ayden

Bella's driving me crazy tonight. She let that barstool jerk flirt with her, buy her drinks, and ask her out. And all I was thinking the entire time was—*I should be the one she's flirting with. I should be the one taking her out. And I desperately want to be the one taking her into my bed.* All of which is ridiculous to even contemplate because Bella Wesley may be beautiful and sexy as fuck, but she and I are best friends. Not lovers. And until this week, I haven't allowed myself to think of her that way. Ever.

Next to me, she stumbles and I catch her with my hand,

keeping her upright as we cross the empty Main Street. She leans into my side, and now—*Christ*—I can't get out of my head the thought of stopping in the middle of the sidewalk to kiss her. Which is nuts on an average day, but right now? I'm leaving town and moving three thousand miles away. Talk about complicated.

As we turn onto Bella's street and head for her house, she snuggles further into my arm, and my heart lurches in my chest.

Outside of my four cousins and Jenson, for as long as I can remember, Bella's been the one constant bright light in my life. If it weren't for her, I may not have been brave enough to accept the incredible job offer in L.A. Sure, two of my cousins live out there, and I'm closer to them than I am to my own brother. Knowing Colton and Dylan will be around to hang out with is awesome. But if Bella hadn't already taken the risk to live somewhere other than Lucky Bay, I never would have considered moving so far away.

Besides, I need this job. When I told my boss what was going on, he put in a call for me. And while the idea of leaving Bella is gut-wrenching, I need to take care of my mom and brother.

And the truth is, I don't think all of Bella left California when she returned to Maine. When I'm in L.A., I'll be able to feel her spirit out there, like she'll still be with me somehow.

She struggles to unlock her front door, and I take the key from her gently and let us both inside. I pour her a glass of water and make her a snack, and I'm putting them on her bedside table when she returns from the bathroom in a t-shirt and sweatpants. She's no longer wearing a bra, and the outline of her breasts shows through the thin fabric of her shirt. I swallow and try not to stare, but her nipples are saluting me.

"Bella." My voice comes out too harsh. "Get into bed."

She climbs in, and I pull the covers up to her neck. "Sweet dreams."

I kiss her cheek and smooth back her hair and then turn out the bedroom light. As I leave her house and head for my own place a couple blocks away, I feel an emptiness fill me. It's unsettling, and the thought of Bella returning to Los Angeles enters my brain.

Part of me feels like a selfish bastard for wanting her to come there with me, but the other part of me knows she'll never be happy if she doesn't try again. Her dream is music. All she ever wanted was to be a singer. And I would love nothing more than to help her get that dream back.

I run my hand down my face as I jog up my front steps and unlock my door.

Maybe there's a way...I don't know how yet, but maybe Bella could actually move out west again, and I wouldn't have to leave my best friend behind after all.

CHAPTER SIX

Bella

I wake up Wednesday morning to a text from Ayden.

Stop by my mom's this morning if you can before work. I leave at ten for the airport.

———

As I walk up the long driveway to Ayden's mother's house, my heart is heavy. In just a short while, Ayden and I will be saying goodbye for real. Ayden is my go-to, and the idea of him not being here anymore sends me into a sea of sadness.

I stop short to touch up my lips with the pink lipstick I just bought. As I run the lipstick over my bottom lip, unbidden thoughts of Ayden kissing me flash through my head. I push them away immediately and shove the lipstick into the back pocket of my black jeans.

I'm going to kill Tari. She's gotten me on a dangerous track of thinking about Ayden in a romantic sense, and that can't happen. Okay fine, I can't actually blame Tari. The truth is, all these sexy Ayden thoughts have been coming mainly from my own newly-warped brain.

Being with Ayden has always been easy. Being with boyfriends has not been easy, and the one time I thought it was, I shouldn't have. Trevor should have come with a huge warning sign on his forehead so I would have known better and walked away quick.

I smile as soon as I catch sight of Ayden packing up his car. He always comes here right before he leaves on a trip, to reassure his mother that he's going to come back and not disappear into the air, or the sea like his father did.

"Hey," Ayden calls out, and I feel my heart lighten. It's amazing how just one little word can do that to somebody, can make you feel something when you haven't been feeling much of anything.

I wave and walk closer, as close as I can without touching him. As usual, Ayden's dark messy hair is half-hidden underneath his Sox cap, and my gaze shifts from his worn jeans up to his fitted green shirt. I get lost on his mouth for a few extra seconds before finally raising my gaze to meet his. We lock eyes, and he lifts an eyebrow.

"You still drunk?" he teases.

I playfully tap his arm. "No, I'm doing fine. And I'm sorry about the other night. I got emotional and..."

He cuts me off. "No apologies, B. Not to me."

His deep blue eyes with more than a hint of green swirl with emotion, and I realize for about the millionth time why so many women have gotten lost in them over the years. I know I should count myself lucky that I'm not one of those lost souls, but sometimes I regret making that childhood pact. Maybe Tari's right. Maybe this really is my last chance to see if Ayden and I could be perfect together, perfect as more than best friends.

I brush off my private thoughts and smile. "The Lucky Bay Clam Festival won't be the same without you. I'll need somebody new to eat fried clams with and ride on the state's oldest carousel."

Ayden touches my cheek. "I'll be back for it. In fact, Peter said that's where we should have our double-date."

"Seriously? That sounds like a long-ass date if you ask me."

"We can cut out early if Jenny and the tool are boring us." He winks at me, and I cross my arms over my chest.

"*Trey*—not tool—does not bore me," I say.

Ayden smirks. "Right. So why were you worrying about the length of the date? You and I always spend the entire day together at the clam festival. In fact"—he takes a step closer to me—"we usually go out afterwards too."

"That's different."

"How?"

"You and I are..." I stumble. "We're...us."

He taps my nose with his finger. "Exactly."

I try to tamp down how incredibly hot I suddenly am while Ayden fixes his landscaping bag in the front seat of his age-old sedan. He bends over to shift the bag across the seat, and the way his jeans hang low on his hips and then hug every inch of his perfect ass...*God, shut up, Bella.*

"Will that all fit in the overhead?" I pick up his coat from the driveway of his parents' house. I should say his mother's house; his father's been gone for nearly fifteen years now. And yet, I feel I'm being disrespectful or something, like I've forgotten about him. Like I could.

Ayden takes the coat from my hands and tosses it into the back, right next to a duffel bag. "I hope so." He reaches over and brushes a stray hair back off my face. I reach for my bun automatically in an attempt to fix it.

He stuffs his hands in his pockets, a sure sign that he's nervous about something. There's a long pause and then—

"Come with me, Bella."

And suddenly it feels like we're talking about more than just this trip.

I stare at him. "I...can't."

Ayden doesn't say anything; he just waits quietly for what we both know is coming.

"I can't leave my mom. Not while she's so...unbalanced."

"She needs professional help, honey," he says in a gentle tone. "You can only do so much."

"She sees a psychiatrist weekly," I say. "What are you saying— she needs to be locked up?"

I nearly choke on the words, and Ayden reaches for my hand.

"Of course not," he says. "I just mean you can't sacrifice your life for your mother, Bella. One day, maybe she'll realize that too."

I go silent, not sure what to say to that.

"Okay, do me a different favor." His energy shifts, and he grins at me in an obvious attempt to lighten the subject matter.

Too grateful for the change in topic to worry about whatever he's going to say next, I look at him expectantly. "What is it?"

"Don't go on any dates while I'm gone."

I burst out laughing.

But when I look back at Ayden, his jaw is tight, and his eyes are clear and focused on me.

"You're serious?" I ask him.

"Yes, I'm dead serious."

"Why? You never like my dates anyway."

He steps closer to me. "Because I'm asking you not to."

Irritation flares through me. "Oh really? And what about you? You'll be in L.A. for days, and no doubt hordes of women will be hitting on you."

"I swear to you that I won't touch another woman while I'm gone."

What?

I reach out and touch his forehead. "Are you feeling okay?"

I stare up at Ayden's face, searching his expression. His cheeks flush ever so slightly, but he doesn't give anything else away.

Fishing for clarity, I say casually, "But you've been sort of dating Jenny..."

He shrugs. "Sort of."

Does "sort of" mean *"Jenny and I are fucking?"*

I push onward. "And she's who you're taking on our double date?"

"I guess so."

"Okay. Well, I'm taking Trey. As you know, we're sort of dating also."

Oh my God, this is not a pissing contest. *Shut up, Bella. Just shut up.*

Ayden throws out a quick grin and returns to his usual laid-back mode. "Bella. Wait for me to come home. Even though we're rooting for each other, this is still a competition, right?"

I narrow my eyes. "So me not going out on any dates while you're away is all about you wanting to win your dare and making sure I don't 'get ahead' of you."

He shifts so he's leaning against his car. "Not only that, no. We're also supposed to be helping each other, aren't we? Since we both admittedly suck at this dating thing, I thought it would be best if neither of us gets off track while we're apart."

My voice softens. "Of course. That makes sense."

"Great." Ayden flips his baseball cap backward and leans in to kiss my cheek.

And just like that, I vow to stop being jealous about Ayden's girlfriends. The reason Ayden and I made that promise to only be friends is for moments like this—so we can be there for each other, no matter what. I love Ayden far too much to risk losing him for a few days of good—okay, I'm sure it would be fucking *amazing*—sex.

I smile up at him brightly, and he cocks his head like he's trying to figure out what just went on in my brain. I lick my lips involuntarily, and Ayden abruptly pulls me closer to him in a tight embrace. My hand automatically goes to his chest where I feel the hard thumping of his heart. His arm wraps around my waist, and his fingers find their way to the gap between my tank top and the waistband of my fitted jeans. When he touches my hot skin, I bite back a gasp.

"We'll figure out the details when I come back." His voice in my ear is low and filled with promise. "And you didn't call that redhead from the bar last night, did you? He's definitely not close to good enough for you."

Before I can answer him, his brother pushes open the screen door of his apartment that sits on top of the detached garage next to the Wild house. His mother opens the front door of the house a second later like she's been listening for signs of Michael's leaving.

"Michael? Michael! Wait!"

Ignoring her calls, Michael storms down the wooden stairs to his truck with his mother's shouts following him.

"Michael Patrick Wild, I do not want you going out on the water today! It's supposed to storm later—remember how your father died?!"

"How could I forget, Ma?" Michael screams back. "You only mention it every fucking day!"

Ayden lets go of my waist, and I step back from him as Michael walks past us without a word and gets into his truck. Ayden stares after his brother, his only visible reaction the clenching of his jaw.

Next to the front door of the Wild's saltbox home, the anchor from Mr. Wild's boat rests against the wall. A gift from the crew who lived.

Anna Wild kneels down in front of it now and crosses herself as Michael peels out of the driveway. "Hail Mary, full of Grace, the Lord is with thee. Blessed art thou..."

I fight the urge to cross myself. When she's finished with the prayer, she stands up and turns toward us.

"Hi, Bella, honey!"

I wave at her. "How are you, Anna?"

"Wonderful. Did Ayden invite you to the party?"

Ayden groans. "Ma, I haven't had a chance yet."

Anna waves a finger at him. "Tell her all the details! Bella, it won't be the same without you—make sure you save the date! It's the day before July fourth."

"Okay, thank you for the invitation!" I call back to her.

"Ayden, you'll call me when you land, right?" Anna asks him.

"You know I will." He walks over to her and gives her a hug.

I can't hear what she says to him, but I make out scattered words like "be so proud" and "thank you."

I never like to push Ayden, but I'm wondering when he's going to open up and fill me in on exactly what this move to L.A. is all about.

After his mom disappears back inside the house, I wait as he jogs back to me.

"So." I tilt my head to where his mother was just standing. "What was that all about?"

He hesitates, and I know he's not going to answer my question. Instead, he says, "Looks like your mom's not the only one throwing a party this summer."

"Really? Your mom is hosting? With prayer and all?"

"Oh, I'm sure there'll be prayer." Ayden scowls. "It's the fifteenth anniversary of Dad's drowning."

I look underneath his cap at his sad eyes. "Fifteen years," I say softly.

"Yep." Ayden blows out a breath. "Ma, the fishermen who knew my dad, their wives, all decided to hold this party. For Dad and the others from that day, you know..."

He trails off, but I understand. All twelve men who died will be honored. Honored for drowning. For holding onto that anchor and never letting go, not until the bitter end.

"Fuck." Ayden grits his teeth, but the pain is etched all over his face. "I thought I could get out of here before it happened. But Ma made sure to change it when she heard about my new job. She's already told Colton and the rest of the cousins too. So of course they're all set on coming even though I told them I'd kill them if they did."

"I'm sure they just want to be there for you. He was their uncle, you know."

"I know." Three heartbeats pass before he says in a low tone, "Will you go to the party with me?"

"Of course I'll go. You know you don't have to ask, Ayd."

"Yeah." His eyes burn into mine. "But I mean be my date. What do you say?"

Did he just ask me out?

"Um..." I wrap my arms around my stomach.

Ayden's blue eyes sparkle. "I meant like a best friend date," he says. "I trust you, and I know you'll stick by me. I really don't want to go with anybody else. Say yes?"

I reach up and tug at the brim of his cap. "Absolutely. I'll be your date, your best friend, whatever you need, Ayden."

Ayden kisses the top of my head. "Thanks, Bella." He opens his car door and gets in. "I'll see you."

My stomach flutters. "Give everyone my love, and make sure to tell Jasalie I miss her."

"I will." He starts the engine, his eyes never leaving mine as he slowly backs out of the driveway.

"Fly safe, Ayd."

CHAPTER SEVEN

I stand motionless, staring after Ayden's car until I can't see it anymore.

Shit. Ayden just asked me to go to L.A. with him.

And I couldn't say yes.

My chest aches as I walk home the long way by the docks. I stare out at the beach and inhale the salty air of the incoming tide, swallowing down the emotion threatening to clog my throat.

———

Three days later, I still can't get Ayden's invitation out of my head. I spend the morning trying to study for the psychology exam I have next week.

But something's tugging at me, a memory I can't push down this time. I slam shut my psychology book and open up my basement door. I walk down the dimly-lit stairwell and open the large storage closet where I begin to pick through everything I've stuffed in here over the past few years. Something falls on my head, and as it drops to the ground, I realize it's two pictures stuck together back-to-back.

Ayden and I, no more than four years old, are in our swimsuits in the kiddie pool. Ayden's sporting a wide, toothy grin. I look serious, like I'm already practicing posing for the camera. He has his arm around me.

I turn the picture over to look at the second photograph. I'm alone with my guitar. My hair covers my face as I strum so I can't see my expression, how happy I am, but I can remember it like it just happened. Grandpa took that picture—me with my first guitar on my twelfth birthday.

I wrestle with myself for quite a while until the agony of limbo is finally worse than any action I could possibly take. And once I force myself out of my paralysis, I go to her immediately. She's been well-hidden all these years, but I know exactly where to find her. At the very back of the top shelf by the broken mini-fridge I never did take to the dump.

I climb up on a chair and take her down. The cover is so full of dust I start coughing. I open up the latches, pull my guitar out, and bring her upstairs. When I take out the pick and begin strumming, she's so out of tune that my notes sound like a screech owl. One of the frets is broken. And she's awfully musty.

I smile.

I forgot how much I'd missed her.

———

An hour later, I hurry into the Lucky Bay Pool Hall and go straight for the music lounge where I find Guy at the piano. He looks up and a smile spreads across his face.

"Bella Wesley. Good to see you in here."

He steps out from behind the piano.

"Hey!" I give him a hug. "Your hair looks great." I touch his dark waves that hang midway down his back. "I feel like I haven't seen you in forever. Even though we work in the same building."

"You don't usually hang out by the music lounge." His voice is quiet.

"True," I say softly.

He nods at the guitar case in my hand. "I have to say you look good holding a guitar again, girl."

My heart lifts and I smile at him. "Thanks. The thing is, she needs a little help getting back into playing shape. That's why I'm here."

I met Guy my junior year of high school. Tari and Peter were in the middle of a brief break-up, and Tari had an upcoming date with a boy who wanted to play pool. Neither of us knew a thing about it, so we went to the pool hall to try to figure it out.

Guy was older than me by a few years, but he'd seen me perform at an open mic, and he came up and introduced himself. We ended up playing together. He gave me stage pointers, and we both performed for the small crowds that would gather at the music lounge. It was a huge confidence booster for me because Guy had been to New York and Los Angeles and played there, and he told me I had what it takes. And because he could do it and had, I believed him.

He became my music mentor. He helped me with my songwriting and gave me lots of performing advice.

Guy gestures for me to follow him over to the wooden bench by the wall. "What's the problem?"

"A broken fret, and I think one of the knobs may be loose."

I unlatch the case, and together we take a look at the guitar.

"She looks pretty good," he says. "It won't take much to get her back to where she was before."

I look up and make contact with his knowing dark gaze. "I'll pay you for your time. Just let me know when you've finished with the repairs."

"If you want to wait around, it may not take too long."

"I wish I could. But I have to meet my mom. And just the very sight of me holding a guitar throws her into a bad mood."

My mother never liked hearing me sing even when I was a child. She and my father would regularly skip my school performances with one excuse or another. They weren't there when I sang my first solo, when I won first place in the talent competition, or when I was the lead in our town's rendition of Grease. Ayden and his mom, along with my grandfather, Tari and Peter, made sure to attend every one of my events, and while I valued their support more than I can say, their presence also made my parents' absence even clearer.

Mom wanted me to be a scientist, the first female in my family to obtain a PhD. She'd been pushing me toward it for as long as I can remember.

Except music was my dream. And moving to L.A. was something I'd been wanting to do for years. But once I made it there, I was so busy trying to keep up appearances for my parents with the excuse I'd given them in order to go to L.A. in the first place—the opportunity of a lifetime, to study marine biology—that the real me, the part of me I cared about, was drowning. I dropped out of the full-time biology program after freshman year of college, and my parents pulled all financial aid for me to continue classes. They were sure that would bring me back home to Lucky Bay.

But I was stubborn. I got a day job at an advertising firm for a boss who rightfully distrusted me because my heart wasn't in advertising. Bill was awful, but I met Jasalie there. We grew close, and working with her made things bearable. But in addition to my full-time job, I was trying to fit in singing and going to school part-time. Eventually, something had to give. I just didn't expect it would be my boyfriend and my music manager in one fell swoop. I was still short of my college degree when I left California, but this summer, I'll finally complete my coursework. I swore once I graduated college, I'd get a "real" job and stop holding onto my pipe dream of making it as a singer.

"So, anytime you want the stage again"—Guy gestures with his arm—"You got it, honey. Just let me know."

I swallow. Just the idea of it makes me want to throw up. Guy raises an eyebrow at me like he knows.

Performing is a full-on risk. You're either in or you're out. There is no middle ground in sticking your neck out as a performer. And I'm well aware of that, so I've chosen to take the coward's route for the last three years and stay on the ground. If my decision weren't haunting me so much, maybe I wouldn't be suffering.

"I appreciate the offer, Guy. Thanks."

He nods at me. "Take care of yourself, Bella. I'll let you know when your guitar's ready."

Maybe by then, I'll be ready too.

———

When I leave the pool hall and step onto the wooden walkway, I spot my grandfather waving from the docks.

He ambles his way over to me and wraps me in a big hug. I lean under Grandpa's Navy cap and give him a kiss on his wrinkled cheek.

"How'd it go this morning?" I ask him.

"It was a good morning." Grandpa nods and wipes his brow. "Hard time getting all the nets in, though. It's a windy day."

I glance at the big waves crashing onto the rocks. "It is."

Grandpa started going down to the docks after Grandma died. He was retired from banking and bored. He helps some of the local fishermen bring in the nets and anchor the boats. He also helps out with the tourist boat, The Madeleine, mainly because he enjoys meeting new people, and he loves being out on the water.

Grandpa eyes my long black skirt and cream blouse, the kind of outfit I only wear when I eat at a fancy restaurant. "Lunch with your mom, huh?"

I nod. "I'm worried her medication's not working right."

I meet my mother every week after her therapy session. She won't let me come to the appointments; she won't let me take her to the appointments; and she won't let me wait for her within a five-block circumference of the psychiatrist's office. So we've reached a tenuous agreement—we meet for lunch, at which point she's supposed to share with me any changes to her treatment plan.

I've tried to get my dad to come to the lunches as well, but he rarely has "time." He's too busy being a lawyer. Lucky Bay may be split between fishermen and doctor-lawyer professionals, but the two sides are bound together by the strong New England work ethic that pervades here. My father and Ayden's both worked the same hours—all twenty-four.

"Your mother..." Grandpa shakes his head. "She won't talk to me about any of this stuff. I try, but she shut me out the same day she shut out your father."

I swallow. "She stopped trusting men. It's not your fault."

His eyes are filled with sorrow. "She can't handle the pain," he says simply. "Everyone's built differently, Bella."

"I don't know," I say. "I'm not especially gifted in the emotions department myself."

"Bullshit," he says gruffly but with a twinkle in his eye. "You know how you feel. You know what you want. Don't pretend otherwise. Not to me and certainly not to yourself." He clears his throat. "So. You and Ayden."

I look at him in surprise. "That's quite a subject change, Grandpa. What about Ayden and me?"

"Are you two going to be okay? With him so far away?"

"Of course. We did this before, remember? I lived in L.A., and he stayed here."

"Yes, but you were so young. You left here at eighteen; in some ways, the break was probably good for you both. This time is different. You're both mature, and I think maybe it hurts more. No?"

I purse my lips. "I don't think we have a choice but to handle it the best we can."

Grandpa lifts a bushy white eyebrow and glowers at me. "You could go with him."

I roll my eyes. "Why is everyone suggesting that? It's completely impractical."

"Who else is suggesting it?" That eyebrow of his rises even higher on his forehead.

I give him a meaningful stare. "You're too nosy. And too intuitive."

He chuckles. "So Ayden wants you with him, does he? What'd you say?"

I don't answer, but Grandpa reads my expression. "Oh, no, sweetheart."

I throw up my hands. "What was I supposed to tell him? That I failed there once, in a very dramatic, public sort of fashion; but sure, I'll give it another whirl. That makes no sense!"

"What's right doesn't always make sense. Don't use your past to stop your future, Bella. Your mother froze herself in time. You don't have to."

"That's the thing, though—Mom. I couldn't live with myself if I left, and she..."

"Broke down again like she did the last time you moved to California?" Grandpa shakes his head. "Wasn't your fault. You know that. Deep down, you do."

"She's just so fragile right now. I'd like to see her stabilize." I pause and say what's on my mind. "The other thing is, Ayden and I...we're just friends. And moving across the country together feels like something couples do. Not best friends."

Grandpa winks at me. "Sounds like you two have a lot to work out."

Sounds like we do.

I kiss Grandpa goodbye and walk across the square to The Mainer restaurant.

As I reach the front door, I glance through the front windows and see Mom already seated at her favorite table.

My chest aches at the view of my mother's pinched face through the glass. I can feel her pain from here, and I know that loss doesn't always have to come from death. Sometimes somebody lives but is anchored under water all the same.

I suck in a breath and plaster on a smile as I walk through the door and over to my mother's table.

She flicks her gaze to me briefly and taps the round table in a clear gesture to hurry up and sit down.

I nod cheerily as I take a seat across from her. "How are you doing?"

"I'm fine," she says in her usual clipped tone.

I want to ask her to please tell me the truth for once. But I don't.

Instead, I glance up at the chandelier lights hanging from the ceiling. I feel like I'm living in the 1800s when I come here. I turn my attention to the sterile white tablecloth in front of me.

"Beautiful cloth, isn't it?" Mom says, noticing my gaze.

I nod politely.

"They do such a lovely job here."

I look back at my mother, forcing my eyes to focus in a way they've never wanted to. Lucy Wesley looks the same as always—dark hair up in a tight bun, black jacket, and dress pants. Sometimes she wears skirts and sometimes she changes colors, but it's always the same general look—straight-laced, Puritanical, fifth-generation New Englander. But underneath all of that, a storm is brewing. It has been for years.

When I was ten, my dad had affair number one. It went on for months before my mother hired a private investigator and caught him in the act with his secretary at a hotel four towns over.

That event changed my entire life. Before it, my mother was fun and loving with me. She had always been strict and proper and insisted on good manners, but she seemed to like being my mother. After that event, she turned cold and shut me out. Ayden's father had died three months prior, and Ayden and I clung to one another like we had no one else.

We became each other's salvation in a world where we'd lost hope and faith in humanity. And while Ayden couldn't get his dad back, I haven't stopped trying to resurrect my mom. I know the warm Lucy Wesley with the silly sense of humor is in there somewhere; I just don't have a clue how to reach her.

And when affair number two happened while I was away in California, it broke my mother's spirit, seemingly for good.

I came home to an absolute shell of the woman I'd left behind four years prior.

I was furious with my father, who seemed clueless how to help other than to promise me he was in a support group to make sure he wouldn't cheat again. Ayden came by immediately when I called him, and the two of us talked my father into planning an intervention. So what positives came out of that intervention? Other than getting Mom started with a good psychiatrist, not much.

First, she overdosed. To this day, she claims it was an accident. Her psychiatrist sort of agreed. She said my mother did not exhibit specific suicidal tendencies, but that she was confused and hopeless. She took enough pills that she needed to have her stomach pumped, and that experience made her swear she wouldn't do it again.

Nevertheless, she has what feels like a lifelong prescription for antidepressants, and she claims the pills take the edge off. That may be true, but I swear I haven't heard my mother laugh in years. Once in a rare moment, I can coax a genuine smile out of her. But a laugh? I've honestly forgotten what my mother's laugh sounds like.

"So!" I say enthusiastically once the waitress has brought over our food. "What happened at your appointment? Did you tell Dr. Thibbs about my suggestion to maybe switch up your meds?"

Mom digs into her halibut. "I did, and she said she'd look into it."

I furrow my brow. "Will she have a new medication for you by next week?"

"I'm not sure." Mom averts her gaze and reaches for her reading glasses. "I want to go over the party list with you."

"Right now? But we haven't finished discussing your appointment."

She whips a lined pad of paper and a ballpoint pen out of her purse and puts them on the table next to my plate of pasta and chicken. "You said you'd help."

After Dad won a big case protecting commercial fishing on the docks, his stock as a lawyer soared, and Mom got stuck on the idea of throwing a town party for him, an honor previously given only to our mayor. She petitioned Lucky Bay and after much deliberation, approval was granted. It's almost like she thinks she and my father will reignite their love for one another with this party. I've been roped into working on the planning with her because she can't do anything alone, and I didn't have the heart to tell her no.

My mother's so rarely excited about anything, and if planning a party will brighten the darkness she lives in, then I'll pitch in as best I can.

She taps the pad of paper sitting in front of me. "Mirabella, make sure you write down all that I say."

"How about I type it up and email you a copy?" I'm already reaching for my phone. "It will be much faster this way, Mom. Let's step into the modern era together."

Mom's so enthusiastic about giving me her ideas that she willingly endures my teasing. "Number one is place settings."

We chat about the party throughout our lunch, and by the time we've finished eating, Mom's about exhausted her long list of items.

"Now, in terms of music," she says as I stiffen. "Do you have any ideas?"

I try to keep my expression neutral. "I'm not sure."

When Max got me my first solo gig at a new bar in downtown L.A., I relied on Guy's counsel the first time I stepped on stage. Granted, it was in an area of town so seedy the owner wouldn't let me outside until my cab had pulled up and opened the door for me to jump in. But then I got a better gig, and a better one. The thing is, for every small victory, there were about ten times as many rejections—for my demo and a record contract of any kind.

I had a secret fantasy of signing a record deal, getting a number one song on the radio, and then telling my mom everything.

But when that didn't happen, I kept my failed auditions and frustrations to myself. And as the years passed, the lie got easier to keep up. Because once I returned home and stopped playing guitar altogether, I figured why tell her now?

"Mirabella!" Mom waves her hand in front of my face.

I drag my head back into the present and blink.

"We'll need music for the party. I don't know the first thing about this subject. Can you look into it for me?"

"Yes, of course I will. And I'll deal with the catering and florist this week."

Satisfied, she gestures for the check.

We leave the restaurant together, and my mother heads immediately for her car.

"Have a good day, Mom," I call out.

As I walk by the wharf, Michael's boat has just docked. He does a final look-over of the ropes before he turns and walks down the wood boards, away from the sea and back to land.

His expression is tight, and when I call out a hello, he barely acknowledges me.

Something's off. And I bet Ayden's new job has everything to do with whatever's going on with his brother.

I reach for my phone and type out a quick message.

Hey Ayd. Thinking of you—hope L.A. is sunny and warm. I'm going to spend tonight studying for my test; by the time you get back, I'll be halfway to graduating.

His response comes immediately. *My fingers will be crossed for you. Miss you, B.*

My throat clogs with emotion, and I slip my phone back into my pocket without writing back.

I miss him too.

I've missed him every day since he's been gone.

But I have to get used to this feeling of emptiness because soon, Ayden Wild will be gone from Lucky Bay for good.

CHAPTER EIGHT

Ayden

I zip up my bag and leave Dylan's guest room. His and Jasalie's house in Malibu is so big I have to walk past three other bedrooms and down a winding set of stairs before I find him. He's sitting on the couch in his massive living room, making out with his fiancée.

"You ready to go, Ayd?" Dylan says, his attention not on me but on the beautiful blonde in his arms.

I chuckle. "You two freaking make me sick. If I weren't so damn happy for you, I'd throw up."

Dylan's lips return to Jasalie's, the only woman I've ever seen who could make my cousin forget about football for two seconds. He wraps his arms more tightly around her and leans her back against the couch cushions. She laughs and pushes him away.

"Don't be rude to our houseguest." She turns to me, her cheeks flushed with embarrassment and happiness. "We've loved having you here, Ayden. And Dylan's so happy you're moving to L.A."

"So is Colton. And yes, I speak in third person now, apparently." Colton, another one of my cousins and the tight end for the Cougars, strides into the room with his wife, Sky.

I'm close to all my cousins, but Colton and I share something the others don't—we're the only two who've lost our fathers. And because of that ill-fated link, we're bonded together in a different way.

Colton throws his arm around my neck as he pulls me in for a hug. "I know you don't want us to be there in July," he says in a low tone meant only for me to hear.

"I don't." I shove my hands into my pockets. "I understand why you want to..."

"We're going to come anyway," he says, his blue eyes flashing with emotion. "I get your hesitation. I really do; believe me. But I also know..." He takes a deep breath. "I know that in hindsight, you'll be glad we were there for you. Trust me on this one."

We all went to the funeral for Colton's dad. We were teenagers then, and Colton's mom did a great job of organizing the service and family gathering afterward. It was an emotional weekend and weeks afterward, Colton said it was cathartic for him.

My dad's passing was different. I was only ten, and his was the first loss I'd ever experienced. But more than that, the way his death happened didn't leave any time for planning. First his ship was acknowledged to be missing, and the uncertainty and the panic dragged on for days. By the time he was officially declared gone, Ma had no interest in a memorial. None of the other wives did, either. No one had slept much for days, or eaten. So when the news of the finality came, we all just held hands at the dock and one of the fishermen's brothers, a priest, said a few prayers for the dead. There were no bodies to let go of because they were already buried somewhere in the sea. And maybe that made a difference.

"Closure," Colton says as he watches my face. "That's all I mean, Ayd."

I give a slow nod. "I guess I have to trust you on it. I won't keep fighting you. You're all welcome to come to Lucky Bay in July." I lightly punch Colton's massive arm.

When I haven't seen them in a while, which is most of the time, I forget just how ridiculously built my two cousins are. All of us, except for Cam, played football through high school, and Cam's currently a star in the ice hockey minor leagues. So we're all athletic, but Dylan and Colton are in phenomenal shape. Colton's muscles go on forever, and Dylan doesn't have an ounce of fat on him. They claim they're not in playing shape right now because it's off-season, but they could fool me.

Sky's red hair is pinned up on top of her head, and her pretty green eyes sparkle as she gives me a hug. "Have a safe flight home." She turns to Jasalie. "Can I hang out with you? The guys are doing guy things now."

"Of course!" Jasalie pats the free couch cushion for Sky.

But before Sky can take a step, Colton's mouth is on hers, and they're making out like they won't see each other for a month. Then Jasalie's back in Dylan's arms, their lips locked on one another's.

"Christ." I tug at the brim of my baseball cap. "I'll meet you two outside. We've got plenty of time to get to the airport, anyway. As long as I don't miss my flight."

Colton gives Sky one last peck on the lips and breaks away reluctantly. "I'm ready." He grabs my bag and gestures to Dylan, who's miraculously made it off the couch.

"Let's go for a drink before you fly out. Dylan has something he wants to discuss with you, Ayd. Best to do it under the influence. I'll drive."

I jerk my head in Dylan's direction. He just ushers me toward the door. "Not a big deal," he assures me. "But Colt's right. Let's get a drink."

———

"You are absolutely not 'lending' me your apartment," I say, the one beer I had not nearly enough to keep me calm. "I don't want your damn money, Dylan."

The three of us are wearing jeans and t-shirts and aren't exactly dressed for anywhere fancy. This works just fine for us since none of us like formalities. So we've parked ourselves at a hole-in-the-wall bar on the beachfront, a place famous for its burgers and fries.

Dylan knows the owner, who set us up in an undisclosed back room because the place is packed with wall-to-wall customers. So we have some privacy back here, but I know I shouldn't let my voice get too loud. Dylan and Colton are both bulls-eyes for the press, and Dylan is especially wary of publicity.

He's had ridiculous lies printed about him, not to mention stalkers and a particularly scary death threat that almost broke him and Jasalie up for good. Luckily, he came to his senses, but he's always on the alert, and he has a crew of security on his payroll.

Dylan runs both hands through his hair, which is as dark as mine, and lets out a frustrated huff. "I'm not even using the apartment, Ayden," he argues me. "It's literally sitting there vacant. I don't want to rent it out, and I'm not sure about selling it yet."

"Why not?" I ask him.

"Because I haven't tried living in Malibu during a full season, and I want to make sure it works before I get rid of my place downtown."

Well, that makes sense, but...

"The only way I'd consider it is if you let me pay you rent," I say. "You'll be my landlord."

Just like I knew he would, Dylan frowns. "That makes no sense, Ayden." He hesitates. "Look, Colt and I know you took the job out here for a reason. A monetary reason. Right?"

I shrug. "California's weather makes my line of work more stable; that's for sure."

"Right," Colton says carefully. "You can work year-round here. Which is great, but I'm pretty fucking certain you're not planning on keeping that extra cash for yourself. Are you, Ayd?"

I resist the urge to punch him. Colton will keep pushing if he thinks he's close to uncovering something.

"Not ready to get into it," I tell him.

Dylan's gaze hasn't left me or the way I'm anxiously flipping my drink coaster around.

"I'm in an incredibly blessed position where money is no longer a stress in my life," he says slowly. "And I'm not going to sit back and watch you bust your ass for family when I could be helping out, even in some small way. Like with your living arrangements."

I sit back and cross my arms over my chest. Sure, Dylan has a hundred million dollar contract, and I...don't, but taking advantage of our relationship isn't an option.

Colton cracks a smile. "Knew this would be a stand-off."

Dylan and I both glare at him. Colton's smile widens. "And that's why I came armed with a solution."

I raise my eyebrows, and Dylan gestures for Colton to continue.

"You and Jasalie want a garden by your pool, don't you, Dyl?" Colton asks.

"Yeah, but what does that have to do with this?" Dylan says.

Colton waves his hand in the air. "Ayden's a professional landscaper. Hire him to do the garden in exchange for living at your apartment. Everyone's happy."

I look at Dylan, who looks at me. For a moment we stay locked in, assessing each other. Then, he cracks a smile, and fuck, I do too. And just like that, the standoff is broken.

We shake hands. Turns out Colton's right. Everyone's happy.

"So Ayd, the only thing left is to convince your comrade in arms to join you out here," Colton says, a mischievous grin lighting his face. "Dylan's apartment is plenty big enough for two."

I'm already shaking my head. "Bella's not on board."

"You've asked her?" Dylan says.

"Sort of. And it didn't go well. Look, I know Bella. She has responsibilities in Lucky Bay just like I do. And while I need to move to California so I can..." I trail off as Colt and Dylan lean closer like they're ready for me to spill my secrets. "And while I'm able to relocate, Bella may not feel like she can."

"That's bullshit." Colton narrows his eyes at me. "You and Bella can work anything out."

"Even if we could, Bella's not ready to move back to L.A."

"Even with you?" Colton says. "Because you two together..."

"Are only friends," I say firmly. "And that's all we ever should be. In fact..."

By the time I've finished telling them about our drunk dares, Colton's shaking his head.

"God, you're a stubborn ass, Ayd. You can actually sit there with a straight face and tell me you don't want to explode at the thought of Bella with another guy?"

I take a deep breath. "Colt, shut the hell up."

"Ayden," Dylan says in a low tone, "Bella's the only woman you've ever cared for. We all see it. Why can't you?"

Because I don't date women I care for. That's the damn point.

Like he knows what I'm thinking, Dylan continues, "And this whole 'I don't fuck my friends' thing you've perfected—how's that going to work when you want to get married? You're going to end up with someone who's not Bella just to keep her in the friend zone?"

I feel like my damn head is going to explode. "You're giving me a fucking headache," I mutter. "I can't explain my relationship with Bella to you two. I'm happy for you both that you've found Sky and Jasalie, but my life isn't the same as yours. I date casually; the more casual, the better. It's what works for me. So stop pushing me. Bella will find someone, yes. Do I like that fact? Not exactly. But it is what it is."

"Ayd..."

"Discussion over. I need to get to the airport to make sure I don't miss this double-date disaster Bella and I are going on."

"Why did you agree to such a fucking stupid idea?" Colton asks me.

"Because I want to keep my eye on the tool she's going with. I don't trust him."

Dylan and Colton exchange a look I can't decipher the meaning of. It looks a bit like "point made."

Then Dylan nods. "Okay. Discussion over. The apartment is yours. You can start working on the garden once you've moved out here and settled in. But Ayd?"

I narrow my eyes. "But what?"

"I respectfully disagree. I think you should convince Bella to join you."

So do I. But that doesn't mean she and I will be on the same page.

CHAPTER NINE

Bella

Dressed in a new pink top and white shorts with matching strappy sandals, I make it a point to be the first one at the Lucky Bay Clam Festival on Sunday. I had told Trey I'd meet him there for our double date with Ayden and Jenny.

As I reach the town square, the Ferris wheel spins high over the crowd, and eighties music wafts through the air.

Lucky Bay's clam festival is one of the biggest fairs on the Maine coast. Everyone always hopes for a warm weekend, and sometimes we're rewarded. Not this year, though. This morning's been windy and cloudy so far.

I take a seat on the bench closest to the rainbow-colored moonwalk and listen to all the kids screaming as they jump up and down inside. The moonwalk's always been big with kids and teenagers—the kids so they can jump around, and the teenagers so they can flirt and land on one another inside the protective walls but not have anyone think anything crazy's going on. I never went on the moonwalk with a date, but I used to hear about all the girls who dragged Ayden onto it.

Speaking of, I haven't seen Ayden since he got back to Maine. His flight yesterday was delayed due to mechanical problems, so he ended up taking the red-eye and only landed just over an hour ago. He texted me that he was on his way home to shower and change and that he'd be picking up Jenny before coming to the festival.

I pull out my phone and text Tari that I'm already having second thoughts about this double date. Before I can overthink things even more than I already am, Trey slides onto the bench next to me.

"Hey Bella," he says with a smile. "How are you?"

Trey's hair is dark like Ayden's, but while Ayden's is wild like his name, Trey's is super short and slicked down. He has nice brown eyes, a friendly smile, and a trim body. He's handsome in a conventional, boring sort of way. And the truth is he does bore me. Tari was right—I really do pick men I don't give a shit about.

"Hey!" I say to him as he leans in to kiss me.

Well, as he tries to kiss me. He goes for my mouth, but I've already turned to hug him, so he ends up kissing my eye.

"Sorry about that," he says as I back up.

"No, don't be sorry." I lean in toward him. "I'm the one who shifted...ouch!" I cry out as Trey's head accidentally slams into my temple.

While Trey apologizes all over again, saying he zigged when I zagged, I hold my head in pain.

Not a great start.

And of course, in the middle of all this horrible awkwardness and genuine physical discomfort, I hear—

"Bella."

I drop my hands and whip my head around. "Ayden?"

He's standing a few feet away in his well-worn jeans that fit him perfectly and a shirt I've never seen before. It's collared and dressier than usual, almost like a polo shirt. I'm staring at it and wondering when he bought something so out of character just as he says my name again. I raise my head and watch his gaze sweep over me intently. I run toward him, and he closes the gap with three long strides. He scoops me up into his arms, flipping his baseball cap backward so he won't bang me with the brim.

Still keeping one arm locked firmly around my waist, he speaks quietly into my ear. "I missed you, B. How'd your studying go?"

"I'll find out tomorrow. After that, only one more test left, and I'll have my degree. Right before you leave." I pull back to look at him. His eyes are bright, but they can't hide the dark circles underneath.

"You look tired."

"Long trip." He lets me down, and my feet hit the ground. "Haven't slept since yesterday."

I break into a smile. "I'm glad you're here."

"Me too." He tips his head in the direction of Trey. "You okay?"

I flush with heat. "Yes. We banged heads. No big deal."

"As long as you're okay." His eyes search mine. "You want to go to the bar instead of hanging here?"

"I want to stay here," a voice says from behind us.

Ayden and I break apart, and oh...there's Jenny Woods, glaring at me. I thought Ashley was the one who didn't like me, but apparently more than one woman in Ayden's world wishes I would go away.

Her long blond curls hang halfway down her back, and her red maxi dress is the perfect blend of casual yet sexy. I feel completely underdressed all of a sudden.

"Hi, Jenny," I say with a smile. "You look really nice. How are you?"

"Fine. Your head is red." She points to my temple. "What happened?"

"Oh. Um..."

"My fault. I banged into her." Trey's off the bench now. His arm goes around my shoulders, and he draws me closer to him. "Maybe we should walk over to the beer garden behind the Ferris wheel."

Ayden's eyes are fixed on Trey's hand, which is dangling over my shoulder and in the general vicinity of my breast. He's not close to touching it, but Ayden's jaw starts working like he's going to grind his teeth down to nothing.

"Let it go," I murmur to him as the four of us start walking across the lawn. "Good Lord, you're not my big brother."

"Don't you think I know that?" he whispers into my hair. "I am definitely *not* your brother, Bella."

My stomach clenches low, and I have to grab onto Trey's waist to stay upright.

Ayden's dimple flashes like he just got what he wanted, and I glare at him.

For the next hour, we all wander around the festival grounds in an awkward attempt to engage in pleasant four-way conversation. Jenny and Trey do most of the talking; Trey's a big sports fan, and he just came back from a Red Sox game the night before. Jenny's originally from California, and she tells Ayden, at least three times, that she can't wait to visit him out there whenever he wants.

"Cool," is all Ayden says in response, but it's enough to set me on edge.

With visions of Jenny and Ayden fornicating on the beaches of southern California, I stop short at the base of the Ferris wheel.

"Who's up for a ride?" I say in a forced happy tone.

"Oh, I'm afraid of heights," Jenny says as she clutches Ayden's hand.

"That's too bad," I say. "Trey, you want to go?"

"Sure thing."

Ayden catches my wrist as I go to pass him. "We'll meet you back here when you finish."

"Ayd, let's go on the moonwalk together while we wait," Jenny says.

I do a slow turn toward her. "The moonwalk isn't very fun for adults," I say. "It gets really crowded with all the kids, and you'll probably end up falling."

She wraps her arms around Ayden's waist and kisses his bicep. "That's okay. I think I can handle falling with this guy. I know he'll catch me."

"Super. Have fun then." I turn on my heel and head for the waiting car at the bottom of the Ferris wheel.

Trey joins me and pulls the bar down over us. And then we're moving. Up into the air, away from Ayden and Jenny and all the tension between Ayden and me that's so thick I can hardly breathe.

Not wanting to imagine what he and Jenny are doing inside those moonwalk walls, I pretend to be really interested in Trey's long conversation about his volunteer soccer team.

"I love to run," he says. "I could run around all day, and it wouldn't be enough. You?"

"Hmm?" I glance over at him. "Oh, me? I'm not much of a runner, no."

Understatement of my life. The one time I tried jogging with Tari on the beach, we gave up and ended up at Sweets, the local bakery, where we ordered a dozen donut holes and proceeded to eat them all.

"You should start," Trey says. "I mean you're clearly in great shape now, but you're still young. Once you get older, you'll have a harder time keeping weight off."

Huh. "Thanks for the tip," I say. "I'm not going to think about my life in twenty years just yet. I have a hard enough time figuring out what will be happening tomorrow."

"I'm a planner," Trey says as the Ferris wheel mercifully comes to a stop at the bottom, and we climb out. "I like to think about every detail of my future, so I make sure I accomplish everything I want. I don't want to have any regrets on my deathbed, you know?"

I look past him at Ayden and Jenny headed toward us from the moonwalk. Ayden's eyes don't leave mine as Jenny chatters away to him.

"No regrets," I repeat. "That's a good motto."

I never thought the Lucky Bay Clam Festival was especially large, but this year, it feels like we walk for hours from one part of the fair to the other. By the time we reach the live music tent, I'm exhausted.

Tari and Peter are at a table, and they call to us enthusiastically. Tari's long hair is up in a top bun, and her head's resting on Peter's shoulder. I take a seat next to her, and Trey joins me on my other side. Jenny and Ayden sit across from us.

Trey, Jenny, and Ayden get wrapped up in a conversation about the band on stage that's currently playing a cover of a popular country song. Tari and Peter take full advantage of the distraction as they both turn to me and lean in conspiratorially.

"How's the hot double date going?" Peter says in a teasing tone.

"Yeah, fill us in," Tari whispers.

I shrug. "I may cut out early."

Tari's eyes shine with sympathy. "Oh, Bella. I'm sorry."

"It's fine," I say quickly.

"I swear we tried to stay out of your way today so we wouldn't crash your double date," Tari says to me. "We didn't plan to run into you, and that was partly how we ended up in the live music tent. I guess I assumed you wouldn't want to come here. I mean not that I should have assumed or anything. I just figured with the music and all..."

I touch her arm. "Tar, don't worry about it. I've been doing okay with all of that, actually."

Tari's eyes widen. "That's so great!"

"Are you thinking of getting back into music again, Bella?" Peter asks curiously, leaning across Tari.

Before I can answer him, a ruckus across the table gets our attention. Jenny's tugging at the brim of Ayden's cap, trying to get him to take it off.

"No," he tells her firmly. "This stays put."

She teasingly reaches up to pull off his hat. Ayden puts one hand on his head to keep his hat in place and his other hand on Jenny's shoulder. Then, he leans in and blows on her neck until she moans.

Oh my God.

Even though he clearly did it to distract her from grabbing at his most important possession, I still wince like I'm in pain.

But the worst part?

Ayden shifts in his seat until his eyes find mine.

And he locks eyes with me.

The entire time he blows on Jenny's neck, he stares at me. He's so goddamn talented the way he uses his mouth, and the look in his eyes as he watches me watch him is one hundred percent sexual.

He's not even trying to hide it.

My thighs clench together, and I shudder. Because right now I don't want Ayden like a best friend.

Right now, I want to climb across the table that's between us and beg him to please get me off. My hormones are screaming SOS. And the guy next to me—my *date*—isn't even on my body's radar.

I vaguely hear Tari let out a squeak of surprise, but I can't take my eyes off of Ayden. His cheeks flush, and his eyes darken with obvious heat—I feel like he's blowing on my neck. And I'm so hot I feel like I need to rip my clothes off.

Then, just when I think things can't possibly get worse, they do.

Jenny, oblivious to where Ayden's attention is focused, turns her head and kisses him on the mouth. He clearly isn't expecting it because his eyes widen in surprise and he physically backs up. But he's still sitting right next to her, so he can't go far without actually standing up and making it obvious.

So—

He continues to stare at *me* the entire time Jenny's lips are on his.

And Jenny's aggressive. Her hands, with those super-pointy, red-painted fingernails, make their way underneath Ayden's shirt and all over his chest. Not that I can blame her. Ayden's so hot it's ridiculous, and he just blew on her damn neck. If she actually started this whole thing on purpose by trying to take his hat, Jenny's a damn genius.

But Ayden never kisses Jenny back. He just sits there motionless, arms at his sides while she hangs on him, his eyes locked on mine.

His gaze is dark and intense, and I swear my body is going to combust.

I'm honest to God halfway to orgasm without being touched when I hear—

"Hey, Bella."

I wrest my gaze from Ayden's and whip my head around as Guy kneels next to my chair.

"Hi!" I say to him. "Are you performing?"

"Already did. I only played a few songs, and now I'm headed to the lounge. It's going to be hopping at the pool hall later, so there should be a lot of music requests." He nods hello to Ayden, who's somehow separated himself from handsy Jenny.

"Hey." Ayden shakes his hand. "Good to see you."

Guy greets Tari and Peter next and then he turns back to me. "How's your guitar working out? Have you had a chance to try playing with those new strings I put on?"

I actually hear Ayden suck in his breath. His shock is palpable, and I can practically feel him trying to catch my eye.

Making sure to keep my attention on Guy, I nod. "Just a little bit so far. But everything feels great. Thanks again for fixing her up."

He stands up and pats my shoulder. "Come by, and we'll sing sometime."

I wave as he leaves.

And then I turn to face Ayden.

His eyes are brilliantly blue as he fixes them on me. "You're playing again?"

I try to keep my expression neutral, but Ayden's enthusiasm is infectious, and I break into a smile. "I'm dabbling."

"Dabbling's good." His grin grows wider.

Tari grabs me in a hug, and Peter says we're all definitely celebrating my return to music later.

Jenny, on the other hand, gives me the fakest of fake smiles and stares off into space.

"When'd you start?" Ayden asks me.

"While you were in L.A."

"That's great, Bella. I'm proud of you." He looks over at Trey. "Did you know that Bella's a singer-songwriter?"

"No, I didn't." Trey asks me what kind of songs I write.

"Alternative mostly," I say. "But it's kind of a strange blend of country and pop."

"Her style's so unique," Tari says. "She's super talented."

"Cool. Do you write any anthem-type songs?" Trey asks me. "Up-tempo songs that are good to work out to?"

"Um, not so much," I say.

"Oh." Trey sounds deflated.

I glance at Jenny awkwardly, wondering how to include her in the conversation as Ayden leans about a mile closer to me than to Jenny. "So you've been writing again, B?"

I take a deep breath. "Yes. Just a bit."

Ayden's dimple deepens. "That's great."

"Thanks." I inch closer to him.

His eyes are glued to mine, and my pulse takes off. I start to forget about Jenny and even Trey.

The sound of Jenny clearing her throat startles me, but Ayden doesn't react. Her loud cough does the trick, though. Ayden jumps like he forgot she was there.

"I need a drink, Ayden," she says as she glares at him.

"In a minute." He doesn't look at her as he says it. "Bella, once you have some new material you want to play, I'd love to hear your new stuff."

"I need a drink right NOW." Jenny stands up and grabs his arm. "And I think we need some alone time. Just you and me."

Ayden's jaw ticks, but he stands and excuses himself. And he goes with Jenny to the bar. To buy his date a drink like she demanded. Like the gentleman he is, I suppose.

"Bella? Come with me for a sec?" Without waiting for me to respond, Tari urges me out of my chair and tells Trey we'll be right back.

She beckons me over to a private corner of the tent where she starts talking a mile a minute.

"What the hell was that?" she asks me in a high-pitched whisper.

I throw up my hands. "No idea. Nothing?"

"You and Ayden? The flirting?" She gesticulates wildly with her hands. "Holy shit, Bella. That was not nothing. He looked at you like he was going to jump your bones. And you were about to climb him like a damn tree. I nearly came just watching you two."

"It's Ayden. He's a flirt."

"Not with you. And *not* like that."

Of course she's right, but I don't know what to say. I have no idea what's happening between Ayden and me or how to stop what's starting to feel like constant sexual tension.

"And I can't believe Ayden picked Jenny for this date," she says. "She doesn't seem like his type at all."

"I didn't know Ayden had a type," I say, only half-joking. "Pretty sure if someone's got boobs, he's willing to give her a shot."

"I guess you're right." Tari shakes her head. "He just seems lonelier than usual tonight."

"He never really lets anyone new in; you know that."

Ayden doesn't get close to many people. The people who were in his life before his father drowned are pretty much still the only ones he trusts. It's almost like Ayden never really came back into his body after his father's death. The shock shot him out like a rocket taking off into space. If you're not really here, you can't really die.

"Did you see how royally pissed off he was when she tried to take off his hat?" Tari smiles. "Remember when you took his hat the other night at the bar? He loved every second of you wearing it on your head—he even gave it back to you!"

"That's because I know what the hat means to him."

Ayden was supposed to go with his father on the boat that day, but they had a fight the night before about a television show Ayden wanted to stay up and watch. His father said if Ayden stayed up he'd be too tired for the next day's work, and he'd have to sleep in.

To get Ayden to agree to go to sleep, Mr. Wild gave him a Red Sox hat he bought when he went to a game down in Boston the week before with his fishing crew. He said he was going to save it for Ayden's birthday, but he decided to give it to him then instead. Ayden fell asleep wearing that hat and swearing he'd get up in time to go with his dad on the boat.

But he didn't. And his father drowned. His mother calls it a blessing from God, but Ayden carries the guilt in his heart.

I look at Tari. "Jenny doesn't understand. So Ayden would never trust her with the hat."

"Hmm." Tari cocks her head at me. "You really are the only woman he truly trusts. You know that? And I don't think that will ever change."

I put my arm around her and turn her around. "Maybe not, but this is all getting too heavy for me. And I have a date to get back to."

CHAPTER TEN

Ayden

From my spot at the edge of the live music tent, I watch as Bella and Tari return to their seats at the table. My eyes follow Bella when she turns to greet Trey, and he puts his arm around her.

Maybe I'm dreaming it, but it almost looks like she draws back from his touch. And I know I'm not imagining the feeling of relief that shoots through me that she's not touching him back.

Jenny's in the bathroom, reapplying her lipstick that she claims wore off from all our "kissing."

I never even kissed her back, but she did enough writhing around for three people.

And normally I would love the fact that a woman I was out with is so into me. I like women. I like it when they have a good time, and I like making sure they have a good time.

But tonight, my attention has only been on one woman, and she's not my date.

That staredown Bella and I were engaged in earlier? Fuck, her eyes were liquid with desire. I didn't imagine *that*. And I nearly exploded at the way her lips parted, and she sucked in a mouthful of air like she was desperate for a hit—of *me*. And I ached to give her everything she needed. I wanted to spread her out on the table and bury myself inside her. I craved my tongue between her legs so I could taste her. And I desperately needed her naked and writhing beneath me while I tangled my tongue with hers.

I was so hard I didn't think I'd be able to get up from the table. I had to adjust myself before I stood in order to avoid looking obscene.

Walking around with an erection because of your best friend is not the most comfortable scenario. Especially when I'm out with another woman.

What the fuck is wrong with me?

Kissing Bella Wesley is not on the table.

It's not an option. Not if I want to hold onto the best relationship in my life.

But right now, I can't be rational. And if I see Bella alone, I will strip her bare.

I feel like I'm going to fucking explode. There's only one solution—leave with Jenny now.

Take Jenny to bed tonight.

Get out all my sexual frustrations with my date, the woman who told me as we left the table that she's been wanting to fuck me all day and she doesn't know how much longer she can wait. She said she's not looking for anything with strings; that she knows I'm leaving, and she's cool with casual. She's everything I typically look for.

Jenny's the safe choice. The smart choice.

I make my way closer to the table, noticing how Bella's turned completely toward Tari now.

"Stalking your best friend isn't a good look." Peter slaps my back and leans against the pole next to me.

"I'm not stalking her. I'm keeping my eye on her."

He chuckles. "Is that what the kids call it these days? That little stunt you pulled back there was you keeping an *eye* on her?"

"Fine. That was...unplanned." I cross my arms. "How bad did it look?"

"Dude, you were practically propositioning Bella while your

date was *kissing* you! It looked bad. Hot but bad. The good news? Bella was right there with you. I thought she was going to crawl across the damn table in about two seconds."

I thought so too. And that thought makes me crazy for her all over again. In that moment, she looks up from her conversation with Tari.

Right at me.

And my heart hammers in my chest.

When my phone rings, I ignore it.

But Peter doesn't. He grabs it out of my pocket and swipes the screen before I can stop him.

"Colt, hey. It's Peter. Good, good," he says with a grin at me. "Listen, you Wilds are missing one hell of a show up here in Lucky Bay, Maine. Your cousin and his non-plus one are eye-fucking each other while they're out on a double date with other people."

I grab the phone out of Peter's hand and give him the finger as I bring it to my ear. "I have it under control," I say to Colton.

"Sure you do," he says.

"She's better off with someone who will be there for her in the long haul," I say. "Even if he is an arrogant tool who doesn't get her at all."

"Are you fucking hearing yourself right now?" Colton says. "You think you're not going to be there for her?"

I'm not about to get into the reasons why with him, so I simply say, "You don't get it."

"I don't have to get whatever bullshit excuse you've hard-wired into your brain. I knew this dare crap was going to blow up in your face. And you deserve it. I've never seen two people so in denial. You and Bella are two stubborn fools."

"Colt..."

"Ayd. You've got less than two months left there. Make it count for you, not against you."

Fuck. I run my free hand down my face.

"Maybe by the time we get there, you'll have figured your shit out," he says in a softer tone.

Doubtful, but Colton's always been the optimist of us.

Bella

I need to get out of here before Ayden and Jenny return. God knows what will happen if we continue with this double date.

I slump back in my chair and look over at Trey, who blessedly asks me if I want to go grab some food.

"Sure." I say goodbye to Tari and follow Trey toward the food trucks.

Ayden and I are definitely never double dating again.

"Lemon cheesecake," I say as Trey and I walk away from the festival and take seats on the beach. "I've never had it before."

"And chocolate gelato," Trey says as he dips a spoon in and takes a bite. "Something sour, something sweet."

I guess we all need that balance. Without the sour, I won't appreciate the sweet nearly as much. Tonight has definitely been more sour than I'd hoped for. Trey's a talker, and I'm fine to be a listener, but we don't seem to have anything in common. He likes sports and alcohol and...I'm not sure what else he likes. We never leave those two topics.

With the sounds of the breaking waves close by, he leans in to kiss me.

The tide is high, and even without looking toward the ocean, I can tell that the waves are huge. Growing up by the ocean, I learned to hear the waves, to recognize the difference in sound between the gentle small ones and the pounding big ones. This beach setting *could* be very erotic if I were here with the right guy.

Of course, there's always my imagination to help me out in these moments.

I can do this. I can lose myself temporarily. I lean into Trey's kiss, waiting for a spark as his lips touch mine. Nothing. Instead, I'm bombarded with thoughts of Ayden. Of his mouth and how it would feel to have his teeth nibble at my lips. Of his tongue and how expertly I'm sure he'd use it. I'm so wired I nearly moan out loud but not because of the man next to me.

What is happening to me? Trey's certainly attractive, but I can't stop thinking about a completely different guy, the one who's supposed to be my best friend. *Not* my lover. Never my lover.

I may be a shitty dater, but usually I'm at least able to have some fun. Today though, no matter how hard I've tried, this date hasn't worked.

"Trey, I'm sorry." I pull away. "I think I need to call it a day. I'm just super tired."

But after I say goodbye to Trey, I don't go home. I can't possibly go home and sleep after that...that *event* with Ayden.

I walk purposefully across the town square, relieved I don't run into Ayden and Jenny.

When I reach the pool hall, I slip inside. Instead of going toward the back room where I work, I turn left and keep walking toward the sounds of a piano playing, not stopping until I can peek inside the half-open door of the music lounge.

Guy's alone. The crowds haven't made their way here this early yet. I lean too far forward and bang my foot against the door jam, causing him to look up at the noise.

"Hey." He waves me inside.

"You sound awesome," I tell him as I walk up to the piano.

"Thanks, Bella. I'm making a brand-new demo."

I shudder involuntarily.

He notices. "Kind of sucks."

"Yeah." I smile at him. "But I'm so proud of you."

"You're a fighter too you know," he says as he reaches for his water.

I look at the music sheets he has spread out in front of him now. Beatles, Beatles, and more Beatles. "Wait a minute. Where are your songs?"

"At home," he says. "Thought I'd relax for the night and play something that's already made it big."

I take a seat on the stool by the piano.

"You sing; I'll play?" Guy says as he starts tapping out a melody. "Like old times."

I hesitate and glance back at the open door. "I'm not sure I'm ready for anyone else to listen."

"So lock the door."

I shoot Guy a grateful look and walk over to the door. By the time I've turned the lock and returned to the stool, he's already started the chords.

I stumble my way through the first verse, but by the chorus, I'm feeling the music. I relax as I sing, and when we finish, I exhale in relief, feeling like I've broken through some sort of barrier.

"You still got it, you know." He raises his eyebrows.

"Yeah, right." I start fiddling with my hair.

He pulls a card out of his pocket and hands it to me. It's a business card.

"Sea Urchin Club & Lounge." I look up. "So?"

"It's a new place in Portland. Just opened last weekend. They're looking for acts. They have slots for performers," he says to my blank look.

"I don't perform club music."

"It's a club and lounge, and they need early evening slots. Your style's fine for that. You're like acoustic rock. I know the manager. Ask for Dan, and tell him you know me."

"I'm done with performing," I say.

"Oh, yeah? That's not what it sounds like. You still sound great, Bella. Seriously."

"I don't think I'm ready for a real gig."

"I know you don't. That's why I'm saying it."

I look at the card in my hand. Sea Urchin Club & Lounge. Dan

Dwynn, Manager. My heart comes up into my throat at the very thought of getting back out there again. But I thank Guy and take the card.

And then I head home.

The second I'm alone in my bed, memories of tonight with Ayden come flooding back. The way his hot gaze fixed on me—I've never had someone focus on me like that.

I sigh. And right now, he's with Jenny. Doing God knows what. I don't want to admit how much that burns. But it does.

I force myself to ignore the ache in my chest, along with thoughts of Ayden and Jenny having hot, sweaty sex, and I turn over and fall into a fitful sleep.

———

Ayden

I swallow down the rest of my beer, wanting nothing more than to get out of here. Once we left the festival, Jenny insisted on going out to eat at some formal sit-down place when I thought all we were doing was grabbing a drink. I'm not dressed for the place, but Jenny doesn't seem to mind. All she wants to do is put her hands on me.

On my face, on my chest, and especially on my hat, which she keeps trying to remove with alarming insistence.

Then she moves on to more interesting areas. Her hand slides down my torso and onto the top of my jeans where she keeps going until she's cupping my crotch.

In the middle of the restaurant. If I wanted her, I would throw down some bills and rush home with her to my bed. That *had* been my plan.

But...

It's like my dick went to sleep when Bella left the festival.

And it feels...wrong to hook up with Jenny.

So I take her hands off me and ask for the check.

Telling her I've got a sudden headache from the jetlag and lack of sleep, I drop her off at her place.

"You sure you don't want to come inside?" Jenny asks me at her front step. "I promise I'll make it worth your while."

Her hand slides to my dick again.

After what happened between Bella and me today, I'm desperate for a release. And I'd like nothing more than to lose myself in someone else. I *need* to lose myself in someone else so I don't screw everything up and slam my mouth over Bella's the next time I see her.

But I can't bring myself to even kiss Jenny good night.

I remove her hand and kiss the back of it quickly. "I'm sure. Thanks for today. Sleep well."

I can feel her glare on my back as I walk away and get into my car. And I kick myself because I had a sure thing, a way to protect my friendship with Bella, and I just walked away.

When I reach my house, instead of pulling into my driveway, I keep driving until I reach Bella's street. And then, before I can stop myself, I go by her house. The lights are out and her car's in the driveway, but that doesn't give me the relief I'm hoping for. She walked to the festival, which means she and Trey could still be out, or together at his house. Or maybe they're at her house and already in bed. I clench the steering wheel with both hands at the very thought.

I have to see her.

But I can't stop by now; if she's with Trey, I'll want to kill him.

And if she's home alone?

I'm so tightly wound right now; I won't be able to stop myself from touching her.

I force myself to pull away from her driveway, and I drive home.

I'm desperate to know if she spent the night with Trey. But it will have to wait until tomorrow.

And there's only one way to find out for sure.

Put my job skills to good use.

CHAPTER ELEVEN

Bella

Whirrrrr!

Without even opening my eyes, I groan at the sound that won't stop.

I put the pillow over my head and try to go back to sleep.

Whirrrr!

The annoyingly grating mechanical sound is growing closer. It sounds like it's right outside my bedroom window.

I open one eye and glance at the clock on my bedside table. Not even seven freaking a.m. What is that damn noise?

Wait a minute.

That sounds like a lawnmower.

But I don't use a landscaping service.

I get out of bed and throw open the window shade.

And suddenly, I'm staring at Ayden's bare, muscled back and his perfectly sexy jeans-clad ass.

Crap.

I really should have used my vibrator more than once last night.

I'm still far too turned on to be meeting Ayden face-to-face.

And the hardest part is that I'm turned on for *him*. No one else. Just Ayden Wild.

He makes a turn and heads toward the house. I try to duck but it's too late.

He lifts his head, and his piercing blue gaze hits me straight on. I shift my eyes downward, but all I see is a six-pack of sweaty abs staring back at me.

I jerk my head back up, and my eyes hook into Ayden's again.

Everything that happened last night passes between us.

Ayden's cheeks flush as he raises his hand in a wave. A cocky wave if I'm not mistaken. He *knows*. He knows how much he turned me on last night inside the music tent.

And I know it too.

Oh, this shouldn't be weird and awkward at all.

Sure it won't.

I pull the blind back down on the window and open my dresser drawers. I grab a pair of pink and white striped shorts and an off-the-shoulder slouchy blue sweatshirt that says Lucky Bay across the back. I dress quickly, throw my hair back into a messy ponytail, and step outside in my bare feet.

Ayden shuts the mower off and slowly heads toward me. I make it down my front steps and partway across the lawn before we meet.

"Hey, B." He reaches out and tugs at my ponytail. "Did I wake you?"

I put my hand on my hip. "What do you think?"

He puts his hands into his back pockets as a slow grin takes over his face.

"And something tells me you wanted to wake me up early this morning." I cock my hip. "You want to tell me why?"

He opens his mouth, but I cut him off.

"See, I'm pretty sure I know the answer to my own question."

He's still smiling. "Oh, really?"

"Yes. You wanted to make sure I didn't spend the night with

Trey. And so you figured if you came over early enough, you could catch me with him. Or not, as the case may be."

Ayden glances toward my bedroom window, and I exhale. "He's not here, Ayden. And I wasn't there either. I spent the night in my house—alone."

He blows out a breath and takes off his hat. Tossing it onto the ground, he digs his teeth into his bottom lip and stares at me.

Don't ask him. Don't ask him.

"I took Jenny home last night," he finally says.

My heart sinks.

Ayden's studying my reaction. "I kissed the back of her hand at the door, and I told her good night."

Hope soars within me, and the knots in my stomach—the ones I felt all night when I envisioned Ayden and Jenny together—disappear.

Ayden's eyes flash. "Bella."

I weigh what to say next. "You were staring at me, Ayden," I murmur.

"I know." His words come out thick. "Don't you think I fucking know that? And I'm sorry I made things uncomfortable. I never meant to do that."

Emotions I never allow myself to feel come up into my mouth, and I can't hold them back. "We don't usually act so...possessive or jealous. Why now?"

He reaches for his hat and shoves it back on his head. "I'm honestly not sure."

I peek underneath his Sox cap to see his expression, but he pulls it lower over his face. I resist the urge to grab the damn hat off his head and fling it down the street.

I tap my toe on the grass. "Look, I'll always be on your side. Just like I always have been."

I can see his throat working as he swallows hard. "Why do I feel like you have more to say?"

"I'm not sure how to say what I'm feeling without blowing up our friendship. And nothing's worth that to me. Not even..."

Not even mind-altering sex with you.

Oh, God. Why won't my hormones stop shouting at me? Ayden and I work as best friends. We wouldn't work as lovers. We're both terrible in relationships, and if we ever crossed that line with each other, no doubt we'd screw it up and destroy our friendship forever.

"Bella." Ayden's tone is solemn. "Last night was...it could have been..."

"A terrible mistake." I make myself say the three words one of us has to say before this boat leaves the dock and heads for the open seas. I lock my knees together, willing the need between my legs to stop calling to me. My nipples are coming to attention too, and I hurriedly cross my arms over my chest. Just because I want to climb Ayden right now and rip his jeans off of him is no excuse. We're friends. That's it.

Ayden's lip curves up as he watches my movements. "A mistake," he repeats. "You really believe that, Ms. Wesley? Can I put you on the stand and have you take an oath?"

I kick his foot lightly. "Shut up."

He's full out grinning now. "Because I'm sensing some major conflict going on between your body and your brain. Am I right?"

"Ayden Wild, stop messing around about this. This is us."

He's still grinning, but the pain swimming in his eyes tells me he knows exactly what I'm getting at. "No one knows that better than I do, B." He pauses. "Do you remember why we made our pact when we were thirteen years old?"

I startle at his question. "Um...of course I do."

Is he going to...

"Because I kissed you."

Okay, so he is going to go there.

"I kissed you, and do you remember why?"

My voice comes out strangled when I answer him. "You said you wanted to make sure that your first real kiss was with me. And that mine was with you."

"That's right." Ayden smiles, and his ocean blue eyes shine as brightly as the sun over our heads. "To this day, it's still the best damn kiss of my life, Bella."

Shit, shit, shit. I squeeze my thighs together, trying desperately to shut down the sensations hitting me between my legs. Maybe if we just have sex once...we could get it out of our systems, and then I'd no longer crave him like I am. Because I am craving Ayden Wild, and it's torturous.

"But I get it," Ayden continues. "I understand why we met up the next day and made the pact. It was a way for us to make sure what happened between us never happened again. I get why we did that."

My next words float out into the air on a breathy half-moan. "You do?"

"I do." His mouth shifts to a frown. "Because we never would have made it through high school intact. Somewhere along the way, I would have hurt you. I would have rather died than do that, but I know myself, Bella. Look at my dad and what he did to my mom."

I jerk to awareness. "What are you talking about, Ayden? Your father drowned. He didn't hurt your mom—or any of you—on purpose." I put my hand on his bare arm and shake him gently.

Ayden's eyes go blank. "My dad may not have meant to break my mom's heart, but he did. My grandfather—same thing. He may not have planned on skipping town the day he found out his company had gone bankrupt, but he did, and my grandmother was left all alone with six boys. Luckily, most of them were already men, but she had to grow old alone."

I keep my hand on his arm and step closer to him. We're inches apart, our eyes locked on one another. "Ayden, listen to me. You're not cursed. Your paternal line is not a curse. Okay? That's not why I agreed on the pact. I agreed because—"

"Because you'd lost faith too," he says, his mouth moving closer to mine until I can feel his breath on my lips when he talks. "When your dad cheated on your mom and she caught him, you lost them both. And you didn't ever want to feel that kind of pain again."

I can't breathe because his lips are now so close. I nearly lean forward and press my mouth against his.

"Breathe, Bella." Ayden steps back so that he's now a foot or so away from me.

I take in a deep gulp of air and let it out.

His dimple deepens. "Feeling better?"

I'm too turned on to laugh it off. "Yeah."

He takes my hand in his. "We were right. We're still right. As much as I hate seeing you with other guys, we're best friends, and we need it to stay that way."

I cough out an answer. "Exactly."

His eyes darken until they're nearly liquid. "Let me ask you one thing, though."

"Okay."

I'm surprised at the vulnerability in his face when he says, "Do you regret me staring at you like that last night?"

No. Not for one damn second.

And I can't possibly lie to him about it either.

I shake my head.

His expression relaxes. "Me neither. And about last night..." He steps so close to me I can see the green in his eyes. "That was the hottest two minutes of my life."

I gasp. "But we didn't..."

"I know. We didn't even fucking touch." His breath ghosts my cheek as he leans closer. "That being said, we can't afford to fuck up what we have."

I nod, unable to tear my gaze off of him. "Right."

He lets out a heavy breath. "So we'll still keep going with our dares this summer. But I think we can agree that double dating is off the table."

"Absolutely. And in the short term, we should probably really focus on finding...you know..." I trail off.

"Finding what?"

"Physical companionship," I say stiffly.

"You mean fuck other people?" Ayden says in a neutral tone.

My face goes nuclear. "Sure. That." *Even though the thought of you touching another woman is crushing.* "Maybe then things will go back to normal between us."

He nods, his expression completely shuttered. "Okay. Will do."

Super.

"I should go..." he says, gesturing toward his car.

"I need to get going," I say at the same time.

Three beats pass as we stare at each other in silence.

"Bella, I truly do wish the best for you on your search for your forever guy." Ayden's voice cracks as he says it, and his gaze on me is so hot I feel like I'm burning up.

"I wish the same for you. And whether my plus one ends up being a tool from the bar, or yours is the town whore, I'm sure everything will work out the way it's supposed to."

Ayden huffs out a short laugh. "Christ, Bella."

"As long as we're clear."

"Crystal."

We stand awkwardly, with me wondering if it's even possible to gracefully exit this conversation, when Ayden catches my wrist and runs his thumb over the soft inner skin. His blue eyes lock onto mine when he murmurs, "I have to tell you, Bella—I hate seeing you date. I've always hated it."

My mouth drops open. "You have?"

"I have." He lets go of my wrist abruptly, and I immediately feel the absence of his warm skin on mine. "But it is what it is. The reality is exactly what you said. You're going to meet someone and marry him someday. And I'll do my best to tolerate the guy."

His jaw locks up the way it always does when he's upset, and I know he's baiting me. He's been like this since we were kids. And I've always been a sucker for it.

"You mean the way I tolerate your multiple women?" I say too loudly as Ayden turns away to grab his lawnmower. "You drive me nuts!"

Ayden stops cold but doesn't turn around.

He walks across my lawn and disappears inside his car.

Fighting back tears, I go inside and pull out my guitar and notepad. I can't drink or date this kind of pain away. The only kind of outlet I can think of for this kind of pain? A good old-fashioned love song. And the lyrics are already forming on the tip of my tongue. I just have to write them down.

Ayden

It takes every ounce of strength in me to keep my back to her. Because if I turn around, I'm going to back her up against the side of her house and slam my mouth over hers.

I stalk over to my car and get in, not looking over at Bella once. My hands shake the entire way home, and when I get inside my house, I immediately turn the shower water to cold. I don't know how to get her out of my system. I don't even know if I want to anymore.

CHAPTER TWELVE

Bella

Over the next few days, Ayden and I try to move past what happened between us at the festival.

We don't see each other socially once. He still brings me to my mom's on Tuesday, but we make sure to avoid discussing our love lives. Neither of us brings up the dares, even in a joking manner. To make matters worse, I'm afflicted by the torturous game of what if.

What if Ayden's found someone? Who is she? Is he fucking her? Does he want something serious at last?

In a strong effort to stay distracted, I keep ridiculously busy. I study my ass off, so much that I'm certain if I do nothing else between now and my final college exam, I'll at least pass. I help my mother with her party planning; in fact, I'm so helpful that we complete her list far ahead of schedule. Except for the music, Mom's thrilled. I find her a DJ, but she's not satisfied. So finally, I tell her to talk to Guy about other options.

She does, and apparently she's so swept off her feet by Guy that she asks him to perform at the party.

"Just a few songs," he says to me. "The DJ will do the rest. And I want you to sing with me."

I freeze as I'm walking out of the lounge. "No. Absolutely not."

"Why not?"

"Because." I turn around to face him. "My mother doesn't like it when I sing."

"You've already mentioned that," he says. "Which is why you have to do it. Which is why you *need* to do it."

"Guy..."

"Bella. Don't let her stop you from coming all the way back."

I tap my foot on the linoleum floor and stare at his determined gaze.

"You're right," I finally say. "God, you're like the big brother I never had. Being an only child has its perks you know."

He chuckles. "We'll pick our selections this week and start practicing."

I wave and head for the door. "Sounds terrifying. See you."

The concept of singing in front of my mother has its benefits. I don't want my father's party to be the first time I perform in public again, so I take the leap and go to the club in Portland for an audition. The club owner hires me to sing every Thursday at six p.m., and he asks me to start that night.

So without a chance to back out, before I know it I'm up on the stage. The crowd is small—okay, really small, like ten people—but I sit on the stool, and I sing my own songs. I filter in a few popular cover songs as well, and overall, I'm cheering inside.

Because I did it.

I got back on the stage.

And yes, it feels just as terrifying and just as incredible as I thought it would.

I text Tari as soon as I'm finished, and we meet for a celebratory glass of champagne.

But while I'm happy with my return to singing, my dating situation feels dire. I've gone on a record number of bad blind dates for me and thanks to Tari, who seems to know an inordinate number of single guys, I could keep going on dates all summer. But I'm starting to feel hopeless.

From the accountant who asked me in the first half hour if "the shades match the drapes," to the wrestling coach who tried to teach me to arm wrestle right at the restaurant dinner table, I'm not feeling it with any of them.

With the intensity of what happened between Ayden and me, I wasn't necessarily expecting I'd meet my soul mate in the next week. But I *was* hoping to find someone to fool around with. Even if it was casual.

After every bad date, I go home and write in my bedroom. I write songs about life, about feeling stuck, and I write about Ayden.

I break things off with Trey for good. I can't possibly go on another date with him after that double date fiasco, and ending things with him is a relief.

I fantasize constantly about Ayden blowing on me and kissing me, and yet I can't even kiss my dates good night at the damn door when they walk me home. But it's more than a lack of chemistry. This strange feeling of guilt comes over me every time one of my dates leans in to kiss me. Guilt like I'm freaking *cheating* on Ayden. All I want is to relieve my sexual tension so I can hang out with my best friend again. Instead, the tension is escalating, until I'm freaking dying for Ayden. Suddenly, it's like no one else will do.

Despite the obvious tension between Ayden and me, when we're at Al's Coffee House after my mom's on Tuesday, he asks if I'll help his mother choose photographs for the video tribute she's organizing for Mr. Wild's memorial party.

Of course I say yes, and when I arrive at the Wild house the next day, I'm surprised when Ayden, wearing a t-shirt and board shorts, answers the door.

"Are you helping with the photos also?" I ask him. "I thought you'd be anywhere but here today. You've already helped your mom so much with the party."

He shrugs noncommittally. "I'm just going to hang out with you and Mom while you work if that's okay."

"Sure." I resist the urge I have to throw my arms around him and tell him how much I miss him. "We haven't gotten to hang out much this week."

"I know." He leads me into the living room where Anna Wild greets me with a warm hug.

While Ayden takes a work call in the other room, I sit with Anna on the couch and glance at the coffee table in front of me. Photographs are covering every square surface—black and whites, candids, and portraits, all of Ayden and Michael and their parents. Some feature the boat Mr. Wild drowned on, and there are a few of the boat Michael fishes from now. A couple pictures show Ayden working, shovel and rake in hand.

"These are amazing, Anna."

She nods, her eyes filling with pride. "Hal loved his camera. And he taught me how to use it early on, so I was able to get a lot of photos of him as well."

Anna makes a joke about her husband's sense of humor. "He loved to tease me with that darn camera. He'd catch me first thing in the morning when I looked a mess."

I laugh with her, and we're still laughing when a quick kiss lands on the top of my head.

I crane my neck and smile at Ayden standing behind me. Out of my peripheral, I catch Anna Wild beaming at us.

I scoot over. "Come sit down, Ayd."

Anna heads for the kitchen to get us all some tea, and I impulsively grab two photographs and hold them in front of me side by side, one of Ayden landscaping, and the other of Michael holding up a huge net of fish and grinning. They look oddly symmetrical, almost like both are paying homage to their father. I'd never noticed before.

Ayden looks over my shoulder. "Michael and me."

Anna walks into the room carrying a tray filled with a pot of tea, Irish scones, two teacups, cream and sugar.

I smile. "That looks amazing, Anna."

She laughs and reaches to fix her long dark hair. Then she smooths her apron over her housedress. "One of my mother's gifts was definitely hospitality." She looks at the pictures in my hand. "Those two are peas in a pod, aren't they?" she says as if reading my mind.

"You know I don't think I ever noticed before," I say to her. "I feel silly."

Ayden frowns. "We're not that similar."

"Oh, Ayden, please. You two try to hide it with the best of them." Anna gestures to the table. "As you can see, everything's a bit of a mess."

"It looks like you've got a lot of material." I pick up a photograph of Ayden as a baby. "So cute."

"And here's one of you and him, Bella," she says, handing it to me.

This picture is older than the one I have at home, but Ayden and I are still in our swimsuits. This time we're at the beach. I've got a pail in one hand, and with my other hand, I'm dumping a shovelful of sand on Ayden's head while he's intently digging in the sand in front of him.

Ayden chuckles. "You were a little angel with a devilish streak."

I laugh as I put it back on the table.

"You were always so adorable, Bella," Anna says as she pours us each a cup of tea. "Your blond hair, those gorgeous eyes. You took my breath away."

Ayden winks at me. "All the boys had crushes on little Bella."

I elbow him in the ribs, and he laughs.

"Thank you, Anna. You're so sweet to say that." I pick up my cup and pour a touch of cream into it.

Ayden's phone starts beeping.

"Sorry." He looks at the screen. "My boss again. I'll be right back." He walks out to the balcony with his phone.

"Ayden and Michael just refuse to look at this stuff," Anna says to me once he's gone. "They're both angry with me for having the party at all."

I take a sip of my tea. "Well, everybody grieves in their own way."

"I know, and I realize it's not easy for them. Two boys, and their daddy gone before either of them are teenagers. They don't see the point in dredging all the pain back up." Anna wipes her eyes with her apron. "I just don't want them to be numb to it is all."

"I understand."

She looks at me closely. "Ayden's going to miss you something terrible when he leaves."

I force a nod. "I'll miss him too, of course. But we've been apart before. Everything will be fine."

"I don't know what he would do without you, Bella." Anna shakes her head softly. "You were there for him when I couldn't be. The way you stood out on the pier with him and held his hand, night after night, while we waited for news of my husband..." Her voice breaks. "You were just a little girl, and yet you made sure he didn't get lost in the shuffle. I couldn't tell you then what that meant to me, but I hope you realize how much I appreciated what you did."

I swallow and reach out to hug her. "Of course I did," I say. "Ayden's held my hand my whole life too."

And right now, I miss him. I'm right here in town with him, and I feel like we have to treat each other like strangers.

My mind is racing, and I need help. From outside of our small town where everybody knows everybody. So, as soon as I leave the Wild house that afternoon, I call up an old friend.

Ava Sparks answers on the first ring.

"How are you, Bella?" she says in her usual caring tone.

And immediately, I relax.

Ava and I are from two different small towns on coastal Maine. We met years ago when we were competing in the same local talent contest. She's a singer too; well, she used to be. Like me, she walked off the stage one day due to circumstances that make mine seem microscopically small.

"I'm kind of a mess," I admit. "How are you doing?"

"Pretty good," she says. "Nothing new or exciting. So tell me what drama you're dealing with."

She's laughing so hard when I finish telling her about the double-date that she can't even speak for over ten seconds.

"I know," I say. "It's so bad it's comical."

"You know what you need?" she says. "A night out. And I have just the plan."

CHAPTER THIRTEEN

Later that night, I sit on my favorite stool next to Tari at Lucky Bay Bar. I'm not in the mood to be out. But when Ava told me California Blue Shaw, her husband, London, and his best friend, Diego, were coming up to Maine to visit for a night, I agreed to meet them all for a drink.

"You said Peter and Ayden are definitely going to Portland tonight, right?" I confirm for the fifth time.

Tari nods confidently. "Definitely. Peter had an evening meeting down there for work, and Ayden offered to drive down with him."

That's good. Ayden and I need time away from each other, at least when we're in bars. Meeting him at his mom's today was fine. Meeting him where alcohol is involved—not fine.

"Are those your friends?" Tari asks me, craning her neck to see the door. "I think I spot Ava."

I look with her, and my angle is unobstructed. "If you mean the four gorgeous people that just strolled into the bar, yes, that's them."

Ava's blond hair is thick and long, and she's model thin without trying. I've seen pictures of her when she was little, and she was always a beanpole.

She's quite a contrast to California as they walk toward us side by side. Cali's of shorter stature and she's got curves for days, and having a baby has accentuated them only in the best way.

Following behind them are two handsome men, London and Diego. With his dark hair tied back in a short ponytail and a stylish long-sleeved shirt and black pants, London looks like the hot, cocky billionaire that he is, but he's also big-hearted and kind and sweet.

Diego is a chef in Boston's North End. He's dressed casually tonight in worn blue jeans and a cream shirt. He has blond spiked hair and brown eyes that seem to notice everything.

"Wo-ow." Tari inhales. "Look at those hot guys. If I were still single, I swear, I don't know which one I'd want more."

"London's taken, so you'd have to go for Diego."

"Fine by me," Tari says with a giggle.

Diego grins as he walks up to me and kisses me on the cheek. "Good to see you again."

"You too. Welcome to Lucky Bay." I smile as I introduce him to Tari, and then I stand up to greet the others.

"How are you?" California hugs me tightly. "Ava said you've had a weird summer."

Ava puts her finger to her lips. "I didn't give her any details. You can share the dirty parts."

I laugh. "Unfortunately, the story's pretty boring. But I'm happy to have a night to just hang out with you."

California's green eyes study me. "Are you dating somebody?"

I wave my hand in the air. "I've tried. God, how I've tried. Ayden and I have this dare going..."

Her teeth flash in a brilliant smile. "Now this sounds interesting. How is Ayden?"

I reach for my drink. "That question does not come with a one-word answer."

California hops onto a stool and turns to me. "Awesome. A good love saga."

"Exactly," Ava says.

"I wouldn't call it a love anything," I protest.

California smiles as London leans over and kisses her on the head. "You sound like me before I gave up my stubborn ways."

California and I met in less than perfect circumstances—I was accompanying Ava to a support group for children of familial suicide. Ava didn't want to run into anyone she knew, so we left the state and drove down to Boston instead, and California was at the meeting. She was no stranger to mental illness and the way it can destroy a family, and the three of us hit it off and have remained friends. She and London started dating during that time, and the idea that they're now married nearly makes my head spin. I'm so happy for her, and no one deserves happiness more.

After catching up with Ava and Cali for a bit, I turn as Diego and Tari engage in a spirited conversation over which is the best Italian restaurant in Maine.

"My uncle and I like to do market research for the restaurant," he says when Cali asks him how he knows what's going on in Maine.

"In other words, they like to eat their way through New England," London says with a grin.

"God, what a great part of the job," Tari says with a sigh.

"It really is," Diego agrees. "But I love just about everything to do with my job. I'm a lucky guy."

I excuse myself for the restroom, and London's phone starts buzzing at the same moment. I gesture for him to follow me to the hallway so he can have some privacy, and then I leave him for the ladies' room.

When I come out a couple minutes later, London's just pocketing his phone.

"My brother," he says by way of explanation. "He's doing a kick-ass job with the family business, but he's still learning the ropes."

He and I start walking back toward the bar together, chatting along the way.

"Cali mentioned you and he are co-CEOs," I say. "That's a lot of responsibility."

"Sure," London agrees. "But these are first-world problems."

I laugh. "That's true."

As we weave through the tables, I can't help noticing the number of heads turning our way. London Shaw is definitely a man who attracts attention. And he doesn't even notice. His gaze is focused solely on his wife, whose bar stool is just coming into view as we get closer.

I smile, happy for Cali that she has such an amazing husband, but then, my gaze snags.

On the baseball-cap wearing, blue-eyed man currently standing in the doorway of the bar and glaring at me.

Ayden's here. And judging from the looks of him, he's not too happy to see me.

Ayden

My first thought is—

Bella's on a date.

This must be her attempt to find *physical companionship* as she put it the other day.

I changed my schedule around so I could sit at my mom's today and sift through old photographs, all because Bella agreed to come by and help. The intoxicating scent of her hair made me jealous of all the guys she's no doubt been going out with all week. And I can't ask her a damn thing. Because we promised we wouldn't, a decision I'm regretting.

I've jacked off to images of Bella every fucking night. Never before did I allow myself to put her into my fantasies, but now she's the only woman in the reel.

I want her so much I can barely stay still.

So when I see her with another guy, the irritation that shoots through me is immediate. And I'm well-aware it's unwarranted. I have no claim to Bella, and she's dating like she said she was going to.

But I'm taken by surprise as the guy puts his hand on her arm and ushers her ahead of him through the milling crowd. And I lose it.

Ignoring Peter's call to stop, I push through the throng of people.

"Bella." I block her path as I reach her.

Her cheeks flush in a cross between amusement and irritation. "Ayden."

I look over at her date. "I don't think we've met," I say in a clipped tone.

Bella rolls her eyes and turns to face the guy, who's smirking. I'm about to wipe that arrogant smile off his face when Bella says, "London Shaw, meet Ayden Wild. My overprotective best friend."

London's dark eyes narrow. "Just friends, huh?"

Bella sends me a meaningful look before adding, "London is California's *husband*."

There's no way for me to keep my face from revealing my shock. "You're Cali's husband?"

London extends his hand. "Good to meet you, Ayden."

"Shit. Nice to meet you." I shake his hand quickly, and we go join the others at the bar, where Tari and Peter are bent over laughing.

"Jealous much, Ayden?" Tari gets out through her peals of giggles. "And what are you and Peter doing here anyway?"

"Portland was boring," I say. "We missed Lucky Bay."

Bella raises her eyebrows at me. "Really. You missed Lucky Bay that much? How long were you gone—a few hours?"

"What can I say—I love my home."

"Plus, someone was wondering what someone else was doing tonight," Peter says in a stage-whisper voice to Tari. "I couldn't keep him away."

Tari pats Peter's chest. "Sure you couldn't. You're as bad as he is, and no doubt you egged him on all evening."

Before I can respond, Ava and Cali step closer to say hello.

"Sorry about the misunderstanding," I murmur to Cali. "Bella and I have a bit of a bet going on this summer."

"I've heard something about that," she says with a smile.

After London introduces Peter and me to Diego, the four of us step a few feet away from the women, who are gushing over pictures of Cali and London's new baby daughter that Cali's showing on her phone.

"I'm not usually such an ass," I say dryly.

Peter snorts. "So he says."

But London regards me with a serious expression. "No worries. I remember what it was like."

"Yeah, two years ago London was Boston's number one player," Diego cuts in with a punch to London's arm. "He never went out with the same woman twice."

Looking at the guy, that's not hard to imagine. London's in great shape, and he's clearly confident as hell.

I accept the shot of whiskey Peter hands me, and tip the liquid down my throat. It burns, and I drop the glass onto the bartop before saying to London, "Is that right?"

London shrugs. "California changed everything for me." He looks over at his wife, and his expression turns downright mushy and affectionate. I would throw up if it weren't for the very obvious twinge of envy in my gut. "We were next door neighbors who formed an instant dislike for one another. Plus, I had issues with commitment."

Diego murmurs, "Not your fault, though."

"Doesn't matter," London says matter-of-factly. "I pushed every woman away."

"All that family and marriage stuff," Diego says with a wave of his hand. "Not going to happen for me. The women I've met have ruined my interest in any of it."

Peter chuckles. "The dating scene's been that bad, huh?"

"Man, I like to say that my best girlfriend has always been Bucca's," Diego jokes.

"His uncle's restaurant," London explains. "D, you need a

fucking online dating profile—first and last criteria will be—*loves Italian cooking. Especially mine.*"

We all laugh as my gaze slides over to Bella. "So, how did you and Cali get past all of the crap and end up where you are now?" I ask London.

"Honestly, I don't fucking know exactly," he says. "Except that California made me feel things no other woman ever could. She got through to me, and I couldn't let her go."

My eyes haven't left Bella's, who's staring back at me with an intensity that burns me up inside.

Could I let Bella go? Maybe I should. It's the right thing to do in order to preserve what we have. But I don't want to let her go.

I don't even know that I can.

CHAPTER FOURTEEN

Bella

"You two are making things harder than they need to be," Tari insists when I meet her to sunbathe.

It's now been ten days since our double date fiasco. I haven't seen Ayden since the other night at Lucky Bay Bar, which was incredibly awkward. We barely talked—Ayden hung out with the guys, and while I had a great time with Ava, California, and Tari, I hated the tension between Ayden and me.

From my position on my stomach, I turn my head to face her. "We are?"

"Yes." She picks up a handful of sand and we both watch as the granules slide out of her hand and fall back onto the beach. "Look at this sand leaving my hand. It's the passage of time. Here we are at the beginning of July already, and you and Ayden are running out of days to hang out."

"It was just...that moment between us at the fair was..."

"Relationship changing." She nods, and I see the understanding in her face. "I know. Going from best friends to more is scary. But don't let one moment stop you from hanging out together."

I swallow. "Ayden's probably out having the time of his life anyway. We agreed to find people to date and have sex with. I'm sure he's having an easier time with the sex part than I am."

"I wouldn't be so sure about that." Tari giggles. "Peter's as much of a steel trap when it comes to Ayden and his dates as I am about you and yours. But I overheard him on the phone with Ayden last night."

"You did? What'd he say?" I prop myself up on my elbows and lean closer.

"He said, and I quote, 'Tari won't tell me a thing about Bella. I swear I know nothing.'"

I stare at her beaming face. "That's it? How is that enlightening?"

Tari rolls her eyes. "Because! It means Ayden's thinking of you. *You*, Bella. Not the women he's on dates with. Get it?"

"I suppose. I just wish I could talk to him about all of this. I miss him."

"So let's get together tonight. The four of us, like old times, at the beach."

I suck in a breath and blow it out slowly. "Okay. Yes."

———

Ayden

"So." Peter clicks his shot of whiskey to mine as we sit at Lucky Bay Bar. It's still early, and the bar's pretty much empty. "You and Bella."

I shake my head at him in warning. "Don't talk about Bella. Any other woman, fine. But not her."

He laughs as he swirls his whiskey before swallowing it down. "You're touchy this week, Ayd."

He's right. I can't get Bella out of my head.

"And that little scene the other night?" His eyes brighten with mischief. "Could have sworn I was going to have to pick you up off the ground after you went after an innocent man. A *married* man who wasn't on a date with your girl the way you thought he was. But London was amused, of course, and so was I."

I swallow down my shot and turn to Peter. "I know. It's just that Bella and I…it's driving me fucking nuts," I admit to him. "We…" I shake my head in frustration.

"It's you and Bella." Peter claps me on the back. "You guys have always been a package deal. So what's the problem? If you want to move things in a new direction…"

"It will change absolutely everything between us," I say. "We swore on our lives we'd never go there with each other. What if we try and it blows up in our faces?"

"Or…" Peter throws some bills down on the counter and we stand up to leave. "What if you get everything you never thought possible because you were looking at all the wrong women?"

I've definitely been looking at the wrong women. For the past ten days, I've been on one date after another, all in the hopes of finding someone to take home with me so I could get out of my system—once and for all—the image of Bella, hot and bothered across from me, inside the festival tent.

Nothing's worked. Not one woman has grabbed my attention. And it's not their fault; it's mine. I've been distracted and irritable. I've been a terrible date; I may be picking up the tab and walking the women to their doors, but I'm a shitty companion. I've kissed each one on the cheek and told them good night, and then I've called Peter so we can meet up for a drink.

I've worked so many extra hours my boss refused to let me come in this morning. And I've helped Ma with her party planning every free moment I have. She's been thrilled with the extra set of hands, but even she asked me what was wrong. When I told her nothing, she just patted my cheek and told me to talk to Bella.

After Peter waves goodnight, I walk by Bella's street on my way home. My hand twitches at my side, desperate to go knock on her door. I ache to touch her. I can hardly stop myself from going to her house, running my fingers through her long blond hair, and putting my mouth over hers. I've never dared to think of being with her in any permanent way, not until she said she was ready to find her plus one. That's when a light bulb went off inside my chest —the only plus one I ever want to see her with is me.

When I went by her house to mow her lawn ten days ago, I contemplated asking her what she thought about us, about the possibility of us dating.

But the look of pain in her eyes when I brought up her parents and why we came up with our agreement in the first place—I was afraid she'd pass out from holding in her breath.

So I didn't ask her. I could already tell the answer.

She's not ready. And I'm not sure I am either. Not for the kind of feelings that will come up if we date. Because Bella and I would be combustible together. The one time we kissed, we were just kids, and yet it's stuck with me all these years. Her tongue was fire, and the way her hands felt wrapped around my neck...

She got inside me with that one kiss, and she's never left.

And I can't imagine leaving her. The very idea of it rips my insides in half.

But right now, I need to try to fix a different problem. I have to talk to my brother and attempt to settle this issue between us once and for all.

———

I knock three times on the apartment door over my parents' garage. Just when I'm starting to worry that he never came home, my older brother jerks open the door.

We stare at each other for a few seconds before he lets out a groan and gestures me inside.

"I'm not changing my mind," he says immediately.

I put up my hands in surrender. "Truce, Michael. I'm not here to fight. But I do need you to agree to take the money I'll be sending back once I move. I don't want Ma feeling caught in the middle of our war."

He's already shaking his head. "No fucking way. I'll find a way to pay Ma's mortgage for her. I live with her, not you. You got the job out west—good for you. Use the money for yourself."

"You're so goddamn stubborn," I tell him.

He gets up in my face and shoves a finger into my chest. "I'm looking out for you, baby brother."

"You're not," I say, enjoying how his dark eyes blacken with anger. "You're letting your pride get in the way of me trying to help. Look, my job will make a lot more money than your boat's currently pulling in."

He shoves me hard, but I get right back in his face and hold him tightly against the wall. "What are you so pissed off about?"

He pushes me off of him, and I take one last look at him before I head for the door. I'm not going to get anywhere with him like this.

"Nice talking to you, brother," I throw over my shoulder as I leave.

———

Bella

After Tari and I leave the beach, I head to town for my work shift. I'm sunburned and dehydrated, so I stop at the small grocery store at the edge of the square.

I walk through the beverage section. I've just grabbed a bottled water when I hear, "Mirabella. I didn't know you shopped here."

Making a slow turn around, my gaze lands on my mother. She's pushing a small cart in front of her.

"Hello, Mom. I didn't know you shopped here either."

Her eyes are puffy beneath all her mascara. "I don't normally," she says. "I like the specialty store over in Ludslow. Everything is prepared ahead of time; you just pick it up, and you're done."

I nod, remembering those dinners.

"But your father has insisted on eating fish once a week," she says. "So there's the fish store on Main, which is very fresh, or there's this place. This is more convenient for me. I'm picking up frozen fish in preparation for next week when he returns from his business trip."

I look at her puffy eyes again. "Have you been crying?" I ask her.

Mom backs away from me immediately. "Have a nice evening. See you next week."

"Mom!" I chase after her and her cart. "What's going on?"

"Mirabella." Her voice is shaky, but she keeps pushing the damn cart away from me. "Please leave it be."

"I want to help, Mom," I say in as low a voice as I can muster. "Please let me help."

"Next week," she gets out in a choked voice. "We'll see each other then."

And she's gone.

Something feels off.

My mother never lets her pain show in public. And she just did.

I pay for my water in the self-service lane, and then I leave the grocery store and watch for my mother's exit.

She comes out a few minutes later, but a store employee is pushing her cart full of bags for her. They walk to her car together, and he loads her bags into the back.

She climbs into her car and pulls out of the parking lot. She never sees me lurking on the sidewalk.

I'm going to be late for my shift if I follow her. But tailing her home won't help anyway; she'll just kick me out.

So I turn around and head for the pool hall to clock in. Once I'm inside the cashier's booth, I take out my phone and scroll through my contacts until I find her.

Dr. Marianne Thibbs.

Mom warned me to never call her therapist. She said it was breaking all sorts of confidences to do so. But the look on her face —I don't know what else to do.

The call goes to voicemail.

"Dr. Thibbs, this is Bella Wesley. My mother, Lucy Wesley, is one of your patients, and I was calling to check on her progress. I know she had discussed changing her medications with you, and I understand all of this is confidential, but if you could please return my call when you have a moment, I'd really appreciate it."

Because it's summer and Lucky Bay gets a ton of tourists, the pool hall is already packed. I put my phone down and try to focus on my job.

CHAPTER FIFTEEN

Work keeps me preoccupied for my entire shift, and when I clock out late that night, Preston's still holding court behind the bar.

"Tell anyone you see I'm still serving," he calls out. "We won't be shut down for at least another hour!"

"Have fun." I head down the hall and wave at Guy sitting at the piano.

He nods at me. "What's up, Bella? You look stressed out."

Normally I'd never open my mouth to Guy about my love life. But I'm knocked off tonight, and the idea of seeing Ayden in a few minutes has me shaking.

So I step inside the lounge and stand by the piano while I fidget with the hem of my shirt. "I just can't stand this tension with Ayden. Can't stand the way we've been dancing around each other all summer."

"Really." Guy raises an eyebrow. "Looks like you can stand him pretty good. Looks like you have for a long time from where I'm standing. And the feeling's mutual, by the way. He's crazy for you, Bella."

"How do you know that? He dates every available female in Lucky Bay."

Guy leans his elbows on the top of the piano. "That doesn't mean shit. What you two have is different, and you know it."

"He just...he's all I think about these days."

Guy chuckles. "That's all that matters."

"How long have you been with Melody?"

"Eight years."

"And you still like her? You don't like secretly hate her but stay with her anyway?"

"No." His eyes light up as he smiles. "I love her more now than I did when I met her. Drives me mad sometimes, but she's the only one I want." He taps the counter with his knuckles. "Don't give up on love just because you saw a shitty example."

Unexpected pain hits me at his words.

"You want to sing a little? Maybe some more practice for my dad's party?"

"Sure. Sounds great."

I turn back to close the door behind me, but Guy calls out my name.

"What's wrong?"

He raises his eyebrows. "Time to unlock the door, Bella."

I freeze. "Guy..."

"You're ready. You may not think so, but you are."

He pauses with his fingers over the keys, as I stand frozen by the door with my hand on the knob.

This is different than singing to a bunch of strangers in Portland; this is much closer to home and much more intimate.

And much, much scarier.

So I do for myself what Ayden would if he were here—

I dare you, Bella.

I take a deep breath and let go of the handle, and then I leave the door open as I walk over to Guy and take a seat on the stool next to the piano.

He nods at me and breaks into a cover of one of our favorites, a Don Henley classic. He plays, and I sing, and when we finish, he breaks into another cover.

I keep my back to the open door. I hear some cheering in the hallway, most likely from drunk customers leaving the pool hall.

After three songs, Guy glances behind me and covers the microphone with his hand. "You got yourself some fans, honey. How about we give them a real show, for one song only?"

My face must show the panic I feel inside because Guy chuckles. "There aren't that many people. Just a few drunk stragglers who heard us as they went to leave. Let's give them a great finish."

I lift my chin. "Okay. Let's do it."

"That's my girl. How about one of your originals that you've been working on—just give me the chords, and I'll figure it out as you go."

The first song to pop into my head is the one I wrote the night Ayden and I decided to take a break from each other. "I've got one that's an easy three-chord progression," I tell Guy. "It's kind of a sad song."

"I have an idea," he tells me. "When you're halfway, if you're feeling up to it, spin your stool around and face the people that are listening to us. Deal?"

Thanks to my gig in Portland, I've faced an audience since the last night I performed in L.A. But tonight, in my hometown where everything is more intimate, I feel especially vulnerable. Visions of Trevor and Max in the crowd race through my mind. I try to erase that memory and my mother pops into my head instead. The tight bun, receded eyes, and pursed mouth. *Shit.* I break into a strangled cough.

"I'll try," I promise Guy right before I start to sing.

After I get through the first chorus, I take a deep breath and spin my stool around. A small crowd is scattered throughout the room, some at the small round tables and others just standing with drinks in their hands.

My eyes widen in surprise when I see Tari and Peter sitting at a table in the corner. I thought they were already at the beach, but they must have popped by to pick me up. Tari has a big smile on her face, and she waves at me. I smile at her and then my gaze travels past them, all the way to the back. And my heart lurches into my throat.

Ayden's here.

He's leaning against the open doorway, hands in his jeans pockets, baseball cap pulled down over his mess of black hair. When I make eye contact with him, his lips part and his eyebrows shoot up as if he's as surprised to see me as I am him. He locks eyes with me and doesn't break the contact.

Shaking more from the lyrics than from the fact that I'm performing, I deliver the final chorus just to him.

Wild boy,
I'm wild for you,
Good man,
I'm good for you.
Wish we could see it
Like they do,
Dream big,
My heart's with you.

I'm so thrown off I stumble through the rest of the song, call out a thank you to Guy, and scramble off the stool and over to Tari and Peter. Peter gives me a high-five as Tari wraps me up in a hug.

"You sounded so great up there!" she says.

I hardly hear her. I'm too busy trying to subtly crane my neck so I can check out Ayden.

"What the hell are you looking at?" Tari says as she turns too.

"No." I tug on her arm. "Don't look there. Ayden's back there."

"Ayden's here? But he said he was going to meet us at the beach. Where..." She trails off and covers her mouth with her hands.

The tap on my shoulder startles me, and I whip around.

Ayden grins as he takes a seat in the chair next to me.

"Hey," I say softly.

"When'd you start singing here?" he asks.

"Tonight was the first time I sang for any of the customers. I've been practicing privately with Guy for a little while."

Ayden puts his hand on my thigh. "You looked amazing."

The heat from his hand burns through my jeans, and I catch eyes with Tari, who tries to stifle her laugh.

Ayden catches himself, and his cheeks flush. "You sounded amazing too," he says as he keeps his hand on my leg. "Was that last one an original?"

I take a deep breath. "Yeah. It's new. I wrote it...recently."

Ayden's dimple deepens. "I like it."

"I'm glad." I inch closer to him.

His eyes are glued to mine, and my pulse takes off.

When Guy calls into the microphone that he's closing up the lounge, Peter stands up. "Let's head to the beach."

Tari and I hang back as the four of us walk through the square and across the docks to the sand.

"Wow," Tari whispers in my ear. "Your performance was like a love potion for that boy."

"That song I sang," I say to her quietly. "It says too much. It's called Wild Love as if that isn't obvious."

"And Ayden ate up every word of it," she assures me.

Before I can answer her, Peter and Ayden have stopped on the flat part of the beach right by the ocean.

Ayden removes his hat and unzips his hoodie. Tari takes off her overshirt and cut-offs, leaving her in a cami and boy shorts. And Peter's dropping his shorts and sliding out of his sneakers.

"No," I say automatically, knowing what's coming next. "The water's always so cold at night."

"Come on." Ayden takes off his t-shirt and my gaze lands on his chest.

Good Lord, Ayden's fit. His body doesn't have an ounce of fat. He's all muscle, and he seems to always be tanned. I know he sometimes landscapes shirtless, but that's got to be a God-given gift, the ability to be constantly tanned in Maine.

"Bella." He's staring at me, and I jerk my gaze up to his eyes. "You're swimming, right?"

I look out at the water. Tari and Peter are already waist deep.

"It's not that bad, Bella!" she calls out.

"Liar!" I say to her.

But I take off my shirt. Ayden's still watching me, his mouth turned up in a grin. "Quit it," I say to him, gesturing him away with my hand.

He drops his jeans off his hips and puts them in a pile with the rest of his clothes. Wearing only a pair of mouth-wateringly sexy boxer briefs, he turns away and heads into the ocean. As I watch his ass while he walks away from me, standing there by myself in the half moonlight, I wonder if he's ever wanted me as desperately as I want him right now.

I slip off my shorts and sandals and head for the water.

By the time I get my first toe in, Ayden's already dove underneath a wave. When he emerges from the water, I nearly hurl my body at him.

He looks like a freaking God, all dripping wet and with his briefs clinging to every important part of him. His mouth quirks up at my obvious ogling.

"Dive in with me," he says. "The water feels great."

"Then why are you shivering?" I ask him, reaching out to touch his chest. My hand feels warm against his wet body.

Ayden puts his hand over mine, and I can feel his heart pounding hard. But I take the plunge. I kneel down till I'm half wet. And before I can allow myself to think too hard, I duck my head and dive in.

At first, it's so cold I get head-freeze. But then I start to feel the warmth underneath the cold, and I keep swimming.

Ayden swims alongside me until we reach Tari and Peter on the sandbar.

"I should have brought the beer cooler out here," Peter says.

"Are you crazy?" Tari and I say at the same time.

Peter laughs. "Just wanted to hear you both say that again. That's four years in a row, I think."

The four of us splash around for a while until Ayden turns to me and says quietly, "Come with me?"

CHAPTER SIXTEEN

We swim to shore, and Ayden hands me his hoodie. I put it on and we walk along the beach for a few minutes in silence. No one's around, and the moon is just bright enough to see our way without a flashlight.

When I realize where we're going, I shriek. "The tidal pools?"

Ayden's dimple flashes. "Is that okay?"

I immediately scoot closer to him. He puts his arm around me and draws me into his chest. "Of course it's okay," I say. "I love the pools."

After Ayden's father died, Ayden was so sad, and I didn't have a clue how to help him. I did the first thing I could think of; I asked him if he wanted to take a walk. We left his house and walked to the beach. We kept going until we found the tidal pools. They only exist at low tide after the waves fill up the empty divots of sand, and they're the stillest bodies of water I've ever seen.

We made up our own game that day, a way for Ayden to express his pain when he didn't know how. I asked him questions, and if he didn't want to share, he'd duck. If he wanted to tell me something, he said "truth."

But we didn't just come here after Mr. Wild died. We came here after my dad's first affair, when my mother checked herself into her bedroom and locked the door for over a week, only to come out for food and wine. We came here when I returned from L.A., and I found out my mother was far worse off than she'd been when I left.

As soon as we reach the pools, I immediately walk to the edge of the water and dip my toe in.

"Take off my hoodie," Ayden says, his eyes glued to my chest. "You'll regret it afterward if you don't."

His voice hitches, but knowing he's right, I slip out of his hoodie. Feeling exposed in just my lacey white bra and matching underwear, I swallow as I throw Ayden's hoodie toward him. He catches it in one hand and lays it on a rock, his eyes never leaving mine.

Before he can catch too much of a show, I step out into the pools until I'm in up to my waist. Then I sink in up to my shoulders. Immediately, I feel a release of pressure in my head, just like I always do whenever Ayden and I come here. I feel freed from daily stresses, if only temporarily.

"I hope you already know this, but in case you don't—you have the world's hottest body," Ayden says as he joins me in the water.

I've always been on the thin side, more athletic-looking than super curvy. My breasts are fine but average-sized, and other than my naturally long, slender legs, I've never thought too much about the rest of me. At Ayden's compliment, one he's never paid me before, I immediately cross my arms over my chest.

"Don't be shy," he says in a serious tone. "I'm just speaking the truth."

I pray my voice will sound even when I answer him. "Thank you."

He shrugs casually. "So, are you ready to play?"

"I'm not sure."

His mouth twitches. "Well, too bad. That's what we do out here, right? We call each other out on our shit?"

"We always have."

He fixes his gaze on me with a force that gives me chills. "You're still a star up there, Mirabella Wesley."

I try to look away from him, but he takes my chin in his hand so I can't.

"I'm dead serious, Bella. I heard you singing from outside the room. It's been a long time, but I'd recognize your voice anywhere." He trails off as I swallow. "You were amazing. I'm just happy for you."

I slip my arms around his wet body. "I wanted to tell you."

"I don't mind the secrets."

"I guess I felt so much pressure and scrutiny, as it was, from myself." I take a deep breath. "Ayd, I'm sorry about what happened on my front lawn. I feel like I could have handled things much better."

He stares at me in the moonlight. "I sure as hell could have. We kind of ran scared." His voice is warm like whiskey. "Am I right?"

I sneak a glance at him. "Maybe."

He chuckles, and we lapse into a comfortable silence. Until he says in a gruff tone, "Michael's boat is barely in the black. And my mom's been late on her last two mortgage payments. One more, and they'll have to foreclose."

I gasp. "Oh no. Ayden, I'm so sorry."

He nods. "I didn't find any of this out until after the second late payment. I would have helped her out earlier, but fucking Michael didn't tell me."

"Let me guess; he did it to protect you?"

He nods at me, his expression grateful that he doesn't have to explain further. "Those were his exact words."

"So you got a job that paid a lot more," I surmise. "And you're going to give all that extra money to your mom so she can keep the house."

"Except Michael won't let me. He says he's the one living on my parents' property, so he should be the one to pay the mortgage.

He told my mom if she uses the money I send that he'll personally send it back to me out of his paycheck."

"But if his boat's struggling..."

"He's being a stubborn ass." Ayden shakes his head. "I need to get him on the same page as me. Ma's feeling torn between us, and she doesn't want Michael upset."

I reach out and take his hand in mine. "It will be okay, Ayd. I think Michael will come around. Maybe the memorial party for your dad will help him somehow."

"Maybe." Ayden tugs me closer to him. "So how long are you going to stay in that cashier's booth?"

"Duck," I say before I drop underneath the cool water.

When I emerge, the blue of Ayden's eyes is so dark it looks black, like the ocean when it's stormy. "Bella, you deserve everything good. A forever plus one, and a singing career, if you still want that. Your ex didn't kill your dreams. And staying here won't help you bring them back."

Before I can say anything, he says, "I want you to move to L.A. with me, Bella."

My breath catches in my chest.

I was prepared for Ayden to ask me again. Ever since he hinted at it weeks ago, I knew he'd circle back eventually. I just didn't know when.

And tonight? Tonight, as usual, Ayden's caught me off-guard. So I go on the defensive. "Question: why?"

He backs up a step. "Why what?"

"Why do you want me to come with you?"

His cheeks flush. "That's a stupid question. You're my best friend. And you can pursue your singing dream there. Of course I want you to come."

"So you want us to what—be roommates? Or would I get my own apartment?"

He splashes at the water with his hands. "I don't know. But it would make sense for you to live with me in Dylan's apartment. You wouldn't have to worry about rent, so you could focus exclusively on your music. And it's a two-bedroom. But until now, I guess I hadn't thought it through."

"I don't think you've thought much of it through," I say, feeling the pain slice through my heart like a knife. "Because you've dated every woman in town here, and you'll no doubt do the same thing in L.A. And while that's worked out fine when we aren't actually living together, I have to be honest—I don't know if it will be as easy for me when I'm watching a parade of women come and go from your bedroom."

Ayden's back in my space, his breath hot and smelling like mint. "What do you want to say? Spit it out, for Christ's sake."

My hand grabs at his soaking wet body for support because I truly think I might fall over. "Forget what I said about the women."

"And what?" His eyes zero in on mine. "I need more than that. Tell me."

He's shaking as much as I am, and the emotion swimming in his eyes unnerves me.

God, I was so not prepared for this conversation. But it's here, and it's big, and I have to somehow muddle my way through it. Even if it feels like too much, I need to stand here and face him. "You just...you act like it's so easy for me to pick up my life and move again. I'm not like these women you've dated where if you say jump, they will. I'm never going to be like them, Ayden."

"I don't want you to be like any of them, for God's sake." He takes hold of my arms and crowds me up against him, his breath coming quickly. "You're my...you're the only damn woman who's ever meant anything to me. Just because we swore we'd never fuck..."

I let out a small gasp, and he rephrases.

"Just because we swore we'd never have sex with each other doesn't mean you're not the most important person in my life. You always have been, and you always will be. You have to know that you're everything to me, Bella."

"I do." I clench my teeth. "I absolutely do. And you're the same

for me. Which is exactly why this feels so..." *Explosive.* "Challeng-
ing. I don't want either of us to get hurt, Ayden. And I'm not sure
how to avoid that if we continue down this path. We have to stay
clear-headed so neither of us does something we can't turn back
from. You mean far too much to me to make that kind of mistake."

Without waiting for him to answer me, I duck under the water.
The cold hits me hard, and I pop back up, my hair now slicked
back against my head.

Ayden flicks his gaze to me. "Truth, Bella? I think you're torn."

I shift my attention away from him and stare out at the shore.
The stillness is soothing. "Torn how?"

"I think you want things you don't think you deserve."

I drag my lip between my teeth and turn my head to meet his
determined gaze. "Like moving back to L.A. you mean."

"Maybe. I think it's more than that." His eyes fix on me as he
raises a topic that used to be taboo between us, even out here in
the middle of the pools—"Truth or duck, Bella—I think you want
me to fuck you, but you're scared."

Holy, holy, holy shit. I drop back down under the water, and I
hold my breath as long as possible before I have to pop back up.

Ayden's standing in the same spot he was, waiting for me. "Are
you embarrassed?"

"No," I lie.

"Am I right?"

"Maybe." Another lie. Of course he's right. As if to offer silent
proof, my gaze slides to his mouth, and I'm still focusing on his lips
when he speaks again.

"Truth or duck—how's your dare coming along?"

I break into a soft laugh. "Shitty. Super shitty."

He shoots me a half-grin. "Yeah? Mine too. I'm pretty much
batting zero."

"Me too."

"Truth or duck—did you sleep with the tool from the bar?"

I go back under water, and I come up spitting water. Ayden
rubs my back until I stop hacking.

"Too personal?" he asks me, his cheeks flushing red. "I know we don't usually ask each other that question. But I'll tell you one of my truths, Bella: I've never been this jealous before of men you're dating."

"How come?"

Now he ducks under the water. When he resurfaces, he exhales. "Changed my mind. I'll actually take the truth on that question."

The air thickens. "Y-you will?"

"I will."

I wave a shaky finger in the air. "So-o. Tell me. How come you're jealous?"

He steps closer to me so that our noses are nearly touching. "Because I've never wanted to kiss you as much as I do right now."

My gaze locks in on his mouth. God, his lips are so sexy they should be illegal. I go back under water.

Ayden's dimple is showing when I re-emerge cold and sputtering.

"It wasn't even your truth," he says with a smirk.

I'm shaking, and I deflect. "No, it wasn't. Here's one for you— did you sleep with Jenny Woods?"

Ayden cups my chin in his hand. "No. I've been solo all summer. And I know that's a first for me," he adds when I let out a surprised gasp. "And these last ten days where we only saw each other when we had to? I've been completely miserable."

I exhale. "Ayden, it's been the same for me. It's honestly been the loneliest ten days of my life."

"How come?"

"Because I missed you so much every second."

"Bella..."

"And to answer your question, I didn't sleep with Trey." I hold out my arms in a surrender gesture. "I never want to talk about this stuff, but I will now. Yes, I was angry I had to leave L.A. Yes, I felt like Trevor forced me out. But no, I wasn't sorry we broke up. And not just because he likes men and we were clearly not meant for each other, but because I didn't love him. I thought I did for a moment or two, but I didn't."

"How do you know that?" Ayden's voice drops to nearly a whisper.

"Because I didn't miss him when we were apart. I missed him a little, but not like..."

I suck in a breath and catch Ayden's eye.

"Not like what?" he asks me.

"Not like I miss you."

Ayden swallows hard as his gaze shifts to my lips.

"Ayden..." I struggle to withstand his hot stare on me. "This is so..."

"There you two are!" Tari and Peter wave to us from the shore. "Come on! We've got tequila!"

CHAPTER SEVENTEEN

We all sit down on pieces of driftwood. Tari asks me how things are going with my father's party planning, but Ayden is on my other side, and he puts his hand on my back as he chats with Peter. The sensual heat of his hand through the thin fabric of my shirt takes up my full attention, and I can hardly focus on what Tari's saying.

"Honey, let's get out the tequila!" Tari calls out to Peter.

"Since when do we drink tequila at the beach?" Ayden asks.

"Tonight, my friend." Peter reaches into his bag and pulls out a bottle of tequila, as well as paper cups, limes, and salt. "This is a gift from Timmy for taking over his shift all week. So let's not waste it."

"Oh no," I say. "Every time I get drunk, I always regret it."

"One shot each," Peter says. "That's all I ask."

It feels like a bizarre rite of passage—the four of us standing in a circle and licking salt off our hands, downing the shot, and then sucking on the lime. Tari begs me to have a second shot with her, and I do.

Peter puts salt on Tari's neck and licks it off before his next shot. Tari giggles and tells Ayden to do the same to me. I tell him to stay right where he is. He grins and doesn't take her up on it.

Within a half hour, the three of us are good and buzzed. Ayden stays sober, saying he has to work at six a.m. Tari and Peter giggle their way down the beach, and I sit down next to Ayden. Courtesy of Peter, I'm still holding all the ingredients for another shot, even though I don't plan to use them.

Ayden takes the lime out of my hand and holds it. Then he wets his neck with a touch of tequila, takes some salt out of my other hand, and puts it on his neck.

"I dare you, Bella," he says, his voice barely audible.

His eyes are fixed on mine, but his expression gives nothing away. And I'm too tipsy to think straight. So I finally stop and let go.

I lean over and lick the salt off Ayden's skin. He laughs and pulls me closer. His arm wraps around my back, and I melt into him. His neck is so warm, and he smells so good, like pine and tequila and ocean.

I lick his neck again. And again. And then I suck on him so hard I'm sure I give him a hickey. A sexy, masculine sound escapes his throat, and his arm tightens around my waist.

By the time I pick my head up and swallow down the shot, Ayden's eyes are liquid with heat. His gaze follows my movements as I grab the lime out of his hand and suck on it. When I'm finished, he cups my cheek with his hand.

"Bella. Damn." He leans in so close to me, his face inches away, that for a second I'm certain he's going to kiss me. But his eyes flick down to my empty shot glass, and with a low curse, he abruptly pulls back. He takes the glass out of my hand. "You can't drive home," he says. "I'll take you."

Ayden

I nearly fucking kissed her.

And if she hadn't been drinking, I would have.

Kissing Bella Wesley has never been on the table before.

It just wasn't an option.

Except that things have changed.

When she fucking licked me, I swear to God I nearly came in my pants. Bella and I have done such a damn good job of never crossing the line, but tonight it felt like the line was definitely blurred. And I know I enjoyed that blurring a hell of a lot more than I've ever wanted to admit to.

And suddenly, I don't want to turn the train back around to the safe friend zone. The direction it's going in feels pretty fucking great.

Because I'm the only one sober, I take Tari and Peter home too.

"Bella, let's meet there for breakfast tomorrow," Tari says as we pass Lou's Diner. "We'll pick our cars up before."

"Uh-huh." Bella's head is propped against the door window, and her hair's covering her face so I can't see her expression.

Desperate to be alone with her, I drop off Tari and Peter first even though it's ten minutes in the opposite direction.

After they get out of the back seat, Tari walks around to talk to Bella, who opens her door and nearly falls out of the car so she can whisper something to Tari.

Peter leans his head in the open window of the driver's side and says to me in a low voice, "Trying to talk to her about a lifetime of shit between you isn't the best idea when she's drunk, man. Just saying."

He's right. I know he's right. Doesn't mean I want to listen to him.

"I've got it," I say. "I won't fuck anything up."

He pats my shoulder and walks away with Tari to their front door.

I glance over at Bella, who's tucked her long, sexy legs underneath her. I lean over to make sure her seat belt is on, and pull out onto the road.

"Hey," I call to her softly.

She turns to me, her eyes sleepy and unfocused.

"You want to come over for a while? I've got leftover Thai food in the fridge."

She smiles so sweetly I nearly lean over and put my mouth over hers. "Sounds perfect, Ayd."

When we reach my driveway, I pull in slowly and turn off the car. "Let me help you out."

I hop out of the car and open her door, sliding my arm around her waist when she practically falls into my arms.

I pause outside the car, my face buried in the crook of her neck, inhaling the scent that always reminds me of her, the intoxicating smell of flowers and mangoes and ocean. My hand tightens on her hip, and I actually have to stop myself from pressing my lips to her soft, edible skin. She wraps one hand around my hat, knocking it off my head and onto the driveway.

"Oh, no." She pulls back and her eyes widen. "I keep messing with your hat lately. I know how you hate that."

I bend down to retrieve my hat, and then I tip my head until our noses touch. "Do I seem like I hate it?"

Her eyes become pools of liquid heat. "I...I'm not sure. No?"

I shake my head, keeping my nose on hers. "No. I don't hate it at all when you mess with me, Bella Wesley. Got it?"

I step back just in time to see her tongue darting out to lick her plump bottom lip.

I stifle a groan. She's going to kill me tonight. Right here in my damn driveway. Her nipples are poking through her shirt that provides hardly any coverage at all without her bra in the way. And I know she's wearing no panties underneath those tiny cut-offs that barely cover her ass. I grab her sea-soaked bra and panties out of the car and slip them into my pocket.

Just getting Bella to the door and inside my house without backing her up against the wall and wrapping her legs around my waist feels like a near impossible feat. I'm so turned on right now that my mind has stopped leading the show, and my dick is in full control.

All I can think about is tasting Bella, touching her, and tangling my tongue with hers.

When she looks up at the stars and points out how "twinkly" they are tonight, I take the opportunity of her distraction to cup my crotch and quickly adjust myself.

Then I walk Bella into the house.

———

Bella

Ayden wants me to be comfortable, and he insists I need to shower off the cold ocean water so I won't get chilled. He says he'll lend me a t-shirt of his to wear.

"Ayd, parading around naked is the opposite of comfortable for me."

He licks his lips and stares at me before quickly rustling through his dresser and deciding one of his high school football jerseys is the largest shirt he owns.

I grumble, but it turns out he's right. I take a quick shower and pull on his jersey, and the darn thing comes to the middle of my thighs. I would ask him for sweatpants too, but it's hot out tonight, and he doesn't have air conditioning.

I find Ayden sitting on his living room floor. The lights are dimmed, and I go join him.

"You already sold your couch?"

"Michael wanted it." He chuckles. "Couldn't wait to get his hands on it once he found out I was moving."

He puts a pillow behind my back for me to lean against the wall.

"Hope you don't mind the seating. The rug's pretty soft, right?"

I laugh. "Yeah, it is."

His living room's still pretty full with the TV, an armchair that's too small for two, and two bookcases filled with stuff. But without the couch it feels empty somehow. I can see the glow of Ayden's refrigerator from here. I remember the day his old one conked out and he and I went shopping for a new one. It took us all weekend to find one that seemed worth the hefty price tag.

"What are you going to do with the fridge?" I say softly.

"Try to sell it I guess. Unless Michael wants it."

He gets up and goes into the kitchen to fix us plates of Thai food.

When he returns, we eat quietly, enveloped by a silence broken only by the consistent humming of the refrigerator. The emptier the space around it, the louder it sounds.

"If I promised I'd stay here forever," Ayden begins.

I nearly throw down my empty plate and get up on my knees to face him. "Don't, Ayd. Don't ever promise that."

"But if I did, would it change things between us? I don't know what I even mean, but you and I aren't telling each other everything, Bella. You know that as well as I do. And that song..."

I inhale. "Yes, that song says a lot of important things. About us. But you taking this job, taking a risk like that, is a good thing. Not just for you but for me too. It's the reason I pulled out my guitar again."

"Really?"

"Really."

My hands go to his chest, and I feel it rise and fall.

"Bella." He puts one hand over mine. "Sleep here tonight."

I bite my lip.

"I'll fix up two sleeping bags, and we'll sleep out here."

Against my better judgment—okay, against all my judgment—I agree.

———

I slide into one of the sleeping bags while I wait for Ayden to come out of his bedroom. Just as I'm settling onto my side, he appears in the doorway.

Sweet Lord in Heaven.

He's stripped down to track shorts and no shirt, and he slips off the shorts, revealing black boxer briefs, before climbing into the sleeping bag next to me. I inhale, wondering if I just made a huge mistake. But he scoots closer to me in his bag and drops his arm over my waist, pulling me against him, my back to his chest.

I go rigid.

"Is this not okay?" he says, concern in his voice.

The thing is, it is okay. It's more than okay. The feeling of Ayden surrounding me, holding me, is everything I want.

"No, it...it is okay," I whisper. "Just don't let go of me."

"Never."

My heart is pounding as he snuggles closer.

"Last week, I told Jenny I couldn't see her again." His tone is low.

I can't restrain my noise of surprise. "I thought you usually just kind of let things take their course and fizzle out."

"I do. But it didn't feel right anymore to do that. So I told her we could only be friends. She was pissed."

"You were honest with her. That's all you can do."

He buries his face in my neck and inhales. "You always smell so good, B."

"I do?" My traitorous voice comes out squeaky.

"Uh-huh. Like flowers and ocean and mangoes."

I laugh. "The mango is my shampoo."

He runs the tip of his nose up to my earlobe. "It suits you."

I let out a shaky breath and fidget with my hands underneath the sleeping bag. "Good night, Ayd."

"Good night, B."

Within five minutes, I hear his breathing even out and get deeper, and I know he's asleep.

That makes one of us. I lie awake on the floor of his living room with just the sounds of the refrigerator for company for hours. My hormones are all over the place, and my thoughts are no better. Ayden is the best part of my life. But I can no longer deny how much I want him. And that scares me. Eventually, I drift to sleep.

When I wake up in the morning, Ayden's no longer in his sleeping bag, but he left me a note on his pillow.

Had an early job at a work site. Stay as long as you want. A

I throw on my shorts from last night, but I wear Ayden's football jersey home with me. A smile pulls at my mouth, and I can't stop remembering the feel of Ayden's arm wrapped around my body all night long.

I call Mom to check in with her. My call goes straight to voicemail, but that's nothing unusual with my mother in the mornings. Ellie would have called me if there were a problem, but I still feel unsettled. I decide I'll stop by unannounced tomorrow on my day off, and then I go home to shower before work.

I've just finished with a customer when Ayden walks up to my booth.

"I'm on a quick work break," he says as he leans his elbows on the counter. His fitted shirt hugs his biceps so perfectly my mouth waters.

He hands me the bag he's carrying.

"What's this?" I say, wondering if he bought me something.

"It's your bra and..." He glances over at Preston, who's cleaning a table a few feet away.

"And your panties."

Oh, no. I bite my lip, wishing I could disappear into the booth.

"You left them in my car," he explains. "I brought them into my house with us."

I curse the tequila again.

"I washed them last night," he says. "They were all salty from being in the ocean."

"Oh, God."

"What?" His gaze feels hot on my face. "I didn't mind."

"Well, that makes one of us." I toss the bag as hard as I can underneath my desk.

"Bella. About last night." His words come out choppy. "How drunk were you?"

I pick up my head and look at him.

His jaw tightens. "You did the shot, and you..."

"I know what you meant. And sure, I wasn't exactly sober, but..." I hesitate, but whatever's in my expression causes him to relax.

His gaze searches mine. "Let's talk tonight."

I widen my eyes. "Okay."

"See you soon," he says with a wave.

Holy crap.

I reach for the phone to call Tari.

———

"Oh. My. God. Yes." Tari is leaning so far into the window of the booth that I'm half-convinced she's going to fall on top of me. "Words cannot express how psyched up I am about this development, Bella. You and Ayden. Together at last."

"Tar, Ayden and I are not together. I got drunk, and then I *licked* him." I pull my hair up into a bun. "I'm mortified, and I have no idea what he's thinking."

"Hopefully you'll find out tonight." Her eyes are bright and eager. "And you have to promise to call me first. Not second or third but first!"

"Who else would I call?" I laugh. "You don't have a lot of competition. But, of course I'll call you first," I promise when she glares at me.

"Okay, well I have to get to the Clam Shack for the dinner crowd. Good luck!"

———

My shift is nearly over when my phone rings. I don't recognize the number, but something tells me to pick it up.

"Hello?"

"Bella Wesley please."

"Yes, this is she."

"Bella, this is Dr. Thibbs."

"Oh, hello. Thank you for returning my call."

"You're welcome. I would have called back sooner, but I was in the middle of an emergency all day yesterday. However, I'm afraid I can't give you any information on your mother..."

"I'm aware that your sessions with her are confidential, of course," I say. "I'm just worried about her."

"I understand. Unfortunately, she hasn't been to see me for over three months."

Dread fills my stomach. "What? But she's told me she's going every week."

"This can happen with patients. They cancel but don't want their loved ones to know. Your mother has made a couple of appointments, but then she's called and said she'll need to reschedule. I would like to see her to discuss her medication; if you can persuade her to come to a session, that would be good."

"Yes, of course." I'm already standing up. "I'll most definitely do that. Thank you again for calling."

I call out to Preston that I need to leave early, and then I rush out the door of the pool hall. I jog to my car, and I've just settled into the front seat when my phone rings again.

I glance at the caller ID and nearly drop the phone in my hurry to answer it. "Mom?" I say. "Are you okay?"

"Mirabella." Her voice sounds sluggish and far away.

I press the phone tightly to my ear. "Mom? What's going on?"

"I think I need some help. Call 911. Okay?"

"Mom!" I say frantically. "I will, but can you tell me what's wrong?"

"Took..." Her voice fades, "a few too many...pills."

My hand that's gripping the phone is suddenly sweaty, and my stomach clenches with terror.

"Don't worry, Mom. I'm calling for help. I'll be right there."

I hang up and call emergency services as I turn on the car and race for my parents' house.

CHAPTER EIGHTEEN

Ayden

I've just stepped out of the shower and am drying off when I hear knocking at my door. I throw on a pair of jeans and a t-shirt and leave the bathroom.

Michael's standing on my top step.

"Hey." I open the door wide. "Come on in."

He steps inside and takes a look around. "You need to get rid of any other furniture?" he says with a bare grin.

"I'll let you know." I cross my arms over my chest. "So, what do you want?"

We stand and face each other. Except for his dark eyes and my blue ones, it could be like looking in the mirror. We both got our father's height and our mother's dark hair.

"I came by to hopefully fix this shit between us." Michael shakes his head. "Before the damn memorial party. Ma hates that we're fighting."

"I know." I look at him. "Are you thinking of accepting my offer?"

"You don't get it, do you?" Michael growls. "You and Mom and everyone else want me to quit fishing because it's dangerous."

"I never asked you to quit. I said my extra money will help to lessen the pressure on you so that if there's a fucking storm outside, you can stay home and not worry about the loss of income. All I suggested was you be more careful—on stormy days or when the waves are brutally rough..."

"That's like asking a football player to always throw the ball away when he's being rushed," Michael says. "A quarterback tries to make the best pass. And sometimes that means he's going to put himself in danger of being hit. And sometimes he'll be hit. Right?"

"Except I don't play football anymore," I tell him.

"Because you didn't love it the way I love to fish." He narrows his eyes at me. "And I know you enjoy landscaping and it's a passion of yours. But the truth is, Ayd, there's only one thing you love the way I love the boat. Are you smart enough to know what it is?"

Immediately, Bella flashes through my head. Her long blond, sun-kissed hair that she loves to pull into a messy ponytail or a bun. Her pretty hazel eyes that hold the wisdom of a woman three times her age. Her body that I've fantasized about stripping naked all summer. The way she makes me laugh when no one else can. The thousands of times that she's been there for me when I needed her and only her.

Michael smirks, his dark eyes brightening with stark humor. "That feeling right there? The one that just rushed across your damn mug about a certain little girl who was always your best friend but who's now a beautiful woman? That, my little brother, is how I feel about fishing."

I stare at him.

"I don't have a Bella in my life," he says. "Most of us aren't that lucky. So you better hold onto her, and don't fucking let her go." He claps my back. "And I'm going to do the same with my boat. Okay? Even if it's dangerous, even if it's the biggest risk I'll ever take, I can't give it up."

Feeling like my world is suddenly spinning, I suck in air.

Michael gives me a look. "Just like you need Bella to breathe, I need to fish."

I pull him into a hug. "Just be careful. And take the money I send home and put it toward the mortgage. Deal?"

He punches me in the shoulder. "Deal."

My phone rings as I'm seeing him out the door. I smile when I see Bella's face light up the screen. As Michael climbs into his car, I swipe the screen.

"Hey, B. How are you?"

"Ayd." Her voice is shaky, and fear cuts through my chest. "Are you busy?"

I grab my wallet and keys off the kitchen counter. "No. Bella, what's going on?"

"It's my mom." She's talking calmly, but I can tell she's trying not to lose it. "She overdosed. I'm at the hospital in Portland."

"I'm leaving now." I pick up my sneakers by the door and slip them on. "I'll be right there, Bella. Promise."

———

Bella

I'm fighting with the doctor on call when Ayden arrives. I hear him talking with the nurse at the main desk, and then he's walking toward me down the hall.

"Hey." He rushes over to me and wraps me in his arms.

And I cling to him. I hold onto his familiar t-shirt that smells like pine and ocean and him, and I inhale him. I never want to let him go.

But I have to finish dealing with the reality in front of me.

I pull away from him and return my attention to the doctor, who I've decided I hate.

"My mother has been through several clinical trials previously. Her current psychiatrist is the only doctor I trust to handle her medications," I say firmly. "So no, I do not give you permission to enroll her in your program and give her new drugs."

"Ms. Wesley." Dr. Whatever-Her-Face speaks to me in slow tones like she would to someone who doesn't understand anything that she's saying. "A clinical trial can be of great advantage to some patients. We wouldn't give your mother anything that would put her at risk."

"I understand you mean well, but I already said no," I say with feeling. "I'm waiting for my father to arrive. I know he'll agree with me. We've been through this with my mother before, and we finally found a doctor we all trust. We're going to wait for her opinion on what is best. She knows my mother's history far better than any doctor here."

"Ms. Wesley, until we reach your doctor, would you please be willing to let us experiment..."

Ayden gives the doctor a hard look as he cuts her off. "I think she was pretty clear in her answer, Doctor. The answer was no. It's still no. So if you could please give us a few minutes alone?"

After the psychiatrist has stalked off in frustration, I turn to Ayden gratefully. "Thank you. She's been really pushy about this new round of drugs. What my mother really needs is to see her own doctor, not some stranger who doesn't understand her case at all. Taking her off her own meds can be dangerous if everything isn't properly balanced."

"You're right," Ayden says, and I could kiss him for always having my back. "How is your mom doing?"

"She's awake," I say. "I managed to get to her house at the same time the ambulance did. So I rode with her in the back. She was conscious the entire time, and the good news is that she didn't take that many pills. They made sure to get them out of her body, just to be safe, but she's okay. Physically, she's going to be fine."

Ayden pulls me into his chest again. "That's good," he says into my hair. "That's really good."

"I called my dad, and of course, he's out of town. He said he would get on the next flight out, but he probably won't get here until the morning. I'm going to spend the night here to make sure that doctor leaves my mother alone. The nurse said she could set up a cot for me in my mom's room so I can be with her. And I'm going to wait to tell Grandpa. I don't want to scare him in the middle of the night. I'll go see him in the morning after my dad gets here."

"Have you called your mom's own doctor?"

"Yes, and she's supposed to come in to check on her. If things look good, she says she'll sign her out of here and have Mom stay at her ward overnight, and she'll evaluate her in the morning." I lower my voice. "I hate this unit. It's an inpatient ward. She doesn't need to be in a locked ward. She's not a danger to anyone."

He eyes me carefully. "Even to herself?"

I flinch, and Ayden takes both my hands in his. "Bella. I just want her to be safe. If she needs to stay somewhere until they can find the right combination of meds..."

"No," I say firmly, trying to keep that calm place inside of me I locked into the moment my mother's frail and terrified voice met me on the other end of the phone line when I left work. "My mother is not sick like that. She just needs a little help. She told me..."

My voice nearly cracks, but I keep it steady somehow. "She told me that my father was supposed to be home this week. He promised her he'd be home every day until after his party. But he took a meeting in Chicago last minute, and she was so upset with him. When I saw her yesterday, she had been crying. My mother never cries."

"You saw her? Where?"

"At the grocery store. I called her doctor to check in, but she didn't call me back until today. And that's when I found out my mom's been skipping her sessions."

Ayden frowns. "Shit, Bella. I'm sorry."

"But I want to..." *Kill my father with my bare hands.* "My father's always been so selfish. And I thought he was changing. I don't even trust he's going to show up here."

Ayden kisses the top of my head. "I'll wait with you."

———

Hours later, as the sun's coming up, Ayden and I walk my mother to a transfer car that will take her to Dr. Thibbs's psychiatric care unit.

"It's not a locked ward," I say to Mom as she walks between us, one of her hands holding onto each of our arms. "And you'll most likely be discharged tomorrow, provided you pass the set of tests in the morning. Dr. Thibbs said she thinks your medication was actually causing you to be more imbalanced rather than less. So getting that out of your system should help."

"I think that's true," Mom says slowly. "I should have gone to my sessions." She turns to me as we reach the waiting car. "Mirabella..." She chokes up. "I shouldn't have lied to you about skipping them."

Tears clog my throat, and I take my mother's hand in mine. "It's okay. The important thing is to pay attention to how you feel. Okay? You can feel better again, Mom. I swear that's what everyone wants for you." I pause. "Even Dad."

"Especially Dad," a familiar voice says from behind me.

I turn toward the voice. With gray hair stylishly cut and dressed impeccably in a three-piece suit, my father's only signs of distress are his red-rimmed eyes and his taut mouth.

He bends down to kiss my cheek. "Thank you," he whispers to me.

We help my mother into the car, and I promise to talk to her tomorrow. My father tells her he's going to follow in his town car, and we shut her car door.

Once she's out of sight, I turn on my father. "How dare you leave her when you promised you wouldn't? You know how much she needs your honesty!" I get right up in his face, and his eyes widen. "You said you were in a support group and that you were trying! Why would you lie to her? She needs to learn she can trust you again, and when you let her down, it ruins every step forward she's making!"

"Bella." Dad's voice is shaky. "Listen to me. I'm sorry..."

I hadn't realized I'd begun crying until I feel the hot tears on my face. "I can never trust you to treat her right, can I?"

Ayden wraps his arms around me from behind. "Bella. Honey. Let me take you home."

Dad reaches for my arm, but I jerk it away from him. "Bella. I should have been far more involved than I have been."

"So why haven't you?" I say to him hotly. "I've been watching out for her since I was thirteen years old. Where were you? If you know you should have been there, why weren't you?"

"I couldn't." My father blows out a big breath and looks at the sky like it will have his answers. "I felt so guilty every time I looked at her. And when she's in pain, like..."

"Like on Tuesdays?" I say. "Yeah, that's hard. It's so fucking hard to see her suffering like that. But you wouldn't really know, would you? You've never actually been there on a Tuesday. In three years, I haven't seen you there once."

"Bella..." Dad reaches for me again, but I back up even more into Ayden, who holds me firmly against his chest.

"You *always* have to work late on Tuesdays, Dad. And I always find the time to show up. When I've just worked a double shift and I haven't slept in a day, when there's a snowstorm and it's the last thing in the world I want to do...Ayden and I show up. Whether he had a broken wrist from an accident on the job, or he was sick with the flu, Ayden hasn't missed one Tuesday with me in three years—did you know that?"

Dad's gaze shifts above my head to Ayden. "No. I didn't know that."

"Because you never cared to find out what the hell was going on in your own home. I tried to talk to you about it numerous times, and you always brushed me off. You always said you had it handled. And I *always* gave you a pass." I sweep my arm toward the hospital building. "And now look where we are. *Again.*"

"Bella, I'm sorry. You're right. I can change. Right now."

Before I can tell him he's a pathological liar, Ayden, his arms still around me, speaks. "It has to change, sir," he says to my father. "I know you're a busy man, but your daughter has been carrying this burden for years now. You've got two women in your life, and you're ignoring both of them."

Dad shifts to face Ayden. "Ayden, this isn't your business."

"Like hell it's not." Ayden's arms tighten around me, and I lean back against him, suddenly realizing how exhausted I am. "*Bella* is my business. That makes this situation my business. And she deserves to be treated right."

As my father and Ayden stand across from each other in dead-locked silence, the vein on my father's forehead gets so big I think it may explode. His eyes travel from Ayden's arms around me, to my face, and back to Ayden, who hasn't taken his eyes off of him. They seem to engage in some sort of wordless conversation before my father lets out a deep breath.

"You're right," he says. "And I'm trying. But I obviously need to try harder. I will."

CHAPTER NINETEEN

I stop crying and hold it together as we say goodbye to my father, walk to Ayden's car, and then drive through the city and into Lucky Bay. I stay calm when we stop by Grandpa's so I can fill him in on Mom's situation. Grandpa takes it well, holding me close to him when he hears how I had to call 911.

"You saved her," he says, his eyes watery. "If you hadn't picked up the phone..."

"I'll always pick up the phone," I say to him as I kiss his cheek. "Always."

Promising to keep him updated, Ayden and I say goodbye and walk to his car.

As we back out of my grandfather's driveway, my tears come again. Ayden stops the car by the docks, in perfect view of the lighthouse, and takes me onto his lap in the driver's seat.

"Let it out, Bella," he says as he strokes my hair. "I'm right here."

"You know what's strange?" I wipe my eyes and look at him. "This sounds awful, but for the first time in years, I actually feel... relaxed. Relieved, almost."

"Do you know why?" he asks me.

I do know. And it's awful to admit, but...

"Because I know she's safe. Someone else is taking care of her for once, and I know that at least for this one stretch of time, she can't hurt herself."

"You can't be held responsible for her life like that," Ayden says. "It's far too much of a load, Bella."

"I don't know what else to do. No one else will help her."

He kisses my head. "Maybe someone else will. Maybe this whole horrible experience will turn into something positive."

I glance out the window at the lighthouse. "It's always been my touchstone," I say. "Despite..."

"It's okay," Ayden whispers. "I don't think the lighthouse should have saved my father. A storm's a storm."

"The lighthouse is supposed to be a beacon for the boats," I say softly.

"Nothing's foolproof."

No, I guess not.

———

Ayden drives me home and insists on walking me to my front step.

"Thank you," I say to him, my voice a bare whisper.

"Can I come inside?"

"I'm not going to be very good company, Ayd. I really need to sleep."

"Let me sleep with you." His eyes are stark with pain. "Please?"

Something shifts between us, and the air goes thick with years of things unsaid.

I love you.

"Okay," I say quietly. "Come on in."

We don't speak as I pull back the covers. Ayden takes off his jeans, but leaves on his t-shirt and boxers. I change in the bathroom into a clean t-shirt and pajama bottoms, and when I come out, he's already under the covers.

I slip in next to him, trying to make sure I don't touch him.

But he growls when I turn my back on him, and before I know

it, he's shifted me so my head is resting on his chest. His steady heartbeat settles me immediately; just the feeling of someone so alive and present with me is a relief.

"How are you doing, B?" he says in a low tone.

"I'm okay." I clear my throat. "Ayden. I can't thank you enough. For being there for me last night when I called..."

"You know you don't have to thank me."

"I know. But I still think it's important to let you know how much I appreciate you, Ayd."

He kisses my head. "I already know that, Bella. Get some sleep."

I can't imagine being able to sleep with Ayden Wild in my bed. Besides, I haven't had a moment to process the last twenty-four hours, and I need a little time to accept that my mother just overdosed for the second time in three years. Yes, it could have been a whole hell of a lot worse. Yes, I'm not naïve to how fortunate she is that she actually caught herself in the act of doing something self-harming.

But the fact is...my mother is unwell and needs help. I knew this, but last night took away any optimistic thoughts that she was just going to sail into happiness and bliss.

All these thoughts churn through my mind while Ayden rubs soothing circles over my back...between the dichotomy of his warm body and my overactive brain, I'm sure I'll be awake for hours.

But I haven't slept for over a day, and the need for rest takes over everything else.

———

Something's beeping.

I reach over to my nightstand and bat at the culprit.

When it beeps again, I realize it's my phone.

Ayden's arm is still wrapped around me, and he hasn't budged. I take a moment to look at his long dark lashes and lips slightly parted. I brush his hair off his forehead, resisting the urge to kiss it.

I reach out to grab my phone and glance over at the clock.

Three o'clock. We slept the day away.

Not wanting to wake Ayden, I slip out of bed and head for the bathroom, where I sit on the tile floor and check my messages.

Tari texted. *Honey, how are you? Ayden filled us in on everything last night. If you want to come by for an early dinner, Peter and I are cooking.*

Dad left a voicemail to let me know the good news that Mom is already home. At Dr. Thibbs's urging, Dad's hired a psychiatric live-in nurse to stay with them for as long as Mom needs her, and Dr. Thibbs already has Mom started on a new medication that she thinks will help with her mood swings. Mom has agreed to intense individual therapy, and my parents are going to start couples therapy this week.

A wave of nausea hits me with no warning. Even though I'm not sick. Not physically anyway. Emotionally, I've been holding onto old hurts for a while.

And the memories bombard my mind—

The image of my mother's face when the P.I. showed her the photos of dad and what's-her-face coming out of the hotel.

The gut-wrenching sounds of my mom crying in bed like she was going to die.

The decision I made then and there to never hurt like that, to never put myself in a position to hurt like that.

All of it rushes through me in waves.

And I take it all. For the first time, I feel it all. And once I've sat with all that pain, I'm certain of one thing—

My forever plus one could only ever be one man.

It's always only ever been one man.

He's been with me from the beginning, and if I want to see where we could go together, I'm going to have to risk everything.

A knock on the bathroom door makes me jump. "Bella?"

I stand and go open the door to Ayden, who's never looked as gorgeous to me as he does right now. Hair sticking up, his eyes bleary with sleep, he reaches out to touch my bare arm. "You all right?"

I smile. "I am."

His eyes lock onto mine. "Good."

I tell him about my father's message, and then mention Tari's invitation. "Are you up for dinner?"

"I'm starved," he says. "If you want to go to their house, I'm happy to; if not, we can order in here."

"I think I'd like the company."

———

Tari pulls me into a hug the moment Ayden and I arrive at her and Peter's house.

"Oh honey, I'm so sorry about all of this," she says. "Thank God your mom's okay."

Peter kisses my cheek and ushers me onto the couch. "Take a seat, Bella. You must be dead on your feet." His eyes widen. "Fuck. I'm sorry. That's an awful thing to say."

I wave him off. "No worries. It's just a figure of speech. I'm fine."

Tari immediately brings Ayden and me each a plate of baked salmon and mashed potatoes. "Start with this, and there's plenty more if you want it."

Within minutes, the four of us are relaxing over dinner.

"Bella, how are things going?" Tari asks me.

I fill them in on my father's phone message.

"So basically, my parents will be talking to a shrink practically every day of the week," I say.

"Hey, sometimes people need to get out their pain before they can move forward," Tari says. "What about your dad's party? Did you cancel it?"

"You would think they would, right? But no, they're going forward with it. And Dr. Thibbs gave her blessing. She thinks it's something for them to look forward to together."

"And your cousins are flying in soon for your dad's memorial party, right Ayd?" Peter confirms.

"Yeah," Ayden says. "I'm meeting them at my house in a couple hours. With everything going on, I nearly forgot."

"I can't believe your dad's party is tomorrow night," I say.

Ayden turns to me. "You shouldn't go, Bella. After everything you've been through..."

"Nothing could make me miss your dad's memorial party," I say. "So don't even try to talk me out of it, Ayd, because I never for one second considered not going."

Ayden's eyes turn green. "Bella..."

"I'm your date, and that's that."

He reaches over and tugs at my hair. "Christ, you're stubborn."

I break into a smile. "So it's settled then." I turn back to Tari and Peter, who are focused intensely on their meals. "We're finished with our discussion. Sorry for the interruption."

Tari giggles. "You two are pretty hot when you're arguing."

I give her a look. "Tar..."

"So," Peter says quickly. "How about we make it easier for you, Ayd, and we'll all camp out on the beach tomorrow after the party for your dad?"

"Sounds great," I say. "Except I don't have a tent."

"I have a few, and I know Michael could lend me his," says Ayden. "But that will only be enough for all my cousins." He turns to me. "Dylan said something about Jasalie maybe coming with him and surprising you."

I shriek. "Why wouldn't she tell me?"

"To surprise you, B." He chuckles. "I ruined the moment, though. I just know you've had enough surprises this summer. Especially lately."

"I have," I say softly. "I appreciate you thinking of me like that."

"So that means even more people," Ayden says to Peter. "I definitely don't have enough tents."

"Tar and I have an extra one we can lend you two." Peter points to Ayden and me, and my stomach immediately clenches.

After the night I had, being turned on feels inappropriate. But nothing seems to be able to dowse my attraction to Ayden this summer, and the thought of being alone in a tent with him all night has my hormones soaring.

"Camping out will be so much fun," Tari says.

"It's romantic, baby." Peter kisses her cheek. "Do you guys mind waiting for five minutes while we go find the tent for you?"

I'm already leaning my head back against the couch cushions. "Take your time."

What was supposed to take five minutes in the den turns out to be a half hour, and by then, they're both in the garage, still trying to find their extra tent.

CHAPTER TWENTY

Ayden turns his cap backward, the way he knows I like it and rests his arm over the back of the couch, right behind where I'm sitting.

"I give up," he says.

My face must fill with the alarm I feel because Ayden touches my cheek. "Not like that, Bella," he clarifies. "I mean I give up on the dare. I'm not going to try to find a plus one."

"You're not?"

"No. You want to know why?"

The air around us is now so thick with tension I swear I could reach out and touch it.

"Because I don't need to search for my forever plus one. I found her a long time ago."

My heart climbs into my throat. "Ayd..."

"You're mine, Bella. You're my plus one." He takes my hand in his, and I try to pull away because mine is all sweaty. But he holds on until I stop fighting him.

Before I have time to realize what's happening, he leans in toward me. His mouth lands on my neck, and he kisses the skin lightly. *Oh, Lord.* My stomach flip flops, and I clutch at Ayden's hand like it's a lifeline. He trails a line of kisses up to my jaw, and then he pulls back slightly. His eyes meet mine, and I inhale at how liquid blue his are. Before I can say anything, he tips his forehead to mine.

He's going to kiss me on the mouth. But before I can be sure, the front door rattles and opens.

I jump but don't shift my gaze away from Ayden.

"Okay," I hear Peter say. "So this tent should work—whoa! Sorry, I didn't—" There's a loud crash like he's dropped something. "Holy fuck. Are you two—"

"Yes," Ayden snaps, his eyes never leaving my face. "We'll be out in a minute."

"Sure thing. Take your time. I'll go back to the garage. With Tar," he adds, and I nearly laugh at how jazzed up he sounds.

The door shuts, and silence fills the room.

Ayden's thumb caresses my jaw. "Let's go to your house," he says in a rough tone. "That way, it'll just be us."

"Okay. Yes." I get up off the couch. My neck is cold where his mouth just was, and my legs are as shaky as the first time I stood up on stage alone.

I hurry to the door, assuming Ayden's right behind me when—

"Oomph." I freaking trip on something and fall face first onto the floor.

Ayden's squatting down beside me then, helping me to a sitting position and checking me for injuries. Because apparently Peter was as shocked by what he witnessed as I am right now, and he dropped the tent in the middle of the foyer.

I stand up quickly, murmuring an, "I'm fine. Let's just go."

———

We've just started the short drive to my house when Ayden speaks.

"I remember how you want our first kiss since we were thirteen to be at your front door." His tone is calm and even, giving nothing away.

What?!

I whip my head to face him, but he doesn't expand on his comment.

And I have no idea where he's getting that kind of intel.

When we pull into my driveway, Ayden parks and is around to my side before I've even opened my door. He holds out his hand and helps me out of the car. We walk up my front steps together, and when we get to the top, I turn toward him.

"How do you know that? About the kiss?"

He faces me, leaning casually against the door. "You told me once."

I furrow my brow. "I did?"

He nods. "One night when you called from L.A. You'd performed that night, but you had a few shots after you got off stage. You were drunk, and that's why you don't remember."

Oh, God. "What did I say, Ayd?"

"You asked me if I ever thought about kissing you again. I said, 'all the time.' Something about the way you asked me, you got me to admit what I always denied, even to myself. You said you thought about it too. You said you'd imagined every detail of how you would want it to play out." He reaches out and wraps his hand around the ends of my hair, gently pulling me closer. "You wanted our kiss to be slow but hard. And you had a fantasy of me grabbing you on your front step, pressing you against your closed door, and kissing the shit out of you."

Holy. There are no words.

"Breathe, Bella." Before I can stop him, he's turned me so that my back is against the door. "I can't kiss the shit out of you if you don't take in oxygen."

I inhale. I exhale. And then Ayden's mouth is on mine.

Hard and urgent like he's been waiting for me forever.

And his lips...as good as I remember them feeling, this is so much better. Because back then we were kids. And now...now we're adults. Having an adult moment.

And oh shit, was Ayden Wild worth waiting for.

His lips are soft and probing as he kisses every inch of my

mouth. "You taste so good," he murmurs as his tongue runs along the seam of my lips, asking to be let in.

And I open for him. My tongue tangles with his, and I let out a moan. Ayden wraps his arm around my waist and pulls me flush against him.

He lets out a sexy groan as he pulls my leg up so his hardness rubs against my center. I press fervently against him, my hands tugging desperately at the short strands of hair below his baseball cap.

He grips my hip harder, urging me to move. I buck my hips, my leg wrapping tighter around his waist, and he shifts his hot mouth to my neck where he trails kisses down to my collarbone. His body drives me wild, especially in my core where all I can feel is a pulsating need for more. More Ayden, closer to me, inside me, as far and deep as he can go.

He's bringing me closer, closer, closer. I writhe against him, the need in me so intense that I barely remember we're in public. I'm halfway to orgasming on my front step when my neighbor's car pulls into the driveway next door. With no stand of trees or a privacy fence, the Scotts are getting quite a show.

With a gasp, I drop my leg and rear back. Ayden holds me steady so I don't tip over onto my head.

"Sorry." He clears his throat. "I'm not usually like that."

"Like what?" Sexy, hot, perfect?

"Out of control." The blue of his eyes sears into me. "You make me forget everything but you, Bella."

I fumble for the right key on my chain. "I should go inside. And you should..."

"Go get ready for my cousins." He nods. "I know. I'll pick you up tomorrow?"

Right. His father's memorial party. And then...Ayden and me. Sharing a tent. When I almost just had sex with him in full view of the street? Sharing a tent won't be a problem at all. Right.

"You can tell your cousins about my mom," I say quietly. "And whoever else is with them. Colton's wife and Jasalie—it's all fine."

"Are you sure?" Ayden cups my cheek with his hand. "I don't have to tell them anything at all."

"I know. But I'm really okay for you to. I think it will be easier for me if they know when I see them."

"Okay." He kisses me gently. "I will then."

I nod before I turn and open my front door. I've closed it behind him when I hear him call out softly, "I'll miss you, B."

"Me too." I slide down my door until I'm sitting on the floor of the hallway. My legs feel too weak to hold me up. Ayden Wild's kisses are fire. And I'm burning up with my need for him.

My phone rings and I pull it out of my pocket.

"I figured you'd be calling," I say to Tari with a laugh.

"Bella! Peter said you and Ayden were in a compromising position at our house! And then you left and I didn't want to interrupt anything, but give a girl a break and fill me in already!"

"You've been very patient, Ms. Tari," I say with a smile. "And you're going to like what I'm about to tell you."

She's screaming before I've even finished describing my kiss with Ayden.

"I'm assuming this means you've given up on your dares?"

"Ayden said to me that I'm his forever plus one and I always have been," I tell her. "And the thing is, he's the same for me. I don't know why it took me so long to admit that, but it's the truth."

"Oh. My. God! Ayden is so romantic with you, Bella! I've never heard him talk like that with anyone before. I can't wait to see you guys together tomorrow."

"But don't make a big deal about it!"

After we hang up, I call my parents' home line.

When Dad picks up, I'm so flustered I nearly hang up on him.

My father doesn't answer his home phone. Ever. He's far too busy answering his work line.

"Bella?" he says. "Hello? Are you there?"

"Y-yes. Hi, Dad." I clear my throat. "I wanted to check in and see how Mom's doing."

"Very well," he says. "She's sleeping right now. I just looked in on her. The nurse moves in first thing tomorrow morning. Ellie's already set up the guest wing for her."

"That's great." I freeze. "What about the new pills? Is the nurse going to keep them somewhere Mom can't find them? You know, in case..."

"Yes," Dad says smoothly. "They're already in a locked cabinet and only the nurse and I will have the code to access it. I'll give you the code as well, of course."

"That sounds...much safer than before."

"It is." His voice softens. "Bella, I want you to take the next two days off."

"I do have those days off from work. I requested tomorrow due to Ayden's dad's memorial, and the next day is July fourth."

"No, I mean I want you to take those days off from us, Bella. Don't call or come by. If there's a problem, I promise I will reach out to you right away."

"But..." I clutch the phone in my hand. "Why would I do that?"

"Because you deserve a couple of days off. Okay?"

I swallow. "Okay, Dad. Thanks."

———

Ayden

A few hours and a bunch of beers later, I'm sitting at Lucky Bay Bar with Brayden, Cam, Jenson, and Peter. Dylan and Colton politely finish up taking selfies with a few fans, and then we're left alone. Jasalie and Sky, clearly lying because they wanted us to have "guy time" as Colt affectionately says, told us they were too tired to come out, so they're back at my house.

Brayden and Cam are joking with Peter about his love-hate relationship with the Red Sox, but I'm barely listening. The taste of Bella is still on my lips, and I can't get the image of her out of my head.

Colton lifts an eyebrow. "So, Ayd. You and Bella. How's that going?"

Well, I just kissed her like I've been fantasizing about for years, and my dick can't stop twitching at the memory. My lips can still feel hers, and my tongue...I didn't want to have even a sip of beer because I didn't want to lose the intoxicating taste of her.

Colton's watching me closely. "Holy shit."

Peter chuckles. "They were nose to nose when I last saw them."

Cam calls out for a round of shots.

"We're not drinking a shot about Bella," I say. "This is between me and her. In other words, stay out of it."

"Well, what's up?" Brayden asks me. "Are you two..."

"We're still...working some things out."

Dylan taps his beer to mine. "Did you invite her out to L.A.?"

I give a quick nod. "Like I told you earlier, she's got a lot going on right now. Too much. So don't try to persuade her."

Peter nudges Dylan. "Bella's into it. She just doesn't know it quite yet."

"She's into it—or him?" Cam asks as everyone but me breaks into laughter.

Bella and I are wading into new waters, and I don't want to fuck things up with her. I *can't* fuck things up with her. But that kiss is taking over my brain, and all I want is to taste her again. Everywhere.

Colton assesses me, and like he always does, he finds a way to rein in the Wilds when we need it. In this case, he uses the art of deflection.

"Why don't you tell everyone about your plans, J?" he says to Jenson.

Jenson runs his hand through his blond mess of hair. He may be the only one of us who's not technically related by blood, but he and Colton, who met as kids at a football camp and have been best friends ever since, are as close as cousins. "Not a big deal. I'm leaving Pittsburgh."

"Where to?" I say.

"Back to my hometown. Just outside Philly."

"Tell them why," Colton prompts him.

Jenson looks pointedly at the nearly-empty beer bottle in Colton's hand. "Maybe I need to cut you off, Wild."

My eyes lock with his, and even though I don't know what the fuck is going on with him, some kind of understanding passes between us.

"Something about a girl?" I say to him in a low tone.

He just looks at me. "Something like that."

CHAPTER TWENTY-ONE

The next day, Jasalie and Sky surprise me by showing up at my front door. Jasalie and I scream and hug each other, and then spend a fun couple of hours catching up. She and Sky are so sweet and they brought me flowers to "brighten up my difficult last couple of days" and it felt great to have company. Although my mind is constantly on Ayden. My body wants more of him, and our kiss last night still has me so turned on I struggle to concentrate.

Once they leave to go get ready for the memorial party, I spend the next two hours pulling potential dresses out of my closet.

I change my outfit three times. I can't understand why I'm so nervous, but I want to make sure I'm dressed appropriately for something that's so important to Ayden.

When the doorbell rings, I take one last look in the mirror. I decided to wear my hair down in loose waves, and I have on my favorite silver studded earrings with a matching necklace and bracelet. I like my sleeveless aqua top although I'm worried the long black skirt clings just a little too much to be conservative. At least my black sandals are cute and comfortable.

I open the door, and Ayden is standing in front of me. His eyes match his tie—they're blue and clear, and they're focused only on me. He lazily scans my body from head to toe, causing my stomach to turn over with butterflies.

"Hey, B. You look beautiful." He kisses my lips lightly, and just that bare touch is enough to give me shivers.

His lips brush mine for a second time, and I grab at his suit jacket and take a step back.

My eyes travel the length of him. With his navy coat and pants, white shirt and blue tie, and no baseball hat on his head, he looks so grown-up, so much a man. Not that he hasn't been looking like a man for some time.

But something about him standing on my steps just now— God, he looks gorgeous. By the time I lift my head back up to lock eyes with him, his expression is amused.

"Checking me out?" He grins. "How'd I do?"

I swat at his arm. "You know how hot you are. Let's get going." I grab my dressiest purse off the couch, stuff my keys into it, and make sure to pick up my backpack with my change of clothes for the beach afterward.

Before we can get outside, I trip, this time on an errant sneaker.

I go flying, and Ayden's attempt to stop me has us both landing on the living room floor together, me on my back and him on top of me. Ayden looks down at me, his eyes piercing. He leans down and kisses me on the cheek.

I put my arms around his back and pull him closer with neither of us saying a word. I can hear him breathing though, and I'm sure he can hear my little gasps.

I start rambling. "I just want to get this out there. I know when we kissed, we broke the silly pact we'd made as kids. And I don't regret it for a second. Maybe I should, but I don't."

"Neither do I." Ayden kisses my nose. "Not even a little bit."

"But after everything that's gone on the last couple of days, things have been pretty intense. Maybe it pushed things too far, farther than you want. I guess I'm saying that if you just want to be friends now, that's totally fine. I don't want you to feel like you have to protect my feelings, Ayd."

Ayden's face is millimeters from mine. "What happened between us has absolutely nothing to do with your mom," he murmurs. "I told you Bella; you're my forever girl. I just don't want to screw this up with you. I *can't* screw this up with you."

He brushes my lips with his. I curl my hand around his neck and pull him closer.

"Ayd," I say between kisses. "We should go...we're going to be late."

He wrenches himself off of me and helps me up.

As we make it the door successfully this time, he nibbles at my neck. "I love this outfit, but the truth is I want to take it off of you right now, Bella."

Oh God. I let out a gasp but keep my hands fisted at my sides, determined not to make us late.

"Later," I manage to get out. "Right now, we have a memorial party to get to."

Ayden wraps his arms around me from behind and starts walking us out the door. "We'll get there," he promises.

My mind is already imagining other meanings to that promise. I lean my head back against his chest and let him guide us down the walkway to his car.

———

As soon as we step inside the banquet hall, photos of Ayden's father and the rest of his family greet us. They're placed next to dozens more photographs of the other deceased fishermen and their families. It's an overwhelming feeling to walk right in on them all like that, but Ayden marches right past without so much as a glance. I follow him as he searches for his mom.

Before we get more than a few feet, a man with curly gray hair stops us in front of the framed photograph of Ayden, Michael, and their father. "Ayden Wild," he says, extending his hand. "I was hoping to meet you tonight."

Ayden looks at him as he shakes his hand. "I'm sorry, sir, I don't know who..."

"In a rat's ass I am." The man laughs. He has a dirtiness to him that makes me step back. His breath smells like whiskey and his eyes are bloodshot. "Nathaniel Gates. I was on a different boat that same night. We were the lucky ones."

I look at Ayden and my heart drops. His face has turned pale and he's clenching his jaw.

"Oh." Ayden puts his hands in his pockets. "Well, good to meet you, sir. If you'll excuse us..."

Nathanial steps closer, blocking our path to the door. "Call me Nate. Please. I was a great admirer of your dad. Good man. In fact, he helped me out of a few jams over the years. Lent me some money once after my first wife left me..."

"Ayd!"

I look past Nate as Michael and Anna approach us.

"So I'd like to offer you a favor," Nate concludes. "Take you and your girlfriend here out on a ride on my boat. Got my own skipper these days."

"Um, Ayden doesn't go on boats..." I start to say, but Ayden cuts me off.

"No, thank you, sir." He takes my arm and starts to lead me around Nate.

At that same moment, Colton, Sky, and Cam come through the front doors. Colton and Cam take one look at Ayden and head toward us.

"You don't owe me anything," Nate says, his voice rising. "It's a favor to your dad. I can show you the ropes of commercial fishing if you'd like."

Oh, God. Ayden's jaw clenches, and I wait for the explosion. Michael has now made it into the conversation, and he quickly tries to intercede, saying something about being a fisherman himself so Ayden knows all he needs to know from him already.

"Oh, you don't know everything, Michael," Nate says, reaching into his pocket for a flask. "You're lucky you weren't out on a boat that night, but if you were, and you'd survived it like I did, you'd realize some things. I want to show Ayden here some of what I learned."

He takes a swig of his flask as Colton and Cam flank Ayden, their faces hard as stone. I turn toward the door as Jenson, Brayden, and Dylan hurry toward us and stand behind Ayden. Jasalie finds Sky and they both look on with concerned faces.

"I don't need to learn from you." Ayden speaks quietly, but it feels like he's spitting the words out.

Nate takes it as a challenge. "Boy, you need to be taught some manners. Not having a daddy around may be the reason? I could teach you some manners." He swings out his arm to hit Ayden, but he misses badly.

Michael tries to pull Ayden away, but Nate just steps closer. "Let's see how brave you are, son. I want to take you out on that water. You think your father was braver than me because he died that night? I wish it'd been me sometimes you know. I wish I could've just felt the darkness for good rather than those cold waves brushing over the bow and me ducking down like a coward, crying for a God to save us...and then the Coast Guard found us. Just in time. We were the last ship rescued that night. Your daddy wasn't lucky like I was—we said their boat was cursed, and God help me—"

Ayden turns back now to swing at Nate, and I gasp, but Michael's got his brother in a death grip. The Wild men, along with Jenson, edge in closer behind Michael and Ayden as the level of tension in the hall rises to the ceiling.

"Stop," Michael says as Anna puts her hands over her face and begs for the fighting to stop.

"Ayd! Stop," Michael says again as he pulls him back.

"You need to get out on the water, boy!" Nate's face is red and he's spitting as he shouts.

"Ayden doesn't need to get on your fucking boat!" I hear myself shout back.

Anna begs me to calm down. But I push closer to Ayden. I get in between him and Nate as I say, "Ayden understands plenty, and he's braver than anybody in here!"

Two strong arms wrap around me from behind, and I'm carried back a few steps.

I twist my neck and make eye contact with a grim-faced Colton.

"Let Ayden and Michael handle it, Bella," he says in my ear.

"But this guy...he's..."

"I know. But this is their fight. We can't get involved. Hal may have been my uncle, but he was their father, and we need to let them decide how to handle this guy."

He's right. I nod, letting Colton know he can let me go. He does but keeps one arm securely around me just as Jasalie and Sky slide in on my other side and Jasalie takes my hand.

Someone's finally gotten the attention of security, and they begin to escort Nate out of the building.

Michael relaxes his hold on Ayden and they lock eyes. After a silent moment, they turn in unison and both reach out to stop Nate from leaving.

Michael leans in close to Nate and says something to him in a low voice. Then Ayden does the same. Nate's eyes water, and he puts one arm around Michael's neck and the other around Ayden's.

Nate whispers something to both of them and then produces a card from his pocket and hands it to Ayden. Then he pats Ayden on the cheek and leaves the building.

———

Ayden

If someone's hurting, don't make it worse. Make it better.

That was my father's motto.

But when that guy swings at me, I want to hurt him back. I

want to destroy him. Why did he get to live when my father, the best man I knew, drowned?

Nate's not taking advantage of his gift of life; he's a drunk and a mean one at that.

But Michael and I lock eyes, and I know he's remembering our father's motto at the same time I do. And I know we need to make this right. Michael tells Nate that he's happy he survived to share the story and I lean in and tell him that living the life our father would have wanted him to is the best way to honor my dad.

"You're good boys," Nate mutters as he wraps his arms around us. "Hal would be so proud. I know he is." He hands me his business card. "We'll talk again when I'm not being a drunk asshole."

Once Nate leaves, I turn around. My mother's smiling at Michael and me proudly and with unmistakable relief. My cousins and Jenson are there, along with Tari and Peter, all of them having my back like they always do. And a crowd of people has gathered, wanting to know what just happened to cause such a scene.

But my gaze keeps moving until I find her.

Bella.

My constant bright light in a sea of dark, the person who was with me after my father passed, who held me up when I felt like drowning, who stopped by my house every day after school the rest of the year to make sure I was okay.

My best friend, my angel, and the woman I never want to be without.

Her hazel eyes widen as I stalk toward her standing next to Colton, Sky and Jasalie. When I reach her, I bury my face in her neck, trying to block out the rest of the room, wishing we didn't have an audience. I wrap one arm around her waist and lift her up off the ground. I lock eyes with her, never wanting to let her go again.

Without putting her down, I start walking through the crowd and down the hallway. I don't stop until I've pushed open the private bathroom and locked the door behind us.

I lift Bella onto the counter by the sink and lean my hands on either side of her. Then I drop my head as I gasp for air.

"Ayden." Her tone is laced with concern.

"Shhh." I ghost her lips with mine. "No talking. Please."

Except that I have to tell her one thing first. "You're the only one, Bella. You'll always be the only one."

My kiss is sudden and unexpected, and she moans in surprise. I part her lips with my tongue and pick her up off the sink. Her long skirt's ridden up her legs, and I help her pull the fabric all the way up so she can wrap her legs around my waist. I back her up against the door, my hand dipping into the top of her dress so I can touch the swell of her breast. I want to be inside her right now, right this minute.

But I know that can't happen. We'd miss the video tribute, and I would never do that to my mom. So I settle for kissing Bella from her lips to her neck and then down to her breasts. My hand has just snaked underneath her skirt and is heading for the part of her I'm completely obsessed with when—

Bang, bang!

"Ayden!" Colton's amused tone comes through the door. "Whatever you and Bella are up to, the video starts in less than two minutes. Aunt Anna was searching all over for you, but I told her I'd handle it. Thank me later, by the way."

I reluctantly lift my head and call out to Colton, "Be right there."

I let Bella down to the ground and help her adjust her dress. I grab her ass before she can open the door and kiss the back of her neck. "You ready?"

She slaps at my hand and laughs. "Let go of my ass, Ayd, and then I will be."

I let her go, and we walk back into the party.

CHAPTER TWENTY-TWO

Bella

The video tributes leave everyone smiling through tears, and the memorial party ends quietly and without any more drama.

Ayden and I change into casual clothes in the banquet hall bathroom. Then, after helping Ayden's mom carry all her stuff to her car, Ayden and I drive out of the parking lot.

The ride is quiet. By that I mean Ayden's quiet. I drive because Ayden seemed like he needed a little time to process the evening. I ask him what he wants to do now, and he doesn't really give me a straight answer. Assuming that means he wants to go to the beach to hang out with his cousins, I drive us to the docks. Ayden grabs his baseball hat from the back seat, and we make our way to the beach.

Peter produces a football from somewhere and coerces Dylan into throwing with him. Colton and Jenson join in, and soon all the guys are shirtless and sweating as they run all over the sand, tossing the ball back and forth and tackling each other.

"Sweet Lord." Sky pretends to fan herself as she watches the scene in front of us.

"It's like watching a birthday present and Christmas all rolled into one," Tari says.

I laugh because she's right. All the guys are crazy hot, but my gaze is only focused on one of them. Ayden's bare chest is glistening with sweat, and his muscles are rippling as he throws a perfect spiral to Colton. His jeans are hanging low on his hips, and when he bends over to pick up an errant pass thrown his way, I have to hold myself back from stepping closer and grabbing his ass.

Jasalie and I turn away from the group to do more catching up. Her straight blond hair hangs past her shoulders, and her model figure hasn't changed in the five plus years I've known her.

"I like Lucky Bay," she says to me. "You always made it sound awful."

I laugh. "I wasn't expecting to land back here the way I did. But my hometown has always been a touchstone for me."

"That part sounds wonderful. I can't even imagine," Jasalie says, her gray eyes revealing a hint of that sadness I've always seen in them.

We've just started chatting about Jasalie and Dylan's wedding plans when Sky joins us.

"Do you know what you're doing yet?" she asks Jasalie.

"I'm not into the whole public thing, and neither is Dylan. So we may do a private ceremony somewhere, just the two of us. Then we'll have a renewal and reception for family and friends in the fall sometime; we think in Montana. My mom may even come."

"Wow," I say. "Has she met Dylan?"

"Yes, she loved him."

"Anyone with a vagina loves Dylan Wild," Sky says with a laugh. "And a lot of people with penises as well."

Jasalie blushes. "I can't believe how lucky I got. But God's plan is often a surprise, I guess."

Sky nods. "I'd say that's the world's biggest understatement."

My thoughts flash to Ayden. The way he kissed me like he'd been waiting for that moment his whole life...a shiver runs through me at the memory.

Jasalie's studying me. "Why do I get feeling we've walked right into the middle of something big?"

I smile.

Colton stalks over to us with a sexy grin. "Hey, Sparky," he says to Sky.

He drops his arm around me affectionately. "I'm sorry about your mom," he says in a low tone. "How are you?"

I force a smile I know he doesn't buy for a second. So I go for the truth instead. "You know, I'm honestly counting my blessings things turned out as well as they did."

His expression is kind but holds no pity. "If you need anything, you know all you have to do is ask. You have my number, right?"

I nod at him gratefully. "I do. Thanks, Colt."

The thing about Colton, and all of Ayden's cousins and Jenson too, is they never say anything they don't mean. I've known them my whole life, and while we grew up thousands of miles apart from each other, they've always been like brothers to me.

He picks Sky up over his shoulder and brings her out to join in the game. She complains the whole way, but Colton gets her laughing, and she stays and lets him teach her how to catch a spiral.

I catch Ayden's eyes on me more than once. I want to offer him comfort, but I don't want to intrude on him and his time with his cousins.

Jenson steps away from the game and nods at me.

"Want to walk to the water?" he asks.

"Sure." I lead him down the shore.

"I was sorry to hear about your mom, Bella. I hope everything works out."

"Thanks Jenson." I look at his face. He has gorgeous green eyes, but they look troubled tonight.

"Is something wrong?" I ask him.

He stuffs his hands in his shorts pockets, his bare chest glistening with sweat. "I have a strange question for you—how did you handle moving back to your hometown after being away for a while?"

"Not well." I let out a laugh, and Jenson does too. "You know it was hard. But a lot of that was because I felt forced back. That wasn't really true, but that's how it felt to me at the time."

He nods. "I'm planning to return to where I grew up. It's just... things are so different now than when I left. I'm a single dad with two kids..."

Something about his tone of voice—it sounds like regret. "Did you leave someone behind?" I ask him. "I don't mean to be nosy. You just...you sound like you might have."

"I did," he says, rocking back on his heels. His blond hair is windblown from the Maine air, and his green eyes flash with pain. "I thought maybe you'd understand what that felt like and give me a little insight on how you fixed it."

"Because of Ayden," I say immediately.

Jenson doesn't say anything; he just looks at me with those green eyes that look like they see everything.

I nod slowly. "The thing is, Ayden and I stayed just friends for a reason. So we couldn't screw up what we have. Crossing that line makes everything more dangerous."

The green in his eyes turns a few shades deeper. "True. But I don't want you to end up with the same regret as me, Bella. When Ayden's three thousand miles away and you're still here, letting him go without giving it a real shot will haunt you. Trust me."

———

Ayden

Bella thinks I want time alone with the guys.

But I don't. What I need is to be with her.

Turns out my cousins know that.

"What the hell are you doing?" Brayden says as our spontaneous game of football dies down and we start putting up the tents.

"I'm camping here tonight," I say. "Last I checked."

"He means, why aren't you with Bella?" Cam asks with a head

tilt toward where she's laughing with Tari over something. "You two look like you've got some things to work out."

I don't answer him while I concentrate on putting the last pole in the ground and making sure it's secure. I drop my bag into the tent, along with the gift I bought for Bella.

Then I walk over to where Dylan's finishing up his and Jasalie's tent.

"Ayd, she's three feet away from you. And in a few weeks, she'll be three thousand miles from you. Don't worry about spending time with us."

"I'm going. I'll catch up with you in a bit."

Dylan chuckles. "I think we can handle it. Go see your girl."

I turn to Colton, who's gathering driftwood for the bonfire. "You were right, by the way."

"Since I'm always right," he says with a smug lift of an eyebrow, "you'll have to clarify that statement."

"What you said in L.A." I nod at him. "You all coming here and being there for me tonight? It *was* what I needed. I didn't know how much."

He claps my back and pulls me in for a hug.

———

Bella

"When Ayden carried you off at the party, it was like something out of a movie," Tari says dreamily. "I was seriously turned on."

Jasalie and Sky break into laughter.

We're all still laughing when Ayden and Cam come and join us. Their t-shirts are back on, and I already miss shirtless Ayden.

"Good to see you, Bella." Cam tilts his head toward Ayden. "Status change yet, or are you and my stubborn cousin both still single?"

I swat at his dark head of hair and he ducks and laughs.

Tari points from Ayden to me. "Seriously, are you two ready to fess up and tell us what's going on?"

Every set of eyes turns to us as silence hits our circle.

Ayden glances at my expression and puts his arm around me. "Not before Bella and I talk."

I mouth, "Thank you" to him.

Tari makes a sad face. "That's no fun. Just remember we're all dying over here!"

"Noted," Ayden says. He brings his mouth to my ear and reaches out his hand to me. "Come with me, B."

As Tari fans her face teasingly, I wave goodbye and follow Ayden down the dark beach. We've only taken a few steps when Ayden, still holding my hand, veers off toward the lighthouse.

I stop short before our feet hit the pier. "What are you doing?"

"You coming?" he says.

I still don't move. "Ayden." He never goes this way. Not once since his father drowned. The pier represents everything painful from that day. Ayden and his mom and brother practically lived on the pier while they waited for news. News that was only bad in the end.

He looks at me with such intensity I swallow. "Bella, are you going to come with me?"

"Um..." I don't want to ask him why now after all these years. It's really not my business, and I don't want to push him like that. "Of course." I keep his hand close in mine, and we walk slowly out to the pier together.

We keep going until we reach the lighthouse, and Ayden stops to look up at it. "The light never goes out." He says it flatly, but I can hear the meaning behind his words.

"Never. Not even when..." I trail off.

"Not even when there's no longer any way to call the sailors home."

I squeeze his hand. "The lighthouse is the first thing I think of when I need hope in this world."

"It's funny. Same for me." He sits down on the dock, and I join him, our feet dangling over the water. "You'd think it would only remind me of bad things, but it's the opposite. It reminds me of my dad, maybe because it's probably the last thing he saw before they hit the open ocean. I kind of wish I'd come out here before now rather than avoiding it all these years."

We lapse into a comfortable silence broken only by the sounds of the waves hitting the craggy outcropping of rocks at the edge of the docks.

"You know what I remember most from that day?" Ayden says suddenly, interrupting my thoughts.

I keep my gaze on the water.

"Besides him dying," he says. "I remember your face when I told you."

I lift my head to look over at him.

"It was so sad," he says. "So scared. And it was…love."

I choke back a sob.

"I knew then that I could never let go of you, Bella," he says. "Not unless you wanted me to."

I inch even closer to him and he pulls me against his chest. "You'll never lose me, Ayden," I murmur into his chest.

He looks down at me. Underneath the lighthouse, his dark lashes cast deep shadows over his cheeks, and his eyes burn into me. His blue eyes nearly turn green with some kind of intense emotion, but I can't get a read on what it is.

"Bella, all I've wanted since we got to the party tonight was to be alone with you."

I tilt my head. "I thought you wanted to hang out with your cousins."

"No. I love them, but I want to be with you. I always want to be with you." He sucks in a deep breath. "No one's ever had my back like you do, Bella. The way you shouted down that asshole…"

"Colton told me to leave it alone," I say quietly. "He was right too. It wasn't my place."

Ayden shakes his head. "I liked that you made it your place. I needed you there. And all I can say is thank you."

I run my hand down the front of his t-shirt, fingering the raised Lucky Bay lettering. "First of all, I think you did thank me when you spirited me off to the bathroom and gave me that ridiculously hot kiss."

His mouth turns up on one corner.

"Besides that, though, you've saved me, stood up for me, and fought for me more times than I can count," I say. "I know your father was your hero, but you've always been mine."

Ayden's jaw is working again like he's trying not to lose it.

"It's okay to cry over him you know," I say. "It doesn't make you weak."

"It's not the right time," he says. "It's never been the right time."

"Because you've always had to stay strong for your mother," I say. "But she's not here right now, Ayd. It's just me. You don't have to be strong for me all the time. Sometimes you help me the most when you're weak."

For the next couple of minutes, we don't speak. I hold Ayden as a few tears slip down his face, and he lets go of the night, maybe finally getting to release the pain he's been holding for the last fifteen years.

"I don't know why I decided to come here," Ayden says as he sits up straight and gestures to the lighthouse. "Maybe to say good-bye."

"To the pain," I say. "But not to him."

"You think he was scared?"

I can't look at him. I know what he's asking, but I don't feel qualified to give an answer.

"I wonder if he had time to be sad for all he'd be leaving behind," he says.

I imagine the boat that night, all the commotion from the storm, and how hard it must have been to see. "I bet it was really dark."

"And really cold."

I turn to face him. "It may have been noisy from the men shouting plus the waves and thunder."

He brings up his legs and crosses his arms over them. "Nate made it sound like there was a lot of time. I always imagined it happening in an instant, you know? I guess it feels easier that way."

"Yeah." I fiddle with the strap on my sandal. "I'm sure it was different for everyone, though. It probably was fast for your dad. You know he was never one to linger."

Ayden rests his head face down on his folded arms.

"I'm sure he prayed," I say. "For all of you and for himself. And God was there too."

Ayden turns his head to look at me. "You think God was there?"

"Yes," I say, and I'm surprised how sure I am of myself when I say it. "I'm sure that God was there. Protecting him."

Ayden reaches out and pulls me close. The emotion swimming in the depths of his eyes unnerves me. I feel like he's seeing me in a way that he never has before. Like in a forever kind of way.

"Ayd—"

His mouth on mine swallows the rest of my sentence. He kisses me urgently, desperately, like we're the last two people on Earth.

When we finally break apart, Ayden pulls off his hat and twists it in his hands. "You think this hat is protection?"

"I think you know that answer far better than I do."

"I think I thought it would protect me from dying," he says. "Like a guardian angel."

He flings the hat into the sea so abruptly I swallow my scream, not sure why I'm reacting like he's throwing away a person.

"What?" His eyes meet mine. "The hat wasn't protecting me, Bella." He takes my chin in his hand and forces me to look at him. "It was keeping me stuck in that moment right before he drowned; that feeling of guilt that if I'd just gotten up that morning and gone with him, I could have prevented the storm from coming somehow. It makes no fucking sense, but I got it hard-coded in my brain."

His eyes look sad but calm. They look like Ayden's eyes again. I hadn't realized they'd ever changed, but I guess one day, fifteen years ago they got murky, and somewhere along the way I forgot they had.

"I'm ready to go," he says.

"Just a second. Come here." I put my arms around him and pull him close to me.

He hugs me back, and I feel silly for fighting back tears. It wasn't my father, after all. I should be the strong one, not the friend who can't control her emotions.

"It's not a bad thing to care, B," Ayden says into my hair. "It's never bad. And you have no idea how much it means to me that you knew him, that you loved him too."

When our lips meet this time, Ayden's kiss is gentle. His tongue dips into the seam of my lips, and my emotions get the best of me. I lean back, breaking the kiss.

Ayden catches my wrist. "What's the matter?"

"Nothing." I swallow. "I...don't know."

"Seriously." His eyes are dark and filled with vulnerability. "I need to know what you're thinking, Bella. Please."

"Do you still feel like you're cursed?" I say the words I've been scared to ask him. "You know, you always swore up and down that you would never get into anything serious with a woman..."

"I've adjusted my thinking around all of that." He runs a finger down my cheek. "Because of you, Bella. You broke through my walls of fear. With everything that's happened this summer, somehow I realized that my decision to stay single and casual was just a way for me to protect myself. Not anybody else. When my father drowned, I was scared to ever feel alive again. And keeping you at a distance while I dated people I knew I could never feel even a millionth as close to—it was the only way I could cope. But the truth is, you're worth risking everything for."

My breath catches in my throat. "Ayden. That makes me...really happy."

Maybe it was the memorial and how much emotion that

brought up. Maybe it was what happened with my mother and how Ayden stood by my side. The way he's always stood by me. Or maybe it's because he's sitting in front of me right now with his heart wide open.

I just know that my guard is down, and I blame the lack of guardedness for what comes flying out of my mouth with absolutely no filter at all.

"I love you, Ayden Wild."

His eyebrows shoot up to his hairline. "Bella..."

"I love you," I repeat. "Not just as my best friend in the world, but as my everything."

Ayden's throat moves as he swallows hard.

"Honestly"—I gesture toward the sea in a motion meant to encompass the vastness of what I feel—"I've loved you my whole life. I just couldn't admit it to myself. Shit." I shake my head. "I know that's far more than you wanted to hear tonight, so please let's table this for a better time."

Before Ayden can speak, I stand up and start moving. I've made it about three feet when his arms come around me from behind. He shifts me to face him and pulls me close. "Why are you running away from me?" His voice is raw and gruff.

I press my chin into his chest and lift my gaze to meet his. "Because I don't want you to say it back right now. Not tonight. Tonight was supposed to be all about your father. I know you, Ayd. I know you need to process this in your own way. So don't say anything. Please. I'm sorry if I've freaked you out. Let's just keep tonight for what it is, a beautiful tribute to your dad. You've waited fifteen years to be able to say goodbye to him, and you deserve the time and space to do that."

"You did so the opposite of freak me out." His hand is trembling as he reaches out to touch my cheek. The gesture is so tender I bite down on my lip. "It's not like that. I just..." He sucks in a breath. "I guess we've both been scared," he says in a rough tone. "Of how big this has always felt between us."

I guess fear of love can be like stage fright. If you don't get up there and show yourself, there's no chance for the love or the rejection. But this isn't just a four by twelve feet piece of wood; this is life, the greatest stage of all.

"I feel alive with you, Bella." The blue of his eyes shifts to a near-green.

His mouth crashes over mine. His tongue moves urgently through my mouth as his hands grip my face and he holds me to him. A moan escapes my throat and Ayden reacts to the sound by shifting his hand to my ass. He presses his thigh in between my legs and I feel his erection on my stomach. We're locked together like we need each other for oxygen, or we'll simply die right here on the spot.

Ayden wrenches himself away from me. "Hold on," he says through heavy breaths.

I stare at him. Does he not feel how amazing we are together, not just the other nights but right the hell now?

His eyes dance with amusement. "Bella." Ayden runs his fingers through my hair. "Trust me; being with you feels fucking perfect. What I meant was this isn't how I want to start things with you. I don't want it to feel desperate. I don't want it to feel like pain."

I try to catch my breath. "So..."

"So let's go back to the beach." He takes my hand in his. "I've got a surprise for you. We're going to have a romantic evening together. Just you and me."

"Like a date?" I say, horrified. "I'm no good at real dates."

"That's because you've never been on a date with me." He grins devilishly.

"Oh, really? Last I checked, you weren't so hot at real dates either, Mr. Wild."

"I think I can be. Will you give it a try?"

I smile back at him. "My first date with Ayden Wild."

He kisses my temple. "That's right. I promise it will be a night to remember."

CHAPTER TWENTY-THREE

When Ayden and I return to the beach, the bonfire's going in full force. I sit down next to Tari, and Ayden kisses my head and says he'll be right back.

"What is Ayden up to?" Jasalie asks me as he disappears inside one of the tents.

"No clue," I say. "He said we're having our first date tonight."

Tari and I sit down on a piece of driftwood, and Sky and Jasalie take seats on the sand. The four of us chat about L.A. and Lucky Bay and how much we love the ocean, no matter what coast we're on.

We're so engaged in conversation we hadn't noticed we're the only people left on the beach.

"It's just us and the bonfire," Jasalie says. "What the heck are they up to?"

Within a few minutes, Peter and Cam are back.

"We have one last tent to set up," Peter calls over to us. "The guys are getting food and bringing it back."

"So my pregnancy test was unclear," Tari whispers to me.

I furrow my brow. "How is that possible?"

"I don't know." She throws up her hands in frustration. "My doctor told me to repeat the test in a day or so."

"That's a good idea," I say.

She and I get so engrossed in conversation about her potential pregnancy that I gasp in surprise when Ayden squats next to me. He's got a paper bag filled with something delicious-smelling in it, and he immediately holds it out to me.

"Hey." His voice is raw.

I snap my head up to meet his blue gaze. "Hey, Ayd." I reach into his bag and pull out a fried clam. "You know this is my favorite. Thank you."

His hand goes to my bare leg. His palm is rough, callused from his work, and I bet it would feel like heaven on the insides of my thighs, or on my stomach, or...

"Oh, look!" Tari stands up so fast she stumbles, but I catch her smile. "Peter brought food too."

Peter and Tari snuggle on the beach with their food, and Ayden settles next to me, his arm going around my shoulders. We eat quietly for a few minutes, making quick work of the clams and fries.

"Miss me?" His voice is teasing.

"Yes," I say as I crumple up the empty food bag. "A lot."

His mouth is immediately on my earlobe. "Me too. I already have our tent ready for us."

"I honestly never even saw you set it up earlier."

He drags his lips across my cheek, and kisses the corner of my mouth. "I did it before we left for the lighthouse. You want to go there now?"

Oh, God, yes. Ayden takes my hand firmly in his and leads me by his grinning cousins, past the bonfire, and over to a tent sitting nowhere near any of the other ones.

"I wanted us to have privacy tonight," he says as he leans close to me and kisses my neck. "As much as we can at least."

Ayden unzips the flap and ushers me in ahead of him.

I gasp as I crawl inside the open flap. Battery-operated, white candles fill the inside of the tent.

"Ayden, this is so beautiful."

He's right behind me, and he gestures to the two sleeping bags open side by side.

"I brought two in case you wanted that. To sleep separately."

"That was thoughtful of you." *Wait, does that mean he doesn't...*

Like he can read my mind, Ayden adds, "Bella, just so we're clear, I want to sleep naked with you."

I swallow my nerves as my heart starts racing.

Ayden and me together.

Naked.

Everything is feeling incredibly real all of a sudden, and while Ayden seems to be taking our "status change" in stride, I feel like I'm going to explode from a combination of lust and terror.

His eyes haven't left mine. "But of course, I'm fine with whatever you want," he adds gently. "That goes without saying."

I clasp my hands together in a useless attempt to stop them from shaking. "I'm just...a little nervous, I guess." A shaky laugh escapes my throat.

Ayden rustles around in his bag for a second and then scoots closer to me. "I got you something."

"You did?"

"Yep." He puts his hands behind his back and grins at me. "Pick a hand."

I laugh. "Left."

"Good guess."

Just like how he always chooses tails when we flip a coin, Ayden always hides presents in his left hand.

He stretches out his left arm, his hand closed in a fist. I reach out and touch his hand, and he shows me what's in his palm.

"A key?"

"That's only part of the gift." He reaches behind his back again. "The other part—is this."

When I see what it is, I put my hands to my mouth. "Our lighthouse?"

The ceramic sculpture is in miniature, but there's no mistaking the Lucky Bay lighthouse. From the pale blue stripes on two sides to the red top, calling sailors home, it's a beautiful replica.

Ayden's eyes are on mine. "You like it?"

My eyes fill with tears before I can hold them back, and I can't do anything but nod stupidly.

"The key is for the door." Ayden takes the key from me and shows me how it fits in the little lock on the ceramic door. "It actually opens. I don't know what the hell you'd put in there, though."

My heart. That's what's always been in the lighthouse. I swallow down the lump in my throat and try to speak. "The image of that lighthouse got me through so many homesick nights in L.A."

"I remember you telling me that." He hands me the sculpture. "Now you'll have an actual physical copy—to take with you if you move, or—"

My gaze darts to his.

"Or," he says carefully. "To keep here with you when I leave. I thought maybe it could remind you of me. You know...if you get homesick for Ayden."

I smile through my tears and put down the lighthouse as I gesture for him to come closer.

He envelops me in a hug, and lifts me onto his lap. I bury my face in his chest, in his shirt that smells so good, that smells like him. All warmth and pine and ocean.

"I can't believe how hard we were working at that dumb-ass dare we made," he says. "Talk about going in the wrong direction."

"I don't know," I say slowly. "The dare brought us here, didn't it? If we hadn't challenged each other to deal with our messed-up love lives, maybe we wouldn't have ended up in this tent together."

"True. But speaking of the dare...you know you never have to worry about me with anyone else." He lifts my chin with his finger and searches my face intently. "Don't you?"

I sigh. "I do. It's hard to watch women hurl themselves at your hotter-than-sin body, but I do."

"Of course I would never betray you, Bella." His expression turns serious. "You know that."

"I know you're not a cheater. Not like..." Now I trail off.

"Not like your father," he finishes. "Absofuckinglutely not."

"Ayden..." I hesitate, not sure how to say it. "Are you sure you're ready to be in a committed relationship? That's never been your dating style. Not once."

His hands are shaking as he reaches for my arm and rubs it gently. "I know. But I want that with you, Bella. Even though I know I don't deserve you, I want everything with you. We can take it as slow as you want. Okay? You can decide no at any point. I don't ever want to hurt you, and I'll do everything in my power to make sure I never do."

Jenson's comment about no regrets flashes through my mind, and I realize he's right. Ayden's moving away. When summer's over, Ayden will be long gone, and unless I can figure out a way to leave my mother behind and go with him, whether he and I are just friends or have turned into lovers, I have to figure out a way to say goodbye to him in the end.

The pain that cuts through my chest is nearly unbearable. But once it passes, I feel freed. Because the truth is, I want to get closer to Ayden Wild than we've ever been.

I lift up my head so I can be sure to see Ayden's reaction when I say, "I want the same as you. Everything."

"Everything." His eyes darken. "You're sure?"

I nod. "Yes. Even though I'm scared out of my damn mind, I'm sure."

Ayden releases a long breath. "That's good. I'm...excited is an understatement."

He hugs me tightly, and I listen to his pounding heart. The air in the tent is so thick I can barely stand the heaviness. And for once, I stop fighting it.

I cup Ayden's cheek with my hand and say softly, "I want you tonight, Ayden."

His blue eyes turn nearly green. "God, Bella—I want you so much I'm shaking."

His mouth covers mine, and we lose ourselves in a tangle of tongues and moans. Then Ayden's hand shifts so that it's between my thighs. My cut-offs are tiny, and the rough pads of his fingers graze my soft skin all the way up to the ridge of my shorts. I bite back on a moan, but this is Ayden Wild. He's spent a lifetime learning to read my signals, and he reacts without hesitation.

"Where do you want me, Bella?" he growls into my ear. "Right here?" he asks as two of his fingers slip inside the leg of my shorts and travel up.

My breaths come in short bursts. "Higher," I get out.

He dips me down to his sleeping bag and lays me on my back. With his eyes on my face, he lifts my shirt and unhooks my bra.

"You know how many times I've pictured you this summer?" he says as he reveals my bare breasts and groans. "It's embarrassing how often I've gotten off to the fantasy of being with you, B."

I cry out as his fingers stroke my hard nipples.

He blows on my hot skin and I shiver. "Endless, countless nights when I wished I could walk over to your house and climb into your bed."

When his mouth goes to my breast, I clutch at his hair.

"You're so beautiful," he says as he licks and sucks at my nipple. "I want to touch every inch of you."

"Oh, God," I say. "Ayd...keep going."

He unzips my shorts and eases them down and off my legs. Then he hooks his fingers into my panties.

"Tell me if you want me to stop."

I nod as he pulls my panties down. When I'm bare before him, he drops his head between my legs. At the feel of his mouth on me, I half-moan, half-giggle.

"What's funny?" His head is back up, and his gaze snaps to mine.

"This is just so...it's you and me." I keep giggling like an idiot.

Ayden shoots me a sexy smile, but then he returns his attention between my legs. And I stop laughing and start moaning. His tongue is everywhere, and it's so incredible. The way he's touching me; I want to completely let go, but I can't.

Ayden lifts his head. "Bella? What's wrong?"

"I haven't um...well, since Trevor, I haven't actually..." I stumble into silence.

Ayden climbs up my body and rests his forearms on either side of me. His eyes flash with confusion. "You haven't had sex since Trevor? I'm sorry—I thought you had."

"I've had sex, yes."

Dead silence hits the tent.

"What haven't you done since Trevor?" Ayden says slowly.

Knowing I'm blushing under his hot gaze, I say quietly, "Come."

He rubs my nose with his own. "You haven't come...at all? In three years?"

"I've come with myself," I clarify. "But not with someone else. I've been too worried about whether or not they're attracted to me. Trevor obviously wasn't, and I missed the signs. Which makes me feel like an idiot. Who could have missed that?"

Ayden captures my mouth in a hard kiss. When he looks at me again, he says, "You're not an idiot. He'd trained himself to cover up his sexual desires. He had years of practice learning to fake who he really was. Do. Not. Blame. Yourself."

I reach my hands behind his neck and bring his face back to mine so I can kiss him again. Then he makes his way down my body, making sure to touch each and every inch of me with his lips. By the time he's back where I need him most, I'm ready for him.

He kisses the inside of each of my thighs and then returns his tongue to my hot center. And he just...doesn't let up. His intensity has my thighs shaking around his head, and still he keeps going. His tongue is everywhere, and when he presses a finger inside me at the same time, it's like a switch flips inside of me.

I call out his name as I come, and I don't stop chanting it until he's lying next to me on the sleeping bag, his eyes locked with mine.

"I've never felt closer to you," he whispers.

"You made that feel so easy." I brush my fingers over his cheek. "I honestly thought I might never orgasm again unless I was alone."

"About damn time. You deserve to let that go and forgive yourself." He shifts onto his side. "You're beautiful, Bella. Inside and out."

I reach for his waistband and slip my hand just underneath. His breath is shaky when he says, "What are you doing?"

"Touching you," I say, as I get onto my knees. "Is that okay?"

When I reach his hardness, he jerks underneath my hand. Ayden chuckles through a groan. "Pretty sure that's a yes."

———

Ayden

Bella's mouth is so hot and wet when she takes me inside that I nearly buck off the sleeping bag.

I reach down and gently pull her off me.

"What?" She looks up at me, her gaze unfocused. "Is that not how you like it?"

I cup her cheek in my hand. "I freaking love it. I love it so much I want it to last more than three seconds." I let go of her cheek and exhale. "Okay. You can keep going. Just...maybe ease into it."

She licks me slowly this time, along my entire length, and I thread my fingers through the long, silky strands of her blond hair. The harder she licks, the more I grip at her hair, and by the time she sucks me fully into her mouth, both my hands are holding her head. Her hair's like a golden halo around her, and she looks like an angel right now, her mouth right where I need her, and her lips wrapped around me. She's my angel and always has been.

"Shit, Bella." I have to fight the urge to thrust up into her mouth. "I've never had something feel like this." I groan as she takes me further in. "You've got the world's sexiest mouth."

She lifts her head. "You can move, Ayd. I like it when you move inside me. Don't hold back."

Her cheeks are flushed red, and her eyes are shining so bright. She's never looked more gorgeous.

"Are you sure? I don't want to hurt you."

"You won't. I want to feel you unleashed, Ayd. I've—" She flushes even redder. "I've fantasized about it."

"B," I groan. "Christ, you're driving me damn near insane." I release my hands off her hair and grip the sides of the pillow underneath my head. And I do as she requested—I let myself go.

For the next few minutes, I'm barely aware of what I'm doing; all I know is I'm making love to Bella's mouth. Her tongue is criminal in the way it moves over me, and all I can feel is her scorching hot mouth taking me deeper. The sensations she evokes as she sucks me off are blinding me with need. And desire. And ecstasy.

My orgasm takes over every bit of my consciousness, and I'm just barely aware of calling out her name as I come. I feel her crawl up my body and unpeel my fingers from the grip I have on the pillow.

"You let go," she says in an awed tone.

"Because of you." I tangle my fingers in her hair and pull her closer to me. "It's always because of you, Bella."

———

Bella

We lie tangled together, the only sounds the ocean waves and our beating hearts.

"I wanted to tell you something," I say eventually into his bare chest.

"What is it?"

"I'm performing once a week at a club in Portland called the Sea Urchin. I just started."

"I'm so proud of you. That's amazing."

"Thanks. It's a good start for me."

"The Sea Urchin, huh? That was always your favorite thing to find when we'd go walking the beach for shells. Remember you called it your good luck sea hedgehog?"

I laugh. "I can't believe you remember that."

"When it comes to you, I remember every detail." He brushes my lips with his, and then he gently plants little kisses all along my bottom lip.

I giggle, but when we make eye contact, the blue in his eyes is on fire. My heart feels like it's going to explode. Ayden lays his hand over my chest.

"You okay?"

I nod.

"Feel mine." He takes my hand and puts it on his heart.

"Pounding," I say in a whisper.

"Just like yours."

I wrap my arms around his back as his lips seek mine urgently. His tongue in my mouth, his hands all over me, all the years of separation drift away.

When his thumb traces my aroused nipple, I arch my back, seeking more.

"Christ, Bella." His breathing is shallow. "You're so under my skin. I can't remember a day when you haven't been under my skin. I've wanted to touch you like this for so fucking long."

I jerk up into a sitting position.

"Sorry." Ayden sits back, giving me space. "Is it too fast?"

"No." I shake my head. "It's not that. I just...need a second."

I close my eyes and breathe. When I open them again, Ayden's watching me.

"When you told me you were leaving, this was the last thing I was expecting." I try not to cry but a tear slips out anyway. "Honestly, I never thought we'd ever be together like this. But now that you're going, and I can't go with you..."

Ayden puts a finger to my lips, and then he says the five most important words I've ever heard in my life. "I love you, Bella Wesley."

"Ayden."

"Shh." He pulls me against him until I'm sitting between his legs. "I know you wanted me to wait to say it. But it feels like I've been waiting forever. I've always loved you, Bella." He holds my face in his hands. "My whole life."

"I love you too, Ayden. So much. I don't know how the hell we can make this last when..."

Ayden runs his lips across my cheek. "Bella. If you find you can't leave Lucky Bay..."

I hold my breath and don't look at him.

"We'll still make it work," he finishes. "Don't make your decision based on us. Okay? Do what's best for you. Moving to L.A. is a completely separate decision from us choosing to be a couple."

I flick my gaze up to meet his intense and determined one.

"It will never be good-bye. I swear on my life, Bella. This—us— is for always. I can always stay..."

"Don't you even finish that sentence," I say sharply. "You are not changing your plans for me. Just like you wouldn't have let me change mine. We'll figure it out, Ayden."

"Long distance, short distance—we're together now. You're mine, and I'm yours."

He says that, but I know us too well. Three thousand miles away is a lot of mileage when we've been together for the blink of an eye. I suck at the dating world, and I need the in-person prac-tice. I'm no good at this relationship stuff, and neither is Ayden. We need to be together. Somehow, that has to happen.

Only, with what just happened with my mom, I have no idea how to make it happen.

"I wish we could make the move to L.A. together. As a couple." I say my dream out loud for the first time.

Ayden plays with my hair as he trails light kisses along my bare neck. "Me too. I want to live with you out there. And not just sharing Dylan's apartment as housemates—I want to share a bed with you too."

"Are you sure? That's a big step, Ayden."

"We've practically been living with each other here our entire lives," he says. "Maybe not as a couple, but we aren't exactly a normal 'boy meets girl' in a new relationship."

"No, we're certainly not. And I want all of that too. I just...with everything that happened this week, I truly don't know that what I want is possible."

"I know. But I have a feeling things will work out in our favor. Somehow. And..." He kisses my head. "That's a separate discussion, isn't it? Whether or not you move doesn't change us right now. We're still on our first date, aren't we?"

"The best first date," I whisper.

"The best first date," he agrees.

CHAPTER TWENTY-FOUR

Bella

I wake up in the morning and smile at the feeling of Ayden's heavy arm wrapped around my body. I'm curled up against his bare chest, his leg in between mine.

After sleeping together like this and exploring each other's bodies last night—I can't imagine the emptiness of Ayden not being in Lucky Bay. And with my mother's current condition, I feel selfish for even contemplating the idea of leaving.

I slip out from underneath Ayden's arm and put on my bikini and a pair of shorts. I unzip the tent flap quietly and step outside. It's a beautiful day, full of sun and not a cloud in the sky. The only clouds seem to be in my own head.

I walk over to where the bonfire was burning last night. Everyone's hanging out eating breakfast.

"Bella! You missed the fireworks last night!" Tari laughs. "Although I'm betting you had some of your own inside that tent. Want to fill us in?"

I stick out my tongue at her. "I'm not spilling anything without Ayden here." I glance around at the curious faces of Jasalie and Sky, not to mention Peter, Jenson, and all the Wild cousins. "Especially not with everyone staring at me."

"Status change will be announced any moment." Cam winks at me. "I called it first."

Peter chuckles as he throws me a muffin. "Just picked them up. There's a hot chocolate for you too."

"Thanks." I've taken one bite of my muffin when Ayden, wearing just his navy blue swimming trunks, takes a seat next to me.

He pats my leg in greeting. "How'd you sleep?"

I smile and hand him a muffin from the bag. "Good. You?"

He leans over and kisses my temple. "Perfectly."

Tari's eyes have grown so wide I'm convinced they're going to pop out of her head. "We've all been sitting here for the past hour with nothing to do but guess about you two." She points between Ayden and me. "Can we call you an official couple yet? Please?"

"Um..." I smile at Ayden. "I don't really like labels..."

"We're a couple, Tar," he says as he cups my face and kisses me.

"Oh, thank God! I'm so happy right now! And you better leave the tent today!" she says. "We're spending the holiday hanging on the beach."

Ayden murmurs into my ear, "We'll hang out for a while. But I have our second date planned for later, so I hope you're free."

I turn to him and smile. "The answer to that question is yes, Ayd. It's always yes."

———

We spend the morning swimming and hanging out on the beach. Tari and Peter leave for a couple of hours, and when Tari returns, she whispers to me that she needs to talk to me.

I look at her flushed face. "You have a secret," I say as I point at her.

Before she can answer me, my phone rings.

I glance down at the number. "I don't know who this is," I mutter.

"Is it about your mom?" Tari asks in concern. "Maybe you should answer it."

"Yeah. Excuse me for a second." I step away from the noisy group and bring the phone to my ear. "Hello?"

"Hi, sweet Bella."

I press the phone closer like I need to be sure I'm hearing right. "Trevor?"

A long chuckle follows. "That's me. Your cheating ex, who you'd probably rather not hear from."

I break into a smile. "How are you?"

"I'm great. How've you been?"

"I'm good. Congratulations on your upcoming wedding. I truly am happy for you, Trevor. I'm sorry I can't make it."

"Thank you. And no worries—I figured you wouldn't be coming back to L.A. anytime soon."

"Actually," I say, not really sure why I'm telling him this, "I'm going to be out there on a visit soon. And maybe someday...I'll be able to live there again."

"Really?" He makes a surprised sound. "Huh. That would be awesome. Seriously."

"Thanks. Honestly, it may not happen, due to some stuff I'm dealing with here. But a friend of mine is moving out there soon, so we'll see."

"A friend as in a boyfriend?"

He apparently takes my silence as affirmation because he laughs. "You've always been a terrible liar, Bella. Who is he?"

"What makes you think you know him?"

"Okay, just tell me this—is his name Ayden Wild?"

My voice goes up several octaves when I say, "How did you know that?"

Another chuckle. "Everything finally makes sense. You and Ayden were always supposed to be together. I knew it before you did."

"You only met him once."

"I didn't have to meet him at all to know the truth. The way you talked about him—your entire face would light up. In a way it never did with me."

"Oh." Then, "I'm sorry if that bothered you. You know, before you were with Max."

"Honestly, it helped me. It made me feel like you and I were the same underneath. We were both lying to ourselves."

I sigh. "I guess you're right. Shit."

"And now," he says in a gentle tone, "we're both free."

"I'm glad, by the way, about what happened," I say to him for the first time. "I'm glad you and I broke up. As painful as it was at the time, and as much as it upended all my plans, I thank God every day for that spotlight. You and I would have destroyed each other, and ourselves, if we'd stayed together in the worst sort of lie."

"That we would have." Trevor exhales heavily. "I thank God too. Our angels were looking out for us that night, huh? When I was too much of a coward to come clean, God did it for me."

"Have a beautiful wedding," I say softly.

"We will. Look me up when you come out here. Promise."

"I will. *If* I come out there."

I can tell he's smiling when he says, "You're meant to be a singer, Bella. And with Ayden by your side, I can't imagine anything stopping you."

As we hang up, I walk back to Tari, who's sitting on the sand alone while everyone else splashes around in the water. Everyone except for Ayden and Peter, who have mysteriously disappeared.

"Everything okay?" she asks me as I join her.

"That was Trevor." I tell her about our brief conversation. "I'm happy he called me."

"Me too." She hugs me. "It sounds like you needed that closure."

I look at her face, which is still flushed. "What's going on, Tar? I didn't mean to put you off with whatever you wanted to tell me."

She laughs as she reaches into her pocket and pulls out a pregnancy stick. "I would say everything is in perfect timing, my dear."

What she's holding up is clearly positive. It's a yes.

My eyes smart with tears as I hug her. Crying is the last thing I ever thought I'd do when Tari found out she was pregnant, but I'm surprisingly emotional.

"You're going to be such an amazing mother, Tar."

She's still laughing as we walk down the beach together. "I still hadn't gotten my period, so I repeated the test at Peter's insistence. This time it was a positive!"

"I'm so happy for you guys," I say.

"Peter's so crazy excited," she says. "He kept saying he was sure this was it. I didn't believe him, of course, but turns out he was right. He's telling Ayden now. I'll have to make sure I tell my parents before the whole town finds out. Because somehow, everyone will know within the day. Even though the four of us won't say a word. It's like law in Lucky Bay."

"So true."

"And I'm starving. Do you want to grab some food and bring it back for everyone?"

"Sounds good. We'll binge again on fried food."

"Hey, it's July fourth."

"With two things to celebrate now," I say to her with a smile.

———

We're all sitting around the campsite eating lunch when Ayden and Peter return with a bottle of champagne. Ayden heads right for Tari.

As he picks her up and kisses her on the cheek, he and I catch eyes. His gaze is locked with mine, and something about the moment—I smile at him, fighting happy tears again.

"What are we celebrating?" Cam asks as Peter uncorks the bottle.

Ayden puts Tari down and points at Peter. "These two just found out they're going to be kick-ass parents."

"Hey, congratulations!" Dylan says with a grin.

Colton follows suit, and soon everyone but Tari has a plastic cup of champagne in their hand.

"To new beginnings," Ayden says as he holds his cup in the air.

I smile at him and raise my cup. "To new beginnings."

———

By mid-afternoon, the tents have been taken down and packed in the back of Peter's truck. Ayden's cousins and Jenson are heading to Ayden's house shortly to pack up and head to the airport, but Ayden and I say goodbye to everyone at the beach.

As we walk to his car, he laces his fingers through mine. "You ready for date number two?" he asks me.

"More than ready."

As we get into the car and Ayden turns the keys in the ignition, I glance at the dashboard.

"Oh, no." I bang the palm of my hand to my forehead.

He jerks his head in my direction. "What's wrong, Bella?"

"I'm such an idiot." I look at him in a panic. "Today's Tuesday. I got confused with the holiday, but that doesn't matter to my mother. A Tuesday is a Tuesday."

Ayden's blue eyes soften. "I know today's Tuesday, Bella."

"But...our date," I say, feeling so sad I can barely finish the sentence. "I'll have to cut it short, Ayd. I'm so sorry."

"Bella. I remembered that today was Tuesday. It's built into our date. Not to worry."

"You built visiting my mother into our date?"

He puts the car into drive and pulls out of the parking space. "Yes."

"But...it's only the second date we've ever had. Going to see my mother doesn't sound very romantic."

"Being anywhere with you is romantic, B," he says to me as we zip along the ocean-lined road.

The intense love I feel for him crashes through me. I don't know how I got so lucky.

"Ayden..." I reach over and take his hand. "Thank you for understanding."

———

Mom usually expects me in the evening, so Ayden says he has dinner reservations for us first. And for that, he says we need to change.

"I think you're sexy as hell in your bikini top and tiny shorts," he says as he takes a seat on my bed. "But this place has a dress code."

"What kind of place is it?" I ask him as I grab a blue sundress out of my closet.

"That..." he says, pointing to my dress. "That will be perfect."

When I come out of the bathroom twenty minutes later, my hair is down and tamed from all the salt water that soaked through it during my morning swim. I'm wearing a hint of lipstick and mascara, and that's it. My face got plenty of color from the day at the beach that any blush would be overkill. And my sundress...well, it has an open back, and the front cuts low in a V-shape. For that very reason, I don't usually feel comfortable wearing it, but I feel comfortable wearing anything—and nothing —with Ayden. I almost feel like I've been saving the dress for him.

Ayden's lying on his side on my bed, waiting for me. He looks up as I enter the bedroom, and his blue eyes turn volcanic with heat.

"Bella. Come. Here."

When I reach him, he pulls me on top of him. "I want to take this off of you right now," he murmurs into my neck. "You're so fucking sexy."

His hands go underneath my dress and straight to my ass.

"Oh God, Ayden," I mumble as he turns us so he can slip his fingers inside the front of my panties.

"Honey, you're wet." He sucks on my neck and then makes his

way along my collarbone. "I have to take care of this for you before we go to dinner. Please?"

"Will we...miss our reservation?" I say in halting tones.

"Not with what I have planned for you. I can bring you there in under two minutes."

I clutch at the blanket on my bed with both fists. "Ayden, please. You're making me so..."

"So what?" he murmurs as two fingers slide inside me.

"Oh God, Ayden. So..."

He starts moving his fingers in and out.

"So God..."

And now his thumb is involved, stroking and playing with me while his fingers are moving inside me at the same time.

"So what, Bella? How does it make you feel when I touch you?"

"So good...oh shit. Ayden, you're...I'm..." My orgasm is so fast and so powerful that I literally buck off the bed.

"So good," he says into my lips as he kisses me hard. "That was so fucking good."

"I know," I say to him. "I love you."

His blue eyes shine with emotion.

"What is it?" I ask him, putting my hand on his cheek.

"I didn't know how much I needed to hear you say those words to me until you did," he says.

"Ayd." I kiss his lips. "You know I've always loved you even before we were a couple."

"Of course. But being friends first and then hearing you say it from this new place..." He shakes his head. "I can't explain how intense it feels."

"I get it." I keep kissing him. "I'm so happy; I can hardly believe this is real."

I reach for his shorts, but he backs away.

"Babe," he says. "We really will miss the reservation if we take any longer."

My body's still on fire for him, but I give him a quick kiss and wriggle out of his arms. "Okay. Let's go."

Ayden stands up, reaching into his shorts to adjust himself. "We'll need to stop by my place for me to change too. And that could be dangerous."

"How come?" I ask him as we leave my bedroom and head for the front door.

"Because," he says as he holds the door open for me and I step through it, "I'm so hard right now that I could injure myself when I put on my pants."

I pat his back. "Poor baby. I can help you out with that."

But Ayden shakes his head. "Nope. We're going to go have a good meal. And then after dinner? That dress is coming off."

I know I'm blushing because Ayden grins and leans in to kiss me as we reach the car. "You're so cute when you're shy. You don't need to be shy with me, B."

"I'm not normally," I say. "But talking about getting naked with you isn't something I'm used to yet."

"Get used to it because I plan on us getting naked together a lot."

And I'm *a lot* fine with that.

———

"This is supposed to be the best Italian restaurant on the Maine coast," I gush as Ayden parks in the lot of Bruscetti's. "I can't believe you thought of it, Ayd."

"We always talked about coming here together some day, remember?" He puts his hand on the small of my back as we walk toward the big wooden doorway.

"I do. I can't wait to try the food."

———

"So what's the verdict?" Ayden asks me as we finish our meal and the waiter brings us an enormous piece of tiramisu to share.

"Amazing." I swallow my first piece of dessert. "And this is so good too. Try it." I put a piece of the tiramisu on my fork and hold it up to Ayden's mouth.

He closes his lips around the fork, never taking his eyes off of me.

"Well?" I ask him, watching him eat the bite of dessert.

"Delicious," he agrees.

I fidget with the napkin in my lap. "Ayd..."

"Yeah?" He takes my chin in his hand so I have to look at him. "What is it?"

"Trevor called me today."

Ayden's eyes narrow. "Why? You guys don't usually call just to chat."

"No. I haven't talked to him in ages. He wanted to say hi I guess. I don't really know why he called, actually. But anyway, he guessed about you. About us."

Ayden nods calmly. "I'm not surprised."

"How come?"

"Because he's a guy. And when he was with you, he was probably thinking I knew you better than he did. Which I do, by the way."

I laugh. "Well, anyway, that was it. I just wanted you to know."

"I appreciate that. Does this mean we're going to have to see him again sometime?"

"Maybe. Now that he and I are each with the right partner, it will probably go a hell of a lot smoother. And it's weird because he called right before Tari told me she was pregnant."

"Why's that weird?"

"Because the only time I've ever taken a pregnancy test was when I was living in L.A. I mean, thank God it didn't look like Tari's did..."

I stop short and cover my hand with my mouth. *Shit.* I've never shared that story with Ayden before, and I can't believe it slipped out now.

I tap my foot on the floor anxiously as I witness a rush of

emotions cross Ayden's face. Shock and fear, replaced by an unreadable expression.

"This is definitely not good second date material," I say with an awkward laugh. "Sorry."

Ayden's throat moves as he swallows hard. "You thought you were pregnant?"

"I suspected," I say quickly. "Just suspected. But I wasn't. So it was nothing."

I wouldn't say it was nothing, exactly. I was beyond relieved, because the idea of being tied to Trevor forever felt absolutely imprisoning. And one month later, he and I were done.

"I didn't keep it from you on purpose." I pause. "Well, that's not true. I did keep it from you. I wasn't sure how you'd react, and it all happened so quickly."

The tension leaves Ayden's face as he pulls his chair closer to me and takes my hand in his. "I would have been there for you, Bella." His tone is guttural. "If you'd needed someone before you knew for sure—if you were pregnant or not—you could have called me."

I bite my lip, and Ayden leans in and kisses my bottom lip, forcing me to release my hold on it.

I squeeze his hand back. "Thanks, Ayd."

I stare down at the table for a moment, desperately needing a change of subject.

Reading me like he always does, Ayden says, "Peter's stoked about the baby. I've never seen him so happy."

I smile. "I cried when Tari told me. I have no idea why. I just did."

"I felt it too," Ayden says. "I never thought I'd really care too much, you know? I knew I'd be happy for them. I just didn't think it would turn my world or anything."

"I didn't expect to be so emotional either. That one time I took the test, I was honestly relieved it was negative."

"Yeah." He shrugs. "But the thing is, you and me..."

I look at him more closely. "You and me what?"

His cheeks flush the sweetest shade of red. "You're the only woman I've ever pictured..."

I let out a strangled gasp. "You always told me you never pictured having kids!"

"That's sort of true." He puts up his hands in a surrender gesture. "I never imagined you and I would break our pact, and I didn't want babies with anyone else. It didn't feel right to even think about it with any other woman. No one except for you, Bella."

"God, Ayden."

"Too fast for date two?" he jokes, his dimple flashing.

I laugh. "Honestly, no. It probably should be, but..." I lock eyes with him. "I want to have a family with you, Ayd. I'm sure this kind of future planning is way not recommended for date two, like you say."

"This—what's between us—has been in the making for our entire lives. That changes things."

Yes, it does. It makes every little thing more intense, and every moment we touch feels like a permanent connection. It makes the idea of Ayden leaving unbearable.

CHAPTER TWENTY-FIVE

Ayden and I pull into my parents' circular driveway at our usual Tuesday time.

"We look a little dressy for our normal visit," I say to him nervously as we head for the door. "Do you think I should tell my mom about us tonight?"

"You mean about our status change?" he teases me. "Cam's got a way with words."

"I may end up using his joke if I get too nervous."

I take out my key and open the front door.

Ellie greets us, as usual.

"Hello Mr. Wild, Ms. Wesley. Your mother is in the den."

Ayden and I stare at each other, his face looking as confused as I feel.

I grab at Ellie's arm before she can turn away. "I'm sorry. Did you say my mother is in *the den?*"

Ellie nods. "Yes. Your father's with her."

I clutch harder at her arm, and a look of alarm crosses her face. "My *father?* Is here?"

"Yes." She slows down her next words, like maybe that will help. "He's...in the den...with...your mother."

Ayden gently removes my clawing hand from poor Ellie's arm.

"Thank you Ellie. We'll go see them now." He puts his arm around me and guides me down the hall.

But I stop halfway through, staring up at him for answers.

"The den?" I repeat, sounding like I'm insanely stupid. "Dad's here? With Mom?"

"What is the world coming to?" Ayden says, and I know he's trying to lighten the mood. "Your mother's out of bed on a Tuesday for the first time in three years." He tips his forehead to mine, his eyes searching mine carefully. "You ready to go find out what the fuss is about?"

I give a quick nod. "Okay."

As we reach the open doorway of the den, both my parents look up from their seats on the couch. Mom's wearing—*gasp*—casual pants and a loose button-down blouse, and Dad's wearing—I nearly fall over—*jeans* and a t-shirt.

"Bella," Dad says, clearly surprised to see me. "I told you to take these two days for yourself."

I think back to our last conversation. "You said to take off yesterday and today, yes. But...," I lower my voice to a whisper, as if that will prevent my mother from overhearing me. "Today's Tuesday."

Dad tilts his head toward Mom. "She's with me. Everything's fine, Bella."

"Mirabella, hello," Mom says in a calm voice. "I'm glad you're here. I have a couple of song requests for your friend, Guy, for your father's party."

"Hi Mom." I can't help the smile that spreads across my face. "You sound good."

She glares at me. "Bella, please let's not do this every time we speak."

"Right, sorry." I unsuccessfully try to stop smiling, and next to me, Ayden's full-out chuckling.

Dad looks from me to Ayden, and even his eyes brighten with humor.

"In terms of music..." Mom prompts me.

"I can talk to Guy for you," I say. "I'll be seeing him tomorrow."

"Okay. I haven't spoken with him since..." She trails off.

And I say softly, "It's okay, Mom."

She nods at me. "Thank you."

Dad puts his arm around Mom, and for the first time, I notice the remote on his lap.

"Were you two watching a movie?" I ask the question like I'm accusing them of just deciding to fly to Mars.

Dad points at the television where I turn to see...Star Wars on the screen.

I whip my head back around. "You two only watch documentaries!"

"First time for everything." Dad shrugs. "I'm finding this movie quite fascinating, actually."

"Oh, it is," Mom says. "Mirabella, you really should see it sometime."

"Mom, I *have* seen it. Like three times. It's been out for..." I cut off. "Oh, never mind."

Ayden takes my hand in his. "Babe, maybe we should continue our date somewhere else and let your parents enjoy their night together."

"Okay," I say.

But before we can say goodbye, my mother lets out a gasp, and Dad's eyes shift from me to Ayden. "Are you and my daughter more than friends now?"

Before I can intercede, Ayden answers him.

"Yes, sir. I'm head over heels in love with your daughter, and I plan to be with her forever."

Dad's concerned expression disappears and is immediately replaced by a look of relief. "Good." He holds out his hand, and Ayden steps forward to shake it. "That's wonderful actually. I just don't want to see her hurt."

Mom's set mouth lifts in a touch of a smile. "I hope you're both very happy," she says awkwardly.

"Thank you, Mom." I take Ayden by the arm, and we make our exit.

But as soon as we're safely inside the car...

"What the hell was that?" Before Ayden can hazard a guess, I keep going. "He was wearing *jeans.*"

"I seriously didn't know he even owned a pair of jeans," Ayden says. "And your mom looked pretty casual herself."

"I know!" I put on my seatbelt but then turn to face him again as he backs out of the driveway. "It felt very surreal, didn't it?"

"Yeah. But I was happy for you. That he was actually following through on his promise to try harder." He puts his hand on my thigh and lightly squeezes.

"Let's hope it lasts," I say, turning to look out the window. "For her sake, I pray that it lasts."

———

Ayden parks his car in my driveway.

And suddenly, date two feels awkward.

Do I invite him in? Maul him right here in the car?

Even though I want to ask him to take me any way he wants, I end up saying, "Will you walk me to the door?"

"Of course."

As soon as we reach the top step, Ayden crowds me against the door. His mouth hovers over mine, a fraction of a centimeter separating us, until he closes the gap and his lips seek mine hungrily. I stop caring about anything—like Ayden leaving town, if I should go with him, or that anyone could drive by and see us. I want to kiss Ayden forever. I never want him leaving my front step.

His hands skim along my hips and over my breasts, ultimately cupping my face. We could make love right here on the steps, and that would be just fine with me. I've never felt like this before when I've kissed anyone, and I feel it with Ayden every single time. It's the most incredible high, and every second his lips burn into mine just makes me want him even more. I slip my hands underneath his shirt and start to pull it off of him. But just as it feels like we really will be naked and intertwined in about two seconds, Ayden breaks away.

"I'm sorry if I'm rushing things, Bella. Do you want me to go?" he says, breathing heavily and backing up so that I can't touch him.

I pull him back to me. "No. Stay."

"Thank Christ. We've waited long enough already." He puts his hands on my hips and lifts me up. I automatically wrap my legs around his waist as he buries his head in the crook of my neck. "I don't ever want to leave you again, Bella. Not even for a moment."

His mouth returns to mine, and with my lips firmly locked on his, I fiddle with my purse, trying to get my house keys out. My back is up against the front door, and somehow I manage to hand Ayden the keys.

He never stops kissing me, never even lets up, as he works the key in the door. He holds me tightly in his arms, and we stumble over the threshold as he closes the door behind us.

We collapse on the living room rug together, and Ayden's hands are already underneath my sundress.

"Bella." Ayden's deep voice rumbles in my ear as he lifts my dress up to my waist. "I want you so much. But tell me if this is too fast, and we'll slow down."

"Not. Too. Fast." My words come out choppy. "Make love to me, Ayden. Please."

He halts, my dress halfway up my stomach. "I literally can't think of anything lately other than making love to you, Bella Wesley."

His hands move lightning quick as he peels my sundress up past my breasts and over my head. It lands next to us on my living room floor. Ayden grabs a blanket off the couch and rolls us onto it, and then he drags my panties down my legs. His groan sends shivers down my spine, and his mouth is between my legs so fast I don't have a chance to close them. Instead, I squirm, trying to shift backward.

"You know I love that," I say. "But you don't have to..."

"Bella." He says my name like a prayer. "Don't. Be. Ashamed." He plants one gentle kiss on my most sensitive spot. "You're beautiful. You're perfect. And you're so damn wet."

His warm breath brushes against the soft skin of my inner thigh. A strangled moan catches in my throat.

And then he kisses me. Right. There. Within seconds I'm clenching Ayden's head between my thighs, and when I come, I see goddamn stars.

He reaches behind his head and takes off his shirt in one motion. I've already got my fingers on his waistband, and I quickly unsnap his jeans and slip my hand inside his boxers.

He's so hard, and as I run my hand up and down his thick length, he pulses against me.

"Bella...fuck." He leans down and groans into my mouth as he kisses me.

He pulls his jeans and boxers the rest of the way off, and then he crawls up my body and leans on his forearms to brace himself over me. I wrap my hand around his erection again, and the moment I touch him, his teeth sink gently into the skin on my neck.

"Shit." His breathing gets erratic as I keep moving my hand. "That feels so good, B. Keep doing that. Actually, don't. I want to be inside you more. But let's move to a bed so you can be comfortable."

He picks me up and carries me down the hall to my bedroom.

As soon as he's on top of me again, I grab a condom out of my drawer and help him roll it on.

And then we're just a tangle of limbs and moans as Ayden Wild pushes inside me for the first time. I cry out in bliss as he enters me inch by inch, and when he pauses to let me adjust, I whisper, "Does this feel different? It does, right?"

"What do you mean?" His voice is raw.

"Than it ever has before? Because it feels..."

His eyes are feral as they fix on me. "Like nothing I've ever experienced. I feel like I'm going to explode." His breath is heavy on my neck. "You're so perfect, Bella. Being inside you is so perfect."

"Can you...move now?"

He kisses me, and pulls back before driving inside me slowly.

Oh, God. My nails claw into his back.

"I love you, Bella," he whispers. "I love you so fucking much," he mutters before he starts to move for real.

I can hear the angels calling to me as we make love. I can hear the ocean waves crashing against the shore, even though we're nearly ten blocks from the beach. I can hear my own heart beating as I feel Ayden's pounding against mine. His breathing gets erratic as he gets close, but he waits for me to clutch at his back and call out his name in ecstasy before he joins me in release. We come together, our eyes locked together.

When we eventually pull apart, Ayden's gaze meets mine.

"God, I didn't know it could feel like that," he says, his voice hoarse.

"You mean sex?"

His smile is beautiful. "That's just it. It's not just sex with you, it's like..." He inhales. "So much more. The most intense experience I've ever had."

We have the whole night ahead of us, and we take full advantage as we make love again and again.

In the shower with Ayden's teeth nipping at my earlobe as he drives into me from behind and sends me into a mind-blowing orgasm and then follows me with his own release.

Against my bedroom wall after we leave the bathroom and can't wait to make it to the bed. Ayden holds my wrists over my head with one hand while he grips my ass with the other and sends me spiraling into yet another climax.

Again when we climb underneath the sheets and Ayden begs me to ride him hard. He comes with me, calling out my name and pulling me down on top of him so it feels like we're one.

I run my hand over his bare chest as we're finally drifting off to sleep. "Being best friends and doing this is pretty incomparable."

His lips seek mine. "There's no comparison to you, Bella. There never was."

Best second date ever.

CHAPTER TWENTY-SIX

The following week passes quickly.

Except for my final college exam, which I pass with flying colors, Ayden and I are inseparable. He even meets me after I pick up my graded test so we can celebrate together.

I wave the test with a big red "A" at him, and he grins.

"I need to release all the stress of being a college student," I say to him when he kisses me outside the school building. "Do you have any ideas?"

His eyes darken with heat. "I have a fucking amazing idea, actually."

I laugh as he puts his hands on my waist and urges me toward his car.

And instead of going to the bar for a drink like we had planned, we go straight to my house. More like, my bedroom, where Ayden takes off my clothes and sinks inside me until I'm screaming his name. Best way to release tension ever.

We stay in bed the rest of the night.

———

The next evening, Ayden, Tari, and Peter come to the Sea Urchin Club to hear me perform. Singing has become fun for me again, and I invite Ayden up for my last song.

"This man has been my muse all summer," I say as Ayden blushes and looks like he wants to be anywhere but on stage. "This next song is all about following your heart."

As I sing Wild Love, I sing it only to Ayden. When I strum the last note, Ayden pulls me into his arms and kisses me, and the whole audience cheers.

Afterward, we go to Tari and Peter's for dinner, and as soon as we're finished eating, I'm cuddling in Ayden's lap on the couch.

"You need a drink?" he murmurs into my neck as he wraps his arms around my waist.

I twist around to kiss his cheek. "I'm good."

"You want something else?"

I nuzzle his neck. "Maybe something else."

He kisses me, his tongue lightly touching mine and his hand slipping underneath my shirt before he pulls back with a smile. "I love you."

Across from us, Peter breaks into laughter. "Get a fucking room, you two."

But Tari squeals. "I love it! Whenever either of you dated in the past, you looked like you wanted to run in the other direction when your date got mushy."

"That's because we were with the wrong people," Ayden murmurs. "This is the only real thing I've ever known. With this girl right here."

As Tari ahhs and takes out her phone to snap a picture of us, I snuggle further into Ayden's lap. I love him. That's all I know. And hopefully that's enough.

———

The next night, Ayden and I stop by Grandpa's.

Ayden gets a call from Michael the second we step inside, and he immediately starts talking to him about the best way for Ayden to send his checks for the mortgage payments. To give him privacy, Grandpa and I step out on the outdoor porch and enjoy the night air.

"Your mother's doing pretty good," he says. "She sounded more stable when I talked to her today."

"Oh, she's still Lucy Wesley," I assure him, and he chuckles. "She can be bossy and cranky and a bit of a snob." I laugh. "But she does seem to be taking well to the new meds. It's only been a short while, so the drugs are still getting into her system while they tweak the particulars, but she says she notices a difference from before. And her therapy sessions, especially the ones she's doing with Dad, seem to be helping. I'm cautiously optimistic."

"And just as importantly, your father seems much more invested in his marriage," Grandpa says. "Did you have anything to do with that change?"

"Not really. Mom's overdose was a big reason." I lower my voice. "Plus, when he needed a push, Ayden may have said something to him."

Grandpa's face lights up. "Ayden, huh? Good man."

"He is."

"And have you given it more thought? Moving to L.A.?"

I fidget with my ponytail. "I'm still thinking. I do want to, but of course, with everything that happened with Mom, I'm more than a little terrified to even contemplate it."

"Have you talked to your father about your concerns?"

"No. Maybe I should. But I don't want to get in the middle of his progress with Mom."

Grandpa nods. "Why don't you leave that part to me?"

"No, Grandpa. You don't have to say anything."

He just gives me that stern look that always tells me to stop arguing him.

Then, glancing inside to make sure Ayden's still on the phone, Grandpa takes full advantage of the moment alone with me.

"You and Ayden seem cozy," he says, his gaze assessing me.

"Just something about the way you are with each other seems different than before. Almost like..."

I feel my cheeks flush.

"Are you two going steady now?" he asks with a twinkle in his eye.

I tap him playfully on the arm. "Stop. We're..."

"A happy couple," Ayden says as he puts his arms around me from behind. "We've been dating for just over a week and I'm going to marry her one day soon."

I drop my jaw as I twist around to look at Ayden. He winks at me and murmurs into my ear, "I'm serious about that last part."

My stomach flip flops and I break into a smile.

Grandpa beams and reaches out to shake Ayden's hand. "You take good care of my granddaughter. She's special."

"I know she is. I will, sir."

"Oh, my God, this isn't the nineteenth century, people!" I throw up my hands. "And I'm right here between you as you talk about me!"

Grandpa chuckles. "You make the perfect couple. The only man I could ever imagine my Bella with is you, son."

I feel Ayden's jaw clench with emotion against my cheek. "Thank you. That means a lot."

———

Ayden drives me to the music lounge so Guy and I can do a final dress rehearsal for our performance tomorrow night. Guy insists Ayden stick around so we'll have practice in front of an audience.

We're still undecided on exactly what our set list is, but we've definitely decided on a song by the Beatles. Guy pulls out his sheet music. "Let It Be. We've done it once already."

"That's fine." I lean my elbows on top of the piano and smile over at Ayden, whose eyes are focused on me.

"And then our second song is set. Except for that one bridge..." Guy shuts his eyes and starts tapping his fingers on the piano.

I sit quietly and let him figure it out. I feel like I have no creative power whatsoever when I think about my father's party.

"Our collab is cool. And I think we can work out the bridge tonight." His lip quirks up. "Angst pop combined with acoustic rock. This has been fun to work with, Bella."

I laugh. "Our two styles mesh pretty well, right?"

"They actually do." He gestures to Ayden. "You ready to be our first audience?"

Ayden gives him a thumbs up. "Go for it."

Our first song goes great.

"That sounded amazing," Ayden calls out.

"Ayden, can you actually sit in the far back of the lounge?" Guy asks him. "We'll run through that same song one more time. I want to see if you notice any problems from a different angle, and I want to make sure you're hearing us okay."

"Sure thing."

Ayden moves to the far back, and Guy starts playing again.

I've just sung the first line when I see Jenny Woods out of my peripheral vision. She's walking down the hall, and she's staring at Ayden. I clench my jaw, prepared for her approach. And it comes. She strolls into the lounge, and with a loud giggle, starts talking to Ayden.

I force myself to keep singing as Jenny ruffles Ayden's hair.

At first, Ayden completely ignores her, but she keeps chatting to him.

And I'm so distracted I'm barely getting words out.

"Bella!" Guy whispers to me. "Don't let her distract you!"

Too late.

I stop singing altogether and stare at Jenny and Ayden like it's a car crash. I feel like I'm back in L.A. when the spotlight found Trevor and Max.

But life doesn't always repeat itself. Tonight, Ayden's eyes never leave mine. He stands up and pulls away from Jenny's hand.

He crosses his arms over his chest, and with his eyes locked on mine, he says loudly to Jenny, "I don't mean to be rude, but I'm hanging out with Bella."

Jenny's eyes widen, but apparently she doesn't give up easily. "Well, are you free tomorrow night? We could maybe hang out again, like old times."

"Sorry," Ayden says. "I've already got a date for tomorrow night."

"What about next week then?" she says, eyeing me.

"Can't," Ayden says as he walks up to the piano and takes me in his arms. "I've got a date then too. In fact, I've got a date every night from now on. Bella's my forever date."

With a scowl, Jenny slinks out of the room.

All the tension leaves my body as I look into Ayden's blue eyes. "You never have to worry," he whispers in my ear as he hugs me tighter to him. "Okay? Never, Bella."

Guy shakes his head at me, and gestures to the sheet music in front of him. "Bella, you can't get distracted like that. I get it, but that can't happen tomorrow."

"I know." I wrap my arms around Ayden's waist. "It won't."

———

I dress for my father's party slowly. I know I'll be on stage, and the entire town will be staring at me, so I choose a simple black dress with black strappy sandals. The dress comes to just above my knee, and it has crisscross straps across the back. I wish I had a necklace that matched, but I'll just have to skip that part. I pull my blond hair up into a high ponytail and take one last look at the miniature lighthouse Ayden gave me, now sitting on my dresser. Just seeing it there helps me feel safe.

A few minutes later, Ayden steps inside my front door and immediately grabs me in a kiss. "You look gorgeous," he says into my lips. "I've never seen this dress before."

"That's because I only wear it for functions I don't enjoy," I say. "You look so sexy, Ayd."

His black dress pants and simple white collared shirt with the top two buttons undone nearly start me drooling. I reach up and run my hand through his mess of dark hair. I'm still getting used to seeing him without his hat.

"Do you miss your hat?" I ask him.

"Not like I thought I would. Besides," he says as he kisses my neck. "I've been a little distracted lately."

I grab my purse, guitar, and song notes. "I'm so nervous," I admit as we walk to the front door.

"Hey. Bella?" Ayden's still standing in the hallway.

"Yeah?" I turn back to face him.

He comes closer to me. "I got you a little something. For good luck."

"Like a charm?" I ask.

"Sort of." He pulls a small box out of his pocket and hands it to me. "I hope you like it."

His hands return to his pockets nervously, and he bites his lip. I open the box, and stare down at a beautiful sea urchin pendant on a silver chain.

My hand goes to my heart. "I love it, Ayden. Wherever did you find it?"

"The little jewelry store on the corner of Main," he says. "I wanted to get you something to remind you of your first gig since you came back here. I don't ever want you to forget your singing gift and how talented you are. So I went looking this morning, and this seemed perfect."

"It is absolutely perfect." I lift it out of the box. "I'll wear it to the party. It will go great with my dress."

I hand it to Ayden, and he carefully puts it around my neck and seals the clasp.

He tugs gently at my ponytail as he presses a sweet kiss to the back of my neck. "You'll be amazing tonight," he says.

I turn to face him, and lift the sea urchin off my chest so I can look at it. "My good luck sea hedgehog." My heart swells, and I raise my eyes to Ayden's. "You're the only person who would ever think to get me a sea urchin, Ayd. I needed this so much tonight." I reach for the back of his neck and pull him close for a kiss. "Thank you," I murmur into his lips.

I hold Ayden's hand as we leave my house and walk out to his car. As soon as we're inside, I start rambling nervously. "My mother's going to pass out when she sees me stand up on that stage with Guy. She thinks he's doing solos." I pause as Ayden starts the engine. "Which he is doing, so I guess that's not all a lie. He just didn't mention to her that I'll be up there for two songs. I just don't want to upset her."

"You won't. And you know this car ride will take about thirty seconds," Ayden reminds me. "Are you sure you're ready to leave the driveway?"

I look at him, nearly in a panic. "I absolutely hate this anxiety," I say. "Hate it, hate it, hate it. This is why I told Guy no. But he insisted."

Ayden sits patiently.

I sigh heavily. "Fine. I guess it's time." I put on my seatbelt and look out the window as we pull out of the driveway and head toward the center of Lucky Bay.

———

The town square is crowded.

"Lot of people here to pay tribute to your dad," Ayden comments as we spot Peter and Tari and wave them over.

"Lot of people willing to enjoy free food and a free party, you mean."

"Bella, do you want us to take your guitar for you?" Peter says to me as they reach us. "We can bring it to Guy in case you run into your mother."

"Thanks." I hand it to them, and as if on cue, my parents come around the corner.

"Hello, Ayden." Mom smiles stiffly. "How are you?"

"I'm good. How are you doing, Lucy?"

She smiles more warmly now. "Very well, thank you. And your support means so much."

I nearly fall over. Mom never disliked Ayden, not exactly. But his family came from the "wrong side of town" as she liked to say when we were kids, and she never seemed to get past his more modest background. But right now, she's looking at Ayden like she's genuinely...grateful.

"I'm happy you're feeling better," Ayden says to her.

"And Bella, you look beautiful." Dad kisses me. "You and your mother really outdid yourselves with this party."

"Mom did most of the work," I say.

———

I sit with my parents and Grandpa through the agonizingly long dinner of salmon and scalloped potatoes.

Ayden's mom comes over to give me a big hug and whisper in my ear, "Words cannot describe how thrilled I am about you and Ayden. You were already a daughter to me, anyway."

I tell her she's going to make me cry, and we laugh before she heads back to Ayden and Michael.

"You seem jumpy tonight," Grandpa says to me quietly. "Boy, this salmon's delicious, isn't it?"

I smile at him. "It is."

"Fresh as can be."

"Your earrings look very nice, Mirabella," Mom says.

"You gave them to me, Mom. You've got good taste."

"Well." Mom blushes and tries not to smile. Then she looks more closely at my hair, and her mouth turns into a deep frown. "You could have gone to Antoine's with me this afternoon. He'd have styled your hair beautifully."

"I'm sure he would have."

Ayden comes up behind me. "You're going to rock it," he says in my ear. "And it's time."

"What?!" I glance up at the stage where Guy is gesturing to me.
"Shit! I didn't even see him!"

Ayden tugs at my ponytail. "Just look for me in the crowd. If you lose focus, keep your eyes on me, babe."

———

"Hey." Guy gives me a high-five. "I got my keyboard, here's your guitar, and I've got the songs. We're ready to go, honey."

"I think I'm going to puke," I say.

"It'll be over before you know it," Guy assures me. "You sitting or standing?"

I smile at him shakily. "I'll stand."

I turn to face the crowd, fixating on my mother immediately. She's noticed me already, and her face is pinched. Every muscle of mine feels frozen solid.

"You've got to look away," Guy says. "Your mom? This isn't the right time to look at her. Turn away, Bella."

And I do. I look away from her. Finally.

I turn to Guy. "Do you do therapy on the side?"

He laughs, and I catch eyes with Ayden. His gaze is intently focused on me.

"Now you're looking at the right person," Guy says. "Keep your beautiful eyes on him. He's a good dude, by the way. I've always liked him." He grabs his microphone to turn it on. "You ready? Once this is on, there's no turning it off."

I take my place in front of my microphone, preparing to turn it on. "Let's do it. Nothing can be worse than this delay."

As soon as Guy calls attention to the stage, the crowd goes silent. But he starts to play right away, and I turn on my mic and join him.

I start out a little shaky, but I'm able to pull it together by the end of the first verse. My voice gets stronger, and I start to relax. I never lose eye contact with Ayden. Through the entire song, he's right there with me, his eyes telling me I can do it.

The Beatles song Guy and I chose is a hit. The music, the duet, it all comes together. People dance while we sing, and clap when we finish.

"My friend Bella's only up here for one more song," Guy says. "We've got something new for you all."

He sings the first verse, and I take over on the second. Guy finishes with *pushing and pulling but something's changing that I can't deny*, and I pick up where he leaves off—*however long we have to wait I know it'll work, I know the stars will shine just for us.*

The combined chorus from each of our songs somehow gels—*I stop and realize what I'd lose, I stop and see how far we've come, babe. We love each other right, we love all night. I'll take the chance if you do too.*

When we finish, after Guy gives me a hug and I turn to wave at the crowd, I sneak a peek at Mom. She smiles at me, like a real smile. I jump off the stage and head for Ayden.

I see him coming from across the lawn. I can make out the blue of his eyes from here. I break into a jog, and when I reach him, I jump into his arms and he wraps me up in a hug.

"You were amazing," he says into my ear. "Blew me away, Bella."

"I love you," I say into his neck.

"Mirabella!"

Ayden keeps me in his arms but turns slowly toward the sound of my mother's voice. I lift my chin as Mom approaches us at a rapid pace.

I say to Ayden, "It's okay. I'll see you in a few minutes."

Ayden puts me down and kisses my temple, then says hello to my mother as he passes her.

"Well, that was a surprise performance," Mom says as she reaches me.

Lucky Bay is my mother's world. It's never really been mine. And as much as I love it here, it's the world I was born into, not the one I want to stay in.

I look back at her, at her eyes that are so receded sometimes it's hard to read them at all. But tonight, I can see something, some sort of life in there. "Surprise," I say, feeling deflated all of a sudden. "I didn't know how to tell you. You've never liked me to sing, you know. And I hate so much to upset you."

"I know." She pauses. "I don't know why it bothered me." She furrows her brow. "I guess it scared me."

I'd been looking away, not wanting to hear her reject me again, but that last part gets my attention. I whip my head toward her.

"Grandma never allowed much expression," she says. "I don't know where you get it from, that talent of yours up on stage. It's certainly not from me."

She meets my gaze, and my heart breaks at the unshed tears in her eyes.

"The medication is helping," she says. "And so is the therapy. It's also brought to my attention how hard it must have been for you all these years. I neglected my own child because I was in so much pain."

I put my arms around her in a hug and then lead her behind a large tree for privacy. "How can I help?" I ask her.

"Be happy, Mirabella. Watching you up on stage, and seeing you with Ayden—you're listening to your heart. You're following your dreams."

I swallow. "Yes. I am."

"Your grandfather spoke to Dad and me. About you moving to California again."

Oh no.

But she smiles. "We will be fine here, Mirabella. If you choose to move to L.A. again, we'll be okay. Your father's going to talk to you about this as well. He wants to pick up the slack for once. So let him help me."

"I'll always help you, Mom."

"I know you will. But you shouldn't have to. You deserve to live out your dreams. And Dad fully supports whatever decision you make. As do I."

I choke back my tears of gratitude and relief. "Thank you Mom. I appreciate that so much."

———

As soon as I get home, I open my garage door. I walk to the far back corner and after several minutes of pushing things aside, like my lawnmower and an old boom box, I find what I'm looking for.

I take it out of the garage and carry it to the edge of my front lawn. I stand there for a moment, glad for the cover of the night. But I've made my decision. In truth, I think I made it a while ago, but I couldn't hear the little voice speaking to me from deep inside. I was too busy being scared.

The dirt is soft and the sign goes in easily. I step back to look.

FOR RENT in big red letters. Yeah, that's about right.

I go inside and pack a bag for Ayden's. And then I reach for the phone. It's after midnight, but I can't wait.

Dad picks up after the second ring. "Hi Dad."

"I thought you'd be calling." His tone is neutral, but I think I hear a hint of—could it be pride?—in it. "I was proud of you today. You have a beautiful voice."

"Um..." I choke down my emotion. "Thank you."

"And your mother said she talked to you at the party."

"Yes, she did. I wanted to ask you, though, if..."

"I'm here, Bella. For your mother. And for you too." He pauses. "Last time you moved, we weren't supportive as we should have been. I don't want you to think it will be the same this time. You're meant to pursue your singing dream, Bella. Plus, I'll have support this time. The nurse is a huge help. And if you need anything..."

"Dad," I say. "What you're doing right now for Mom? That's all I need from you. I can't tell you how much that helps me, to know she has you in her corner. And I do have one more favor."

After I finish with my father, he puts my mother on the phone.

"Mirabella!" Mom exclaims. "Why are you calling so late?"

I choke back a sob. "I just wanted to say good night, Mom. You threw a wonderful party for Dad. You should be proud of yourself."

"Oh." Pause. "Thank you. And are you thinking about moving with Ayden?"

"Yes. I am. But I plan to fly home every three months to visit. I just talked to Dad about it."

"Every three months? You'll come home to see us?"

"Yes. I wanted to see how you felt about that plan. Really be honest with me."

"That sounds fine, Mirabella. It truly does."

"Call me if you need my help. With anything, okay?"

"Will do. Good night, then."

"Good night."

I brush the tears off my cheeks and go pack my bag. Then I drive to Ayden's.

He opens the door before I even knock. "You all right?" he says as he searches my face.

"I am." I kiss him. "And I'm ready. For L.A." I kiss him again. "I'm ready for us."

His mouth lifts in a surprised grin. "Are you sure, Bella?"

I step inside his house and walk with him toward his bedroom. "More sure than I've ever been of anything," I say. "And more scared. But that's part of the fun, right?"

He puts his arms around me as he urges me onto his bed. "It'll be fun, and I'll keep you safe. I'll always be by your side. I can promise you that."

I know he can. He's made good on that promise since I was three years old. As we fall into bed together, I know that somehow, I've figured out how to get myself out of Lucky Bay for the second time.

Sometimes, you have to come home for a while, to the place where you were born, to heal. And it doesn't always mean you failed or you're a coward. Sometimes it's the bravest—and the hardest—thing you can do. Sometimes it's the only way to say goodbye to the past and to move forward. Ayden's officially my plus one now. And I'm his. Forever.

EPILOGUE

Los Angeles, One Month Later

Ayden

Bella turns over in her sleep and sighs. I press a kiss to her bare shoulder, not wanting to wake her but impatient all the same. One last sleep sigh, and she opens those beautiful hazel eyes and smiles over at me. Her golden hair shines in the morning sun pouring in through our windows we forgot to close the blinds on last night.

"You've never looked more beautiful." I kiss her nose. "I love waking up next to you."

"What are you doing up?" She glances at the clock. "It's barely seven."

I kiss her neck until she shivers, and then I keep kissing her, pulling the covers down to expose her bare breasts. I spend time on each one, and Bella squirms and moans beneath me. Then I keep moving south.

Down her stomach, across her navel, and I press light kisses on the soft satin skin on the inside of each thigh.

Then I put my lips where I know she wants me most, and I don't let up until Bella's writhing around my head with her hips. When she goes over the edge, I shift until I'm over her body, bracing my arms on either side of her head. Her hair's now framed out and around her face like a golden halo, and I take care not to land on it with my elbows.

Our eyes lock, her hazel to my blue, and with one thrust, I'm all the way inside her. We both cry out at the same time. Making love to Bella never gets old. Each time, I swear to God, feels better than the last. More mind-blowing. More emotional. More connected. I don't deserve her. But I'm sure as hell never going to let her go.

She falls over into bliss again, and I follow her, calling out her name and burying my head in her neck. Without moving off of her, I reach under my pillow and hand her what's been burning a hole in the sheets for the past twelve hours.

Her eyes get huge as she stares at the ring shining in my open hand.

"Holy shit, Ayden."

I break into a laugh. "Mirabella Wesley, I love you. You're my best friend, my angel, my everything. Will you also be my wife?"

Bella throws her arms around my back, pulling me even closer. "Freaking yes, I will," she says "I love you, Ayd."

I slip the ring onto her trembling finger, and she holds it up to the sunlight. "Gorgeous."

I kiss her. I couldn't agree more.

After I lost my father so unexpectedly, I was so scared of loving anyone again, of letting anyone too close. But Bella's not just anyone. She's everything. She was always mine just like I was always hers. We were too scared of losing each other to realize the truth. But now that we have, we don't have to worry about crossing the ocean of life all alone. Now we can navigate through the storm the way we were meant to: together.

ANOTHER EPILOGUE

Jenson

In five hours and two left turns, I'll be pulling into the town I left years ago, the same place I left my heart. I tuck my two sons into their car seats and buckle them in before I climb into the driver's seat and start the truck. We pull out of my townhouse complex in Pittsburgh, and I head for the highway.

"Daddy, how long before we get there?"

As we pull up at a stoplight, I look at Kyle in the rearview mirror. "A little while. But before you know it, we'll be home. To the home where I grew up," I clarify. "You boys remember the town. You always love visiting Liberty Falls."

"Will we get to play football with your new team like we do here? What if they don't let us?" Connor asks me, as he pulls his blankie tighter around him.

They may be identical twins, but my two boys couldn't be more different in temperament: Kyle's always running three steps away from me, and Connor makes his decisions more cautiously. I'm trying to take a page from each of them and follow my heart without ignoring all sense of logic. Like this move I'm making across the state of Pennsylvania—I've wanted to do it for a while, but I didn't make the leap. Not until right now. My heart pounds at the risk I'm taking, but the woman at the finish line is worth it. She's always been worth it, and she always will be.

"I've already told the head coach how much you love coming to practice. He's looking forward to meeting you both," I assure Connor.

"Will we see Grandma?" Kyle asks.

"We're going to stay with her and Grandpa, like always," I say.

"What about Livia?" Connor asks, staring at me in the mirror with those serious green eyes that match mine in color and intensity. "Will we see her too?"

"Yeah, I want to see Livia!" Kyle chimes in, nodding his blond head vigorously.

My chest tightens. "I hope so boys. I certainly plan on it."

As the light turns green, I put my focus back on the road. But my thoughts are only on one woman.

Olivia Graham, I'm coming back for you, babe. I hope you're ready... because I'm not giving up this time without one hell of a fight.

***

Thank you for reading AYDEN!
Want more of Ayden and Bella? Click **HERE** for a bonus story!
CLICK HERE TO READ JENSON AND OLIVIA'S LOVE STORY!

JENSON

As Colton Wild's best friend, Jenson is an unofficial Wild man!
Jenson and Olivia's second chance off-limits love story is filled with
romantic and sexy twists and turns. JENSON is available **HERE**!

Take a peek at **JENSON**:

It's been years, but they never got over each other ... A SECOND
CHANCE OFF-LIMITS ROMANCE

He's a single dad and she's a career woman ... but their hearts are
perfectly matched.

Olivia

Jenson's not just a former star quarterback turned brilliant football
coach. He's not only an amazing father to twin sons.

He's also...mine.

The problem? He's always been off-limits.

But we always planned to be together one day. Except sometimes plans change. So we both moved on, or we tried to.

But now, after all these years, Jenson's back in town. We're both single. And we can't keep our hands off each other.

Jenson

When Olivia was born, I was told to look out for her, and she was the girl who made me smile when nothing else could.

When we got older, I fell in love with her. And then we broke each other's hearts.

I'm a single father now, with two boys who look up to me. And I'm about to show them how to get the win when the clock's running down and the defense is stacked against you. I'm going to fight for the one thing, outside of them, that's meant the most to me in my life.

I've come back to town on a mission:

To make Olivia mine. Because she and I are meant to be.

But for Olivia and me, meant to be has never been easy...

READ JENSON AND OLIVIA'S STORY IN *JENSON*! CLICK HERE!

BONUS AYDEN AND BELLA FREE STORY!

Ayden and Bella's life as a married couple living in Los Angeles is filled with love and new adventures. They have everything they want...except one thing. Pick up **WILD VALENTINE** as a free bonus short story (complete with an HEA) **HERE**!

ALSO BY MELISSA BELLE

Boston Boys

BOSTON BILLIONAIRE

BOSTON LOVE

BOSTON ESCAPE

BOSTON ROOMIE

BOSTON BAD BOY

BOSTON PLAYER

Wild Men

COLTON

DYLAN

AYDEN

JENSON

BRAYDEN

CAMERON

DECLAN

MICHAEL

Wild Men Texas

WHISKEY GIRL

WARRIOR GIRL

WILD GIRL

Storm Brothers

HUNTER

JARED

MAX

LIAM

Bonus Wild Men Stories

WILD MAN (Colton and Sky prequel novella)

WILD VALENTINE (Ayden and Bella short story)

Sign up for Melissa's Newsletter to get a free story and to receive alerts and updates on upcoming book releases.

ACKNOWLEDGMENTS

Thank you so much for your help with editing and proofreading and keeping me on track to: Jon, Hunter, Dawn, and J.W.

And a special thank you to my parents for all the Maine summers by the beach.

STAY UP TO DATE WITH MELISSA

Do you want to stay up to date on awesome sales, upcoming hot releases, and giveaways? Sign up for my VIP List and get a free story!

ABOUT THE AUTHOR

A USA Today Bestselling author, Melissa Belle is known for her contemporary romance style that's sweet, sexy, and smart. She writes hot, steamy romance with complex heroes and heroines. She spent years in the field of psychology before writing her first novel riding the train around Europe with her husband. Melissa likes cupcakes, road trips, and songwriting.

To receive an email when Melissa releases a new book, sign up for her VIP List!

www.melissabellebooks.com

www.ingramcontent.com/pod-product-compliance
Lightning Source LLC
Chambersburg PA
CBHW060908250626
47159CB00008B/2912